"It is always a pleasure to read a book starring Harry and Mrs. Murphy but *Cat's Eyewitness* is particularly good. . . . Rita Mae Brown delights her fans with this fantastic feline mystery."
—*Midwest Book Review*

"It's terrific, like all those that preceded it. . . . Brew the tea, get cozy, and enjoy. This series is altogether delightful."
—*Kingston Observer*

"Frothy mayhem."
—*Omaha Sunday World-Herald*

"[An] irresistible mix of talking animals and a baffling murder or two . . . The animals' wry observations on human nature and beliefs amuse as ever."
—*Publishers Weekly*

"Delightful . . . Grade A." —*Deadly Pleasures*

WHISKER OF EVIL

"A page-turner . . . A welcome sign of early spring is the latest sprightly Mrs. Murphy mystery. . . . There's plenty of fresh material to keep readers entertained. For one thing, the mystery is a real puzzler, with some subtle clues and credible false leads. . . . [They] have done it again. Give them a toast with a sprig of catnip." —*Winston-Salem Journal*

"Rita Mae Brown and Sneaky Pie Brown fans will gladly settle in for a good long read and a well-spun yarn while Harry and her cronies get to the bottom of the mystery. . . . The series is worthy of attention."
—*Times-Record News*

"Another winsome tale of endearing talking animals and fallible, occasionally homicidal humans." —*Publishers Weekly*

"The gang from Crozet, Virginia, is back in a book that really advances the lives of the characters.... Readers of this series will be interested in the developments, and will anxiously be awaiting the next installment, as is this reader."
—*Deadly Pleasures*

"An intriguing new adventure...suspenseful...Brown comes into her own here; never has she seemed more comfortable with her characters." —*Booklist*

"Another fabulous tale...wonderful...The book is delightful and vastly entertaining with a tightly created mystery."
—*Old Book Barn Gazette*

"Undoubtedly one of the best books of the Mrs. Murphy series...a satisfying read." —*Alabama Times Daily*

THE TAIL OF THE TIP-OFF

"You don't have to be a cat lover to enjoy Brown's 11th Mrs. Murphy novel.... Brown writes so compellingly.... [She] breathes believability into every aspect of this smart and sassy novel." —*Publishers Weekly* (starred review)

"Rita Mae Brown's series remains one of the best cat mysteries.... Brown keeps the series fresh."
—*Charleston (SC) Post & Courier*

"The animals' droll commentary provides comic relief and clues helpful in solving the crime."
—*The Washington Post*

BOOKS BY RITA MAE BROWN
WITH SNEAKY PIE BROWN

BOOKS BY RITA MAE BROWN

Puss 'n Cahoots

RITA MAE BROWN
& SNEAKY PIE BROWN

ILLUSTRATIONS BY MICHAEL GELLATLY

BANTAM BOOKS NEW YORK · TORONTO · LONDON · SYDNEY · AUCKLAND

PUSS 'N CAHOOTS
A Bantam Book

PUBLISHING HISTORY
Bantam hardcover edition published March 2007
Bantam mass market edition / February 2008

Published by
Bantam Dell
A Division of Random House, Inc.
New York, New York

Library of Congress Catalog Card Number: 2006037253

Bantam Books and the rooster colophon are registered trademarks
of Random House, Inc.

ISBN: 978-0-553-58682-4

Printed in the United States of America
Published simultaneously in Canada

www.bantamdell.com

OPM 10 9 8 7 6 5 4 3 2 1

Dedicated in loving memory of
Paul and Frances Hamilton

Acknowledgments

As always, Ruth Dalsky, my researcher, endures all things. It's a good thing she has a sense of humor.

After discussing varying agents of death and destruction with my friend and doctor, Mrs. Mary Tattersall O'Brien, M.D., I'm surprised any of us are still alive.

You know how authors always write "Whatever mistakes are made are entirely my own"? I much prefer to blame the above.

Cast of Characters

Mary Minor Haristeen, "Harry"—A few days shy of her fortieth birthday, she's fit, looking forward to the future, and in love with her husband, whom she's remarried after a former divorce.

Pharamond Haristeen, "Fair"—One year older than his wife, whom he's thrilled to have won back; he's an equine veterinarian and a gentleman.

Joan Hamilton—The proprietor of Kalarama Farm. She's justly famed as an extraordinary breeder of Saddlebreds and is an old friend of Harry's.

Larry Hodge—Joan's husband, as famous as a trainer as she is as a breeder. Larry possesses good humor and can defuse potentially upsetting situations.

Booty Pollard—At forty-one, he is a fierce competitor to Larry Hodge. He keeps a pet monkey, Miss Nasty, as well as snakes. The snakes he keeps at home. He's vain and spends a boatload of money on clothes.

Charly Trackwell—He, too, is in the first flush of his forties, and his ambition grows with each passing year. He is a trainer with an exclusive client list. There are those who think he has an exclusive lover list, as well.

Ward Findley—Younger than the big-three trainers, he shows talent. At twenty-nine, he wants to break into the spotlight but currently he's held back by lack of money. If he can just knock out a big win, he will attract clients with heavy checkbooks.

Renata DeCarlo—A movie star who feels the encroachment of middle age, she has suffered a string of flops. Naturally she's beautiful, but she's at loose ends, unsure which way to turn next. A good rider, she shows Saddlebreds and her trainer is Charly Trackwell. Renata is the jewel in Charly's crown, and she would be the jewel in any trainer's crown.

Paul and Frances Hamilton—In their eighties, they are a long-married couple, parents to Joan. Paul loved Saddlebreds as a boy on the farm. Frances loves people, and the people are at the Saddlebred shows. They have eight children. Joan commands the Saddlebred world. Her siblings pursue other venues.

Manuel Almador—Head groom at Kalarama Farm, he's good with a horse, well organized, and greatly trusted. Manuel is in his late forties.

Jorge Gravina—He understudies Manuel. In his thirties, very responsible, he's well liked and a quiet-living man.

Benny—Ward Findley's jack-of-all-trades. He's a man who married too many times.

Carlos—Charly Trackwell's head man, who knows when to look the other way.

The Really Important Characters

Mrs. Murphy—Harry's tiger cat possesses high intelligence and marvelous athletic ability.

Pewter—Mrs. Murphy's rotund gray sidekick lacks some of the tiger cat's athletic ability, but she makes up for it by being grouchy. However, Pewter is perfectly capable of seeing what humans cannot.

Tee Tucker—The bravest corgi who has ever lived. She loves Harry and Fair, too, and she loves the cats, even if they pluck her last nerve.

Miss Nasty—The monkey is aptly named and is as much of a clotheshorse as Booty Pollard, her owner. She takes an instant dislike to Pewter, and it's mutual. No good can come of this.

Queen Esther—Renata's three-gaited mare is talented, expensive, and beautiful. She's not the brightest bulb on the Christmas tree, however.

Shortro—Renata's young three-gaited gelding is wonderfully intelligent, game, and a good citizen.

Voodoo—Renata's flashy older gelding, who taught her a lot. He was the first expensive horse she bought once she started to make money in Hollywood. Clearly, he won't be the last as Renata means to win, win, win.

Spike—A ginger cat, battle-scarred, who lives in the barn at Shelbyville by the practice arena. He doesn't suffer fools gladly.

Harlem's Dreamgirl, Point Guard, Golden Parachute— Outstanding Kalarama horses.

Frederick the Great—A five-gaited stallion shown by Charly Trackwell. Both horse and trainer are at the peak of their powers.

Callaway's Senator—Frederick's fierce competition. A five-gaited stallion originally bred at Callaway Farm and bought by one of Booty's wealthy clients. Booty believes this is his year to win all the big shows with Senator.

Puss 'n Cahoots

1

Long, golden rays raked the rolling hills surrounding Shelbyville, Kentucky, on Wednesday, August 2. At six P.M., the grassy parking lot of the famous fairgrounds accepted a steady stream of spectators. By seven P.M., the lot would be overflowing and the shift to backup parking would begin. A soft breeze carried a hint of moisture from the Ohio River about twenty-five miles west, which separated the state of Kentucky from Indiana. Barn swallows swooped through the air to snare abundant insects, as crows, perched on overhead lines, watched, commenting on everything. Cattle dotted pastures. Butterflies swarmed the horse droppings at the fairgrounds. While butterflies liked flowers and flowering bushes, they also evidenced a strong fondness for manure. Each time a maintenance man dutifully picked up the manure, a cloud of yellow swallowtails, black swallowtails, milk butterflies, and small bright blue butterflies swirled up from their prize. No matter how lowly their feeding habits, it was a beautiful sight.

"If I weren't in this blasted collar, I'd snatch one," Pewter bragged. *"Maybe two."*

"They are tempting," Mrs. Murphy agreed with the fat gray cat. Mrs. Murphy, a sleek tiger cat, was carried by Harry Haristeen. Pewter was carted by Fair Haristeen, DVM. The cats eagerly awaited the beginning of the first night's competition.

Shelbyville, the second glittering jewel in the Saddlebred world, attracted the best horses in the country. The show commenced a full two weeks before the Kentucky State Fair, the blowout of Saddlebred shows.

The four jewels in the crown were the Lexington Junior League, Shelbyville, the Kentucky State Fair at Louisville, and the Kansas City Royal, the only big show held in late fall, November. All the others were summer shows.

Throughout America, but most especially in Kentucky, Indiana, and Missouri, the Saddlebred shows added sparkle to the season and coins to the coffers. Every town bigger than a minute hosted one, no matter how humble. No one ever accused the Shelbyville show of being humble. A grandstand encircled the immaculate show ring oval. Most of the seating area was covered. The south of the lighted ring was anchored by an imposing two-story grandstand, where food was served if one had a ticket for the feast.

The aroma of the ribs tortured Tucker, the corgi, walking between her two humans. She drooled with anticipation. *"How long before we eat?"*

"I don't know, but I could faint with hunger." Pewter sighed.

"Oh la." Mrs. Murphy thought to say more but realized if

she started a fight she would unceremoniously be taken back to their suite at the Best Western hotel.

Harry and Fair paused to watch horses being worked in the practice ring on the east side of the fairgrounds. Booty Pollard, a famous forty-one-year-old trainer with a fully dressed monkey perching on his shoulder, walked next to a junior riding a three-gaited country pleasure horse. The walk, trot, canter horse was one of those wonderful creatures that take care of their young rider. Fortunately for the junior, this mare's three gaits were smooth. They were leaving the ring. Booty turned his head upon hearing another trainer raise his voice.

Charles "Charly" Trackwell, a big-money trainer and a peacock, shouted at a stunning young woman on an equally stunning chestnut three-gaited horse, Queen Esther. Queen Esther was much fancier than the country pleasure horse Booty's junior was riding. Queen Esther's trot just threw the beautiful woman up out of the saddle. Renata DeCarlo had paid two hundred fifty thousand dollars for the mare. Renata meant to win. She had to work harder than other competitors for the judges to take her seriously, but she liked hard work as much as she liked winning. At thirty-eight—although her "official" bio shaved six years off that age saying she was thirty-two—she was a movie star and there weren't many stars bred in Lincoln County, Kentucky. While everyone wanted to look at her, spectators and judges could be prejudiced. Envy from others found odd ways of expressing itself. Renata often received a ribbon lower than she should have earned. Her gorgeous mare merited being pinned first, the blue ribbon, more often than not. Shortro, her young gray stalwart three-gaited gelding, also endured lower pinnings than was fair.

But Shortro, unlike Queen Esther, was happy if he won a blue, red, yellow, green, white, pink ribbon. Queen Esther always wanted the huge best-in-class ribbon, as did Renata.

Horses, like people, are fully fledged personalities.

"Relax your shoulders, Renata," Charly growled.

"Beautiful," Harry commented.

"Fabulous mare." Fair prudently focused on the chestnut mare, which made Harry laugh.

They passed the white barn closest to the practice ring, the silver tin roof showing some wear and tear. The old barns might need a coat of paint, unlike the grandstand, but they were airy and quite pleasant. The number of competitors was so great that tent barns had been thrown up to handle the overflow. Each day hundreds of horses competed, some being driven in, vanned, for that day only. Keeping track of what horses were on the grounds proved overwhelming sometimes, because not every horse was competing. Some were companion horses to keep the star horse company. The temporary stalls, bisected by two aisles, were also completely full. The great stables marked off one or even two stalls for a hospitality suite, which would be outfitted with canvas panels and drapes in the stable's colors. Many boasted a tented ceiling inside to further enhance the welcoming atmosphere. An open bar and refreshments added to the festivities. Directors' chairs—again in the stable colors—tack trunks, bridle cases, ribbons hanging on the "walls," as well as lovely photographs of clients and horses completed the setting. The labor that it took to create these oases of cheer, along with another stall made into a special changing room for the riders, often behind the hospitality room, amazed Harry each time she visited one of the big Saddlebred shows, which she did once a year. Although a passionate Thoroughbred woman, she loved the Saddlebred. She'd trained a few from Kalarama Farm to be foxhunters. Saddlebreds could jump, really jump, which delighted Harry. The Thoroughbred, with its sloping shoulder and lower head carriage, ideally has a long, fluid stride. The Saddlebred's energy is expended upward, high stepping with some reach, and the head is held high. Go back one hundred fifty years and the two different breeds share some common ancestors.

Joan Hamilton, one of Harry's best friends, was the driving force behind the breeding program at Kalarama Farm. Her husband, Larry Hodge, trained and also rode many of the horses. As often happens in the horse world, when the right two people find each other, a magic glow shines on everything they touch.

On the way to the Kalarama ringside box, Harry and Fair strolled the midway crammed with a lot of stuff you'd like to buy and a lot of stuff you wouldn't. The jewelry shop tempted Harry. She stopped to admire a ring with square-cut rubies and diamonds set in a horseshoe. It was the most beautiful horseshoe ring she'd ever seen.

The ubiquitous funnel cakes cast their special doughy scent over the area, as did hot dogs, ribs, slabs of beef, and delicious chicken turning on a spit. The food shops, jewelry shop, and clothing shops were interspersed with people from the local farm bureau and various civic organizations running the booths, all having a good time. Most of the civic booths were under the grandstand facing the midway. A gleaming SL55 Mercedes lured folks to buy raffle tickets, one hundred bucks a pop, proceeds going to charity. Flattening your wallet proved all too easy walking along this small, seductive thoroughfare.

The uncovered western grandstand loomed over one side of the midway, and there were booths under it, as well. Everywhere you looked, right or left of the short midway, there was a booth. Right in front of the western grandstand, smack on the rail, were boxes, with six or eight folding chairs inside. These, rented by the great stables, were magnets for the spectators. Riders, breeders, and owners usually repaired to their boxes, which unlike the rented stalls did not bear the stable colors but sported a chaste white rectangular sign with the name of the box owner in simple black Roman letters.

Joan leaned forward to talk to her mother, the diminutive, lively Frances, and her father, Paul, as they checked their programs. Paul was one of those people who exerted a warm charisma, drawing people to him. Neither of the elder Hamiltons ever met a stranger.

Harry stepped into the box, Mrs. Murphy in her arms. Fair, Pewter, and Tucker immediately followed.

After hugs and kisses all around, everyone settled in their seats. Cookie, Joan's brown-and-white Jack Russell, squeezed with Tucker on a seat.

When Harry and Fair had arrived yesterday, they viewed Joan's yearlings, mares, and colts, and watched Larry work the horses. Harry learned from watching Larry, who knew exactly when to stop the lesson. So many trainers overtrained, the result being the horse grew sour or flat. Since a Saddlebred must show with brio, overtraining proved a costly mistake.

Frances, wearing a peach linen and silk dress with a corsage, turned to her daughter and said, "Joan, did you show the newlyweds Harlem's Dreamgirl?"

"Yes, I did."

Paul, a twinkle in his eye, twisted in his seat to wink at Fair. "You got the dreamgirl."

Fair slapped the older but still powerfully built World War II Navy vet on the shoulder. "I think we both married our dreamgirls."

"Paul and I married in the Dark Ages." Frances laughed.

"Still a honeymoon," Paul gallantly said.

Joan took off her beige silk jacket as the heat bore down. A gorgeous pin, a ruby and sapphire riding crop intertwined through a sparkling horseshoe, graced the left lapel.

"Joan, did you fix the clasp on that pin?" Frances asked.

"Yes, I did, and it's tight as a tick."

"Good. You know I think that's the prettiest piece of my mother's jewelry."

Joan, knowing her mother wouldn't be satisfied until she had examined the pin, slipped her coat off the chair, handing it to her mother.

Turning the lapel back, Frances fingered the pin. "Well, that should hold it." Before handing it back to Joan, she noted the careful work the jeweler had performed. "You know that's our lucky pin. You wear it when it counts, but always on the last night of the show."

Everyone studied their programs.

"Third class has that movie star in it." Paul read down the list.

The third class was the adult three-gaited show pleasure.

"She's going to have a tough time beating Melinda Falwell." Joan folded back her program.

"Booty's client." Paul named Melinda's trainer, a gregarious man still recovering from a sulfurous divorce last year. The recovery was financial as well as emotional. It was

Booty who Harry and Fair had seen walking out of the practice ring.

Five years ago an intense rivalry set off fireworks in the Saddlebred world as the old guard began to retire or die off, leaving the younger men and a few women in their middle years to come forward in a big way. Larry Hodge, Booty Pollard, and Charly Trackwell had taken up where Tom Moore, Earl Teater, and the late Bradshaw brothers had left off. Pushing behind Larry, Booty, and Charly were men and more women than in previous generations, in their late twenties and early thirties, one of whom, Ward Findley, evidenced special talent.

Saddlebred trainers rode the difficult horses or the horses in the big classes, which would add thousands of dollars to the horse's worth if the animal showed well. In the Thoroughbred world, trainers did not ride in the races. Here they did, which gave the shows an extra dimension. It was as if Bill Parcells played quarterback or Earl Weaver stepped up to the plate.

The amateur riders, coached by the trainers, didn't necessarily ride easy horses, but usually the horses were more tractable and less was at stake. A win at one of the big shows could send a horse's value skyrocketing. Few people are immune to that incentive, hence the enduring appeal of the trainer/rider.

Ward Findley, who was twenty-nine and had close-cropped, jet-black hair and sparkling blue eyes, quickly came up to the Kalarama box, leaned over, and whispered to Joan, "You'd better get to the barn." Right behind Ward came Booty Pollard, his pet monkey on his shoulder. "Trouble," Ward continued. The monkey, Miss Nasty, chattered as she peered at everyone in the box. Miss Nasty loved Booty, but she hated his snake collection, which he kept at home. She, at least, got to travel. Fortunately, the snakes did not. Booty did have peculiar tastes in pets.

Paul, overhearing, stood up.

"Daddy, you stay here. People need to see you and Mom." Joan was already out of the box.

Fair, an equine vet, followed her. Kalarama had their regular vet, but he didn't attend the shows. The organizers kept a vet on the premises so there was no need for each competitor or breeder to tie up their own vet for the four evenings of the show.

Not to be left behind, Harry scooped up both cats, her progress slowed by the two unhappy kitties squirming in her arms.

"If you'd put me down, I could follow just fine," Mrs. Murphy complained.

"She thinks you'll run off," Tucker, excited by the tension in the humans, commented.

"You're a big, fat help," Mrs. Murphy growled.

"I'm a dog. I'm obedient. You're a cat. You're not." Tucker relished the discomfort of her two friends, since they often lorded over her.

The conversation abruptly ended as they reached Barn Five, where three horses were being led into the barn, Charly Trackwell trotting after them, his face grim. They were not Joan's horses.

"Isn't that the chestnut mare from the practice ring?" Pewter studied the gleaming animal, her long neck graceful.

"Yes." Mrs. Murphy was happy when Harry unhitched Pewter's and her leash and quickly deposited them in the hospitality room. Pewter used the opportunity to jump onto the table, snatching a succulent square of ham.

"You're a goddamned diva!" Charly shouted at Renata DeCarlo, who stormed ahead of Charly.

The loss of board and training fees for three horses would hurt Charly a bit, but the real blow was losing his movie-star client.

Joan prudently stood by a stall, since Charly now faced Larry, Renata to Larry's side. Fair stood behind Larry.

"I'm sick of you shouting at me, Charly." Renata, face flushed, was remarkably calm.

Charly turned to Larry. "You're behind this, Hodge. You've been trying to steal Renata away from me since she came to my barn."

"That's not true." Larry kept his voice level.

"You love the glamour. And you'll make a bloody fortune. You always do." Charly, shaking with rage, stepped toward Larry.

Renata grabbed Charly's arm, which he threw off. "You've criticized me one time too many. You're an egotistical shit and I'm sick of it."

Much as he wanted to hit her and Larry, too, Charly managed to control himself. He stopped breathing for a second, then gulped air. "Renata, you redefine the word 'ego.'"

"We can all sort this out tomorrow when everybody has calmed down," Larry sensibly suggested.

"The hell with you." Then Charly wheeled on Renata and pointed his finger right in her face. "I know about you." With that he turned on his booted heel and left.

Manuel Almador, Larry's head groom, watched along with Jorge Gravina, second in command to Manuel. Their distaste for Charly flickered across their faces.

Renata, floodgates now bursting, allowed Joan to shepherd her to the hospitality room. The people who had gathered at the barn's entrance dispersed, a few to follow Charly. They had to trot, since his long legs covered the ground.

As Renata's sobs subsided, Larry, Fair, Manuel, and Jorge consulted one another in the aisle.

"Manuel, you and the boys will need to sleep here all week. Take four-hour shifts. Charly will have his revenge, and I don't want it to be on Renata's horses or ours, either."

Manuel nodded; he knew Charly's reputation.

Handsome Charly, an explosives expert and captain in the first Iraq war, was explosive himself.

"I can check, too. We're just down the road," Fair offered.

"Thanks. The men can handle it." Larry appreciated Fair's offer. He glanced at his watch. "Olive." He named a client riding in the next class. Larry needed to walk with her to the arena, then stand alongside the rail so she could see him. He smiled. "No charge for the extra entertainment."

Back in the hospitality room, the animals listened as Renata ticked off Charly's list of faults, most notably that he was arrogant, didn't listen to her, and was a man, which seemed to Renata to sum up his original sin.

"*Dramatic,*" Tucker succinctly observed.

"*It takes a while for humans to dissipate big emotions.*" Mrs. Murphy sat on the maroon tack trunk piped in white and black. "*Some of them never do. They're still talking about what happened to them thirty years ago.*"

"*Key to happiness, a bad memory.*" Pewter swept her dark gray whiskers forward. The stolen ham, happily consumed, contributed to her golden glow.

Mrs. Murphy's green eyes studied Renata's perfect face. "*A little too dramatic for my taste.*"

The three Virginia animals, along with Cookie, sneezed.

Renata's perfume was too strong for their sensitive noses, but Joan didn't respond to it. The animals marveled at the failure of human noses, even one as delicate and pretty as Joan's.

Finally, Joan calmed down Renata, reminding her that she was riding in the third class. She guided Renata to the dressing room. Renata considered the third class a warm-up for the rest of the week. She needed the taste of competition more than the gelding she would be riding, a flashy black-and-white paint named Voodoo. She could have skipped it but wanted to teach Charly a thing or two. He wasn't going to affect her riding. Renata, ready to wail anew when she realized her tack trunk and clothes were at Charly's hospitality room, was short-circuited.

At that moment, Charly's head groom, Carlos, appeared along with Jorge, Kalarama's groom, with Renata's trunk, clothes, and tack. Not a speck of dirt besmirched anything. She liked Carlos and tried to give him a tip, but he refused. Jorge refused also.

As Renata changed, Jorge tacked up Voodoo, while Shortro and Queen Esther watched. Voodoo, the first good Saddlebred Renata had bought, had a special place in her heart. Voodoo taught her a great deal while forgiving her mistakes.

Joan, Harry, Fair, and the animals walked back to their Kalarama box as the crowd clapped for the contestants leaving the second class.

Paul and Frances were now looking down from the top tier of the main grandstand. The odor of the food had enticed them from the box. Joan settled in her chair. The third class, with a full twenty-five entrants, seemed to go on forever, finally being won by a young lady riding a horse bred in Missouri by Callaway Stables, outside the town of Fulton.

Joan reached around to drape her jacket over her shoulders. She gasped. "My pin."

Harry looked at the jacket, then got down on her hands and knees to inspect the ground. "Oh, Joan, it's not here."

Fair stood up, checking the entrance to the box. "How about if I go to lost-and-found in case it fell off and someone picked it up?"

"It didn't fall off. The clasp had a triple lock." Joan's face, mournful, registered this loss. "Someone took it off."

"Maybe your mother did when she left the box." Harry was hopeful.

A flicker of hope illuminated Joan's beautiful features. "Well, maybe." Her voice lowered. "I kind of doubt it. All these years I've been coming here, I never worried about anything being stolen. I can't believe this." She sighed deeply. "Mom is going to be really upset with me." She paused. "I'm upset."

"Not to be crass, but how much do you think the pin is worth?" Harry put her hand on Joan's shoulder.

"I don't know. Twenty-five thousand? Thirty?"

"God!" Harry, mindful of every penny, now turned whiter than Joan.

"We may find it yet," Fair said comfortingly.

Joan's shoulders straightened. "We might. But I don't know if we'll like what we find with it."

"That's a strange thing to say." Harry's eyebrows raised quizzically.

"I have this terrible feeling..." Joan's voice trailed off.

This melancholy premonition vanished as Miss Nasty,

Booty's sidekick, free at last, rollicked along the top board of the show-ring rail.

How long she'd escaped her confinement was anybody's guess, because she could be stealthy when she wished. Now her desire to be the center of attention overtook her.

Fortunately, the horses for the fourth class would have a five-minute wait as two tractors with drags fluffed up the footing in the ring.

Pewter observed the young monkey. *"Ugly as a mud fence."*

"Must have slipped her chain." Tucker did think it was funny that Miss Nasty waved her tiny chapeau to the crowd.

Cookie, who knew the monkey only too well, replied, *"Miss Nasty doesn't have anything as common as a chain. She's tied with a silken cord that has a gold lock on the end. She knows how to pick it. And she can pick the lock to her cage, too. Booty should keep her in her cage all the time, but he likes to have her with him. She gets into everything. Once she climbed into a car and started it. I heard she let out his snakes, and some of them are poisonous. No one would go to his house until he found them all."*

"People leave their cars unlocked at shows?" Mrs. Murphy registered surprise.

"No big deal." Cookie nodded.

"If Miss Nasty picks the lock on her silken cord, why doesn't Booty use something stronger?" Pewter wondered.

"Oh, he accuses people of freeing her. He can't face how naughty she is. It's a good thing he can't understand what she says. She should have her mouth washed out with soap." Cookie laid back her ears as Miss Nasty approached, paused to stand up and clap, then waved her hat and put it back on. She dropped to all fours, loping along the top rail again.

"Her dress is fetching." Fair laughed at the pink sundress,

which matched her straw hat, a small fake peony attached to the pale green chiffon ribbon.

"She owns an extensive wardrobe." Joan, despite her pin's disappearance, smiled. "When Annie divorced Booty, he acquired the monkey, naming her Miss Nasty in honor of his ex-wife."

"Low blow." Harry giggled.

"Not low enough." Joan's grin widened. "Her dresses and ensembles are copies of Annie's. Annie shopped a lot at Glasscock's, an expensive store in Louisville, so I bet you Booty pays plenty for Miss Nasty's frocks."

"No!" Harry found this delightfully wicked.

"How did he remember what Annie wore?" Fair was puzzled, because he wasn't good at remembering such details.

"Booty is as vain as Charly about clothes. He even remembers things I wore years ago," Joan replied.

"Maybe he's gay." Fair shrugged.

"That is such a stereotype." Harry punched him.

"Booty's not gay, he just likes clothes, fashion. He's got an aesthetic streak. I mean, he wears alligator belts and boots. I expect the belts alone cost three hundred fifty dollars."

"Ex-wife ever see Miss Nasty?" Fair thought that would provoke fireworks.

"She's seen her." Joan's eyes twinkled. "It was not a successful introduction."

"Did they wind up at the same party with the same dress?" Harry laughed.

"In fact, they did. Booty must have called every friend of Annie's he knew to find out what she was wearing. They were in Lexington, and I expect the screams could be heard all the way to Louisville, maybe even down to Memphis. Annie vowed revenge, but only after she'd called Booty

every name in the book and some we'd never heard before."
Joan paused a beat. "Best party I ever attended."

The laughter drew Miss Nasty to the Kalarama box. She
poked her fingers in her various orifices.

"Crude." Pewter wrinkled her black nose.

"Fat." Miss Nasty turned a somersault.

Booty appeared at the in-gate at the other end of the ring
from the Kalarama box. Spying his cavorting pet, he hastened toward her. She stopped, stood up as tall as she could.
She rubbed her chin.

"Miss Nasty, Daddy's coming," Joan jollied her. "Daddy's
wearing a pink shirt to match your pretty dress."

"He'll beat your red ass until your nose bleeds," Pewter, en-
raged at being called fat, predicted.

Miss Nasty extracted something unpleasant from her
nostril, flinging it at Pewter.

The cat lunged forward toward the offending creature,
but Miss Nasty leapt off the rail, scurrying toward one of the
tractors. Skillfully timing her leap, she landed on the back
fender, then reached for the back of the seat and grabbed it
to swing onto the driver's shoulders. He swerved but recovered. He knew Miss Nasty, so he made the best of it.

Booty walked inside the ring. He dangled an enticing
piece of orange. At the first pass of the tractor, Miss Nasty
was tempted. On the second, Booty turned his back on her
to head out of the ring. She succumbed.

Booty swooped her up amid cheers.

"He really is wearing an alligator belt and boots." Harry
gasped.

"You can buy me that for my birthday," Fair suggested.

"I think I'd better buy a lottery ticket first." Harry calcu-
lated the expense of the boots and belt. Then she saucily

said, "My birthday is in five days, but I'll pass on the boots. Pass on the monkey, too."

"*I'll kill that monkey,*" Pewter fumed.

"*You say that about everything,*" the tiger teased.

"*I will!*"

"*You'll have to brave boogers to do it,*" Mrs. Murphy warned.

"*Or worse.*" Tucker appeared solemn.

"*You just wait and see.*" Pewter ignored the teasing.

Harry dropped back to her hands and knees again, looking on the wooden floor of the box. "I swear I'll find your pin, Joan. You know how I get. Don't despair."

2

*T*he air-conditioner hum awakened Harry, who was accustomed to sleeping with the windows open at home, the only sounds being that of the night. Fair, flat on his back, had one arm draped over his massive chest, the other by his side. He slept hard, but like most people in medicine, one ring of the phone and he'd be wide-awake.

Pewter snored slightly as she curled up next to Mrs. Murphy. Tucker, on her side by the bed, didn't lift her head when Harry got up.

However, as their human friend pulled on jeans, T-shirt, socks, and sneakers, Mrs. Murphy and Tucker opened their eyes. Pewter remained dead to the world.

Harry slipped into the bathroom, closed the door, and clicked on the light so as not to wake her husband. She left him a note, which read:

Honey,
Couldn't sleep. Took the truck. I'm going to Barn Five.
I'll probably be back before you wake.

Love,
Miss Wonderful

Then she crossed out "Miss" and wrote above it "Mrs." She propped the note against the mirror, using her makeup bag to hold it.

She clicked off the bathroom light, then felt her way to the hotel-room door. Tucker and Mrs. Murphy, eyes better in the dark than Harry's, walked out with her.

"If you're going, we're going." Tucker blinked, still sleepy.

"Pewter will have a cow." Mrs. Murphy giggled, for the gray cat hated to miss anything, even though she hated to cut short her beauty sleep.

Harry unlocked the door of the F-250, Fair's vet truck, where his medicines, needles, and gauze were locked in a special made-to-order aluminum trunk bolted to the truck bed. Most equine vets used a similar system, since they needed to call on their patients more than their patients called on them. Many a time Fair spread a large plastic sheet on a level part of a pasture and operated on the spot. This ability to act instantly saved lives.

Harry grumbled that they'd spend a fortune in gas driving the eight hours, first to Springfield, home of Kalarama Farm, then on to Shelbyville. They did, but Fair wanted to be able to assist should a crisis occur. Each time they pulled up to the pump, it cost eighty dollars. Harry swooned, then recovered. Fair shrugged, paid the bill, and said the whole world would suffer for depending on oil.

As neither of them had a ready-made solution to this

spectacular global crisis, they kept rolling down Interstate 64.

As the big V8 turned over, the clock on the dash read "one forty-five." Harry adjusted the seat. The truck's captain chairs could go up and down, forward and back, and even alter firmness of the backrest. The pedals could go up and down to adjust to leg length. The truck beeped when one backed up close to any object. Despite sucking gas, the machine thrilled Harry. She drove a 1978 Ford truck, and a few years ago Fair, hoping to win her back, helped her purchase a dually to pull her horse trailer. But her everyday drive was the half-ton pickup, which was a far cry from this tricked-out hunk of metal. However, she loved her old truck. Harry was loath to part with anything that still promised usefulness. Her sock drawer testified to this.

She allowed the motor to warm up, then pulled out of the Best Western parking lot, passed the not-yet-open Wendy's and the tractor dealership she wanted to visit, and turned right on the old main road, Route 60, which connected Louisville to Lexington. Then she turned left at the intersection and drove less than a quarter of a mile to the main parking lot by the practice arena. Charly Trackwell rented stalls in that lower barn. No one stirred, so she drove on the empty paths to Barn Five. She cut the motor and opened the door so Mrs. Murphy could hop out. She lifted Tucker down.

Barn owls flew in and out of the various barns. A whip-poor-will called in the bushes. A horse nickered when she walked into the barn.

Jorge, wide-awake, greeted her as she stepped into the aisle.

"Señora Haristeen."

"Jorge, I hope I didn't disturb you. I couldn't sleep, so I thought I'd check on the horses along with whoever was on watch."

Jorge, in his late thirties, hair already salt and pepper, nodded, a smile on his creased, strong face.

Wordlessly, she followed him as they checked each stall.

"Jorge, how much is Point Guard worth?" She stopped to admire the five-gaited young stallion, who was being introduced to the show world this season. Along with the normal three gaits of walk, trot, canter, Point Guard could do the slow rack and the rack, a specialized gait where the horse lifted his legs high and up. A horse needed an aptitude for this, as well as all the additional training. The effect, when correctly done, was akin to watching a great ballerina leap and seem to hover in the air both effortlessly and endlessly. The rack showed off rhythm, balance, and power.

"Mmm, right now, maybe three hundred thousand." He admired the animal.

Shelbyville would be an important step in Point Guard's career. Joan and Larry hoped as he matured he'd be outstanding, for he had the conformation, action, attitude, and will to win.

Harry marveled that the horses could keep their concentration with thousands of excited humans so close to them that those on the rail could reach out and touch the horses. Of course, if anyone ever did anything so foolish, they'd be thrown out of the Saddlebred world forever. Still, the proximity of the spectators to the competitors was extraordinary and not duplicated in other sports. Football, baseball, hockey, and even basketball kept the fan at a distance from the athlete. Golf and cycling were two of the few sports where a person could get close to the real action. Even in hunter–

jumper classes, humans had been moved farther away from the show ring, except for local shows, where the feeling of closeness, conviviality, and personally knowing the riders and horses still prevailed.

Money changed sports. While it improved spectacle and competition, the fan began to be regarded as a necessary evil. There was money enough in the Saddlebred world if you were good, but the fans were part of the extended family. No matter how big the shows, they kept their hometown feel.

These things flitted through Harry's mind as she studied the big black horse, drowsing in his stall.

"Ah." Jorge smiled. "Big career ahead."

Harry found it difficult to speculate on how quickly the value of a horse could change after even one show, one big show. "Well, if he wins at Louisville, it goes through the roof."

"Not this year. Frederick the Great and Callaway's Senator." He said no more, for those two horses, fully mature and show hardened, would go head to head Saturday night, the last class, the show-stopper class. Charly and Booty rode the two stallions, respectively.

"So if he comes in third, young as he is, that's a huge victory."

"Sí." He nodded. "Sí."

The rumble of a large diesel engine alerted Harry. She stepped out of Barn Five. The motor cut off. Harry couldn't see the truck parked down beside the practice ring. She stepped back into the barn and looked at Jorge.

"Feed," Jorge shrugged.

Tucker and Mrs. Murphy, after ascertaining that no mice

or other vermin could be assaulted, also listened as the motor cut off.

"Let's go," Tucker called to Mrs. Murphy as Jorge walked back into the barn, Harry following.

Tucker, low to the ground, was fast and agile. Mrs. Murphy loved running with the corgi. Both animals possessed curiosity and stamina. Pewter usually spewed an endless stream of complaints. They were glad she was snoring back at the Best Western.

The dewy grass kept the impression of their pawprints. They stopped at the bleacher bench on the eastern side of the practice arena. For many, watching the horses work gave them clues as to how they might fare in their classes.

"Who are those men hopping out of the back of the van?" Tucker, eyes good in the dark, watched the back of a white horse van with green trim.

Mrs. Murphy walked closer. Tucker followed. *"They're young."* She strained to hear, ears forward, but the only sound was their boots tiptoeing into the oldest barn. *"They're Mexican."*

"What are they doing? Maybe they're going to steal horses." Tucker knew humans to be a noisy lot, so if the human animal, especially in numbers, was silent, no good would come of it.

"You don't need that many people to steal a horse." Mrs. Murphy wondered what was going on, too. *"Come on."* She sprinted toward the barn.

Tucker, bigger than the cat, worried that she'd attract attention. She followed but looked for places to duck away.

Mrs. Murphy sauntered into the barn as though she lived there. She checked out the stalls, and as all were wood she could climb up to get out of the way. Just in case.

However, there were barn cats, who immediately tore after her. She ran, because four cats against one is not a pleasing prospect.

"Scram!" the biggest ginger cat screeched.

Mrs. Murphy shot past Tucker, and the corgi turned to keep up with her friend as the barn cats puffed up, stopped running, and whooped their victory.

"See anything?"

"The men are lined up along the wall. Charly Trackwell gave a roll of cash to Ward Findley. Booty Pollard, with Miss Nasty, is there, too."

"Guess it doesn't concern Kalarama or us," Tucker said.

"Guess not. Odd, though."

"Twenty men in the back of a horse van?" Tucker was surprised.

"They looked tired and hungry." Mrs. Murphy wished those barn cats hadn't appeared. She could have listened to what the men were saying.

Harry was glad to see the cat and dog once they were back at Barn Five. "Where were you?"

"Investigating," Tucker replied.

Harry shot Mrs. Murphy a hard glance. "See if I let you off your leash again."

"Pooh," Mrs. Murphy said but thought worse.

Once Harry and the animals had driven off, Jorge briskly trotted to the old barn, just as the big diesel fired up to back out.

3

"What a gorgeous hair dryer." Harry laughed as she and Joan drove along the back roads of Shelbyville in Joan's new Jaguar with its all-aluminum body.

Joan, like Harry, fretted over money. Owning a sports car seemed frivolous, but one day Joan drove into Louisville to run errands and drove out with a richly appointed Jaguar. It was one of the few impulsive things she had ever done. True to form, she suffered a wave of buyer's remorse the next day, which vanished the moment she slid behind the wheel, inhaled the leather scent, and cranked the motor.

"I lost my mind." Joan giggled.

"I need to take a lesson from you." Harry could take being practical to extremes.

"You know what, when you need to let fly, you will. After all, you remarried Fair this spring."

"And look how many years it took me to do it." Harry turned as they passed the back pastures of a farm, the tobacco barns well situated to capture the breezes. "I'm surprised he waited."

"He loves you."

She turned to face Joan. "I have no idea why."

"You're lovable." Joan smiled. "And men want a challenge."

"I provided that." Harry inhaled the thick honeysuckle scent as the long slanted rays of early-morning light reflected off the ground fog in swales over creeks and ponds. She changed the subject. "Did you go to the sheriff about your pin?"

"Yes."

"Mom know?"

"No." Joan hugged a curve, marveling at the car's ability to stick to the road. "She won't notice for a while, because I don't wear the pin every night."

"God, I hope it turns up." She inhaled again, giddy from the odor. "Will Mom have a fit and fall in it?"

"No. She'll look down, fight back the tears, purse her lips. It's worse than being fussed at. The guilt."

"You majored in guilt, all those years of Catholic school." The corner of Harry's mouth turned up.

"I know it! And I still can't rid myself of it. Makes me so mad. Like this car. I earned this car. I work hard. You know I do, and I love driving this thing, but every now and then I think of the suffering in the world and this wave of guilt washes over me. Well, I'm not going to confession over it. I'm not." Her voice was determined.

"I think about suffering, too, but tell me, are we all supposed to suffer? Is that what equality means? We're all dragged down together?" Harry snuggled down in the seat, then sat up straighter. "Any one of those people suffering in the world, if they had the resources, would buy this car. Why spurn happiness? God gave you the chance. You took it."

"Theology by Haristeen." Joan smiled, since she could always count on a good discussion with her friend.

"Logic, not theology. There's precious little happiness in this world. Grab what you can. I don't mean you take away someone else's, but grab what comes to you."

"But that's it, isn't it? If I buy this car I'm polluting the atmosphere. I could send this money to, oh, Uganda and help someone."

"First of all, Joan, that's bullshit. Industry pollutes more than cars. And even if you drove a hybrid, you might not emit as many hydrocarbons, because you'd use less gas and oil, but it would still contribute to global warming. Exhaust is hot regardless of the fuel. You have to drive. When have you ever seen a bus stop out in the country? Right?"

"Right."

"Okay. Furthermore, if you send money to Uganda it will wind up in some corrupt official's pocket. You don't even have to send it to Uganda; think of the millions that disappeared earmarked for the victims of Katrina. Give to charity you can monitor with your own two eyes."

"You got that right." She nodded.

"Every time money changes hands, some sticks. The more people between your dollar and the recipient, the less reaches the recipient. Charity begins at home."

Joan laughed, a big smile crossing her radiant face. "I'm sooo glad I bought this car."

"And in British racing green. Back when auto racing began, those great races over countryside and through cities, each country had its color. Pretty cool, really. The Germans were silver or white or both. France was blue. Italy was red. But British racing green is the coolest."

"Still have your 1978 Ford F-150?"

"My baby." Harry giggled. "Hey, you know I planted those Petit Manseng grapes, don't you?" Harry had hopped to another subject, but Joan was used to it.

"You sent me pictures when you laid out the rows."

"Well, I won't get anything—I mean a good yield—until the third year, but the vines are up and leafy. This is the only time, really, that Fair and I could get away. Did I tell you I snuck out early this morning?"

"Harry, how much coffee have you had?" Joan shook her head in amusement.

"Am I speedy?"

"You and the car."

"Sorry. Too much caffeine, but I have a good reason. Well, sort of a good reason."

"I'm waiting."

"Couldn't sleep. I snuck out, took Fair's truck, and drove over to the fairgrounds. Thought I'd sneak in and see if the watchman was really awake. He was. Jorge. So we checked stalls together, Mrs. Murphy and Tucker ran off, returned, and then I drove back to Best Western. I prudently tore up the note I left Fair, and he's none the wiser."

"He's protective."

"On the one hand, I like it. On the other hand, I don't."

"Harry, you don't always have good sense about danger."

"Getting out of bed is dangerous." Harry didn't take offense at Joan's observation, because it was the truth, but she slid away from total agreement.

"You can't resist a mystery, dangerous or not, so I hope you'll find my pin."

"Is that a challenge?"

"Well—yes."

"Guess I should start calling pawnshops." She paused. "Know what else I forgot to tell you? I'm looking for a young Thoroughbred—the old staying lines, good heavy cannon bone—for Alicia Palmer. She'll pay me to train it as a foxhunter for her. If you see anything out there, let me know." Harry specifically mentioned the old staying lines, the ones that produced great stamina, and a heavy cannon bone, the bone above the hoof in a horse's foreleg. A heavy bone usually indicated a horse wouldn't be subject to hair-line fractures or splints. A steeplechase horse, a three-day eventer, and a foxhunter had to jump. The force per square inch on the foreleg was considerable. A heavy, thick cannon bone was a form of insurance.

"Raced or unraced?"

"Doesn't matter. If it's off the track I usually have to give the animal more time for the drugs to flush out of its system, especially if the animal's been on steroids."

"So much for drug testing."

"Same with human athletes. The more elite athlete can hire a better chemist. We can't stop it, so legalize the stuff. Remember the 2006 Olympics? A crashing bore. They'd weeded out too many people. The public wants the best, and you only get the best with drugs. Simple."

"People can't face the truth."

"Right, so they turn everyone into a liar. I'm not saying drugs that really tear up the body should be legalized, and one shouldn't start these programs—you know, like EPO, where you up the red-blood-cell count with redundant blood—without monitoring by a doctor. And that's another reason to make them legal. Kids in high school start buying this stuff on the black market, and they don't know where they really are in terms of their body's development or chemistry. Doctors can't treat or monitor these substances if people don't come to them, and as long as performance-enhancing drugs are illegal, they won't."

"Harry, we live with such appalling contradictions, I just don't believe people can face the truth—about anything."

"If we made a list of contradictions and you drove in a straight line, we'd reach Nashville before we ran out of subjects."

"Think it was always this way? I mean, do you think it was like this in the sixteenth century?" Joan wondered.

"Yes and no. First off, there were fewer people. Think about it. England had about two and a half million people. There wasn't as much pressure on the environment, and from a political standpoint, there were fewer people to manage or coerce. But were there contradictions? Sure. How about the king being the anointed of God, yet he's a complete idiot? He empties the treasury, destroys the country with ill-advised wars, contracts syphilis from fooling around, and beheads those who can truly challenge his authority. Seems like a big contradiction to me. Or cardinals who amass wealth and earthly powers. Another contradiction. 'Render unto Caesar that which is Caesar's,' et cetera."

"Apart from the lack of good medical care, I envy those people in a way. No TV. No badgering by advertisers. No credit cards."

"The devil invented the credit card." Harry laughed.

Now Joan changed the subject. "You haven't said anything about turning forty."

"Have four more days. Why rush time? It's only August third."

"Harry." Joan's voice dropped, her register of disbelief audible.

"Well, what do you want me to say? Big deal. It's a number."

"Everyone makes it a big deal; it's a turning point."

"I'm ignoring the whole thing."

"Harry, I don't believe you."

"Believe me. I'm not getting sucked into the to-do."

"All right," Joan said without conviction.

Harry changed the subject. "When I was at the barn this morning about two o'clock, it was black as pitch. New moon was on the twenty-seventh, so you know how dark it can be. Well, anyway, I was walking the aisle with Jorge and I heard this big motor, then it cut off. But I didn't hear horses unload. Now, I doubt I would have heard them walk off, but usually someone will whinny."

"Sometimes people bring in horses at night. Less stressful." Joan thought a minute. "Did you hear anything at all?"

"No. I heard the truck come in, a big diesel engine. Heard it cut off. Then maybe ten minutes later, the motor fired up again and the truck drove out, but I didn't see it. You think maybe someone brought in feed or a load of hay?"

"No."

"You're right. They'd still be unloading when I drove out, I expect."

"The hay trucks come early in the morning, but not that early." She paused a long time. "Did Jorge say anything?"

" 'Feed' was all he said."

"But he heard it?"

"Sure. The night was quiet, plus those engines boom."

Joan turned left, roared east, and within fifteen minutes cruised down Shelbyville's Main Street, now one way, which irritated her.

"I know you like mystery." She slowed at the intersection of Sixth Street and Main. "One of Kentucky's most famous murders occurred right there." She pointed. "Used to be the site of the Armstrong Hotel.

"General Henry H. Denhardt, famous in his lifetime in Kentucky, was shot three times by the three Garr brothers. Two hit him in the back, one got him in the back of the head. This was September twentieth, 1937." She pulled over to the curb but left her motor idling. "He crumpled in the doorway of the hotel. Kind of a slimy end for a World War One officer."

"Revenge killing?" Harry, being a Virginian, knew the South well.

"He was accused of killing Verna Garr Taylor. She was a real beauty, according to Dad, who was a teenager at the time. She'd been widowed, and the general—he was about twenty years older—fell wildly in love with her.

"Dad said she was murdered just inside the Henry County line on November sixth, 1936. Said he and his gang of friends even drove to the spot on Highway Twenty-two. It was really a big thing. Made all the national newspapers."

"Did he kill her?"

"Said he didn't, but the evidence pointed to him. He went to trial but got off because the jury deadlocked. Verna's brothers waited close to a year, then avenged their sister."

"Sounds pretty dramatic."

"People still remember. The brothers went to trial. One,

E.S., never made it to the trial because he was put in a sanitarium. Dad said the murder of Verna snapped his mind. He died there within a couple of years, I think."

"Other boys get off?"

"Jack did, because no one could prove he fired a gun. They got off because of self-defense, even though the general was unarmed."

"Rough justice."

Joan frowned for a moment. "Rough justice is better than none."

"I agree there." Harry nodded as Joan shifted into gear and they drove the three minutes it took to reach the fairgrounds.

Once at Barn Five, Joan found Jorge grooming a three-gaited gelding owned by a Kalarama boarder.

He smiled when he saw Joan. "Looking good." He indicated the mare.

"She does. Jorge, when Harry came over here this morning, did you hear a truck pull in?"

"No, señora."

She didn't reply, then smiled and walked the aisle, checking each stall. Harry walked beside her. They didn't speak until emerging on the south side of the barn.

"Maybe he's hard of hearing." Harry couldn't imagine any other explanation.

"He's not," Joan replied.

4

*H*orse people try to get most chores finished before the heat builds up. Lazy, puffy clouds slowly moved west to east, a shimmer could already be detected, and heat wiggled in the air by nine. It would be a scorcher.

The long hoof of the Saddlebred, cultivated for the high-stepping, long-strided animal, ensured shoes would be thrown. In each barn, blacksmiths prized for their skill bent over, hoof on their knees. Heat or not, horses needed shoes. Feed dealers talked to owners, pressing free samples and supplements on them. Delores from Le Cheval, an elegant tailoring establishment, arrived with a gorgeous long navy blue coat for Renata. She left it in the changing room, feeling it would be secure since the Kalarama staff was in evidence. Grooms, handlers, vets, trainers filled the barns; the place hummed like the backstretch at the track.

Harry, Fair, Mrs. Murphy, Pewter, and Tucker sat on an old checkerboard oilcloth under the shade of a hickory. Fair had brought breakfast muffins, jams, and honey, which he spread out on the oilcloth.

"I'll chew through your collar if you chew through mine," Mrs. Murphy offered Pewter.

"But the color of mine looks so good against my fur." The vain gray cat wore a turquoise collar, the leash matching the color.

"You're mental." Tucker watched a swarm of no-see-ums swirl upward, then move along.

Renata DeCarlo drove a new Dodge half-ton, which she parked. Collecting her extra derby and her makeup bag, she walked by the group, stopping to pet Tucker.

"Delores left your new coat in the changing room," Harry told her. "Congratulations on pinning third last night."

"Thanks." Renata smiled. "I needed the workout, and Voodoo gave it to me."

"You're so pretty." The corgi's soft brown eyes scanned the young woman's face.

"I think animals have their own language." Renata, friendly, paused.

"Sit down," Harry offered. "We have hot coffee, lemonade, or iced tea, and I bet if you want to spike it there are any number of people in these barns to help you out."

"Thanks. I'd love a lemonade." Renata smiled at the suggestion of spiking her morning drink and sat on the oilcloth, demurely crossing her legs. "I don't drink."

"Me neither." Harry liked Renata, wondering if someone in her position could ever hope for a fulfilling life.

It wasn't the actress's fault so much as everyone wanting something from her: her body, her time, her money, her work for a good cause. The reality, which eventually smacked every intelligent person cursed by fame, was that few people really wanted *you*. They only wanted what you could do for them.

The cats stared at her. She stared back, then laughed. "Who's the cannonball?"

"Pewter." Fair grinned.

"I am not fat. I have big bones." This had become the gray kitty's refrain over the years.

"And who is the one with the incredible green eyes?"

"Mrs. Murphy. Both of these girls used to work for the federal government." Harry tickled Mrs. Murphy's ears while Pewter kept staring at Renata, trying to decide whether to do something hateful after the cannonball remark.

"In the post office," Fair added. "They helped sort the mail, they rolled the mail carts around, they knew everyone's mailbox."

"Is this their vacation?" she asked.

"No. We quit when a big new post office with lots of rules was built. Before that, the P.O. was a small building with a counter and brass mailboxes." Harry sighed. "It was so cozy. Well, I digress. Sorry. Anyway, new post office, new rules, no cats or dogs in the building."

"I'd leave, too."

"My wife was the postmistress." Fair liked saying "my wife."

"Aren't you kind of young for that?" Renata smiled a gleaming, megawatt smile.

"Uh," Harry faltered, "I'm about forty. Almost," she hastily added.

"Forty for an actress is tough. Roles dry up. Magazines

run articles on the star's fitness routines. It's unbearable. I don't mean turning forty, I mean the way everyone reacts."

"Miss DeCarlo, in your case people will react no matter what your age. The only reason you aren't mobbed around here is this is a horse show, and horse people are different," Harry responded.

"Thank God." She leaned against the trunk. "What wonderful lemonade."

"Mother's recipe, and she said it was her mother's recipe, and so it goes." Harry smiled, pouring more lemonade into Renata's waxed-paper cup. "Where did you learn to ride?"

"Kentucky. Lincoln County. Saw my first Saddlebred before I could walk and, I swear, that was that."

"It's a different seat." Harry mentioned the type of riding. "We ride hunt seat. We foxhunt, so it's not exactly the hunt seat you see in the show ring, but close."

"Never tried."

"It's a big thrill, but anything you love is exciting. Saddlebreds are like ballerinas; I can see why you fell in love."

Booty Pollard sauntered by, dug his boot heels in, and stopped. "Fitting right into the Kalarama family, Renata."

Miss Nasty flipped the bird at Pewter. The monkey wore a light green halter top with a matching short skirt, the green being the same color as Booty's mint-green polo shirt.

Fair stiffened. "Booty, I know you wouldn't want a client like Renata in your barn, now, would you?"

Booty was direct. "I'd kill to have a client like Renata. I'd kill for Renata." He grinned.

"You'd have to," she fired back, which made all of them laugh, for Booty could take a joke on himself.

"Pay attention to me." Miss Nasty clenched her jaws together.

"Drop dead," Pewter replied to the monkey, which set off more chatter.

"Coffee? Iced tea? Lemonade?" Harry shaded her eyes as she looked up at Booty; he was easy on the eyes.

"Nothing, thanks." He noticed Ward Findley leading a quality black mare by the practice arena. He was heading to his green and white horse van. She wore a green blanket piped in white, Ward's colors. "Nice horse. Must be one Ward's carrying to a farm. You know, he does a pretty good business vanning horses. Ever notice how Ward always sticks his whip in his back pocket or his boot? He's kind of like a guy who isn't a very good polo player, so he wears his whites two hours before the match and two hours afterward." He guffawed. "Hey, he's not on food stamps, so Ward's contributing to the economy." He shrugged.

"Right," Fair succinctly agreed.

Mrs. Murphy watched the beautiful mare step right into the van. She said in passing, *"Bet she's expensive. And from the same line as Queen Esther, too. Same head conformation."*

A few strides behind Ward walked Charly, who wasn't paying much mind to Ward. One wouldn't have known Charly was a trainer until it was time to ride. He wore deck shoes, khaki pants, a solid white T-shirt of high-priced cotton. A ribbon belt, deep blue with a red pinstripe, added a little color.

"Mr. Prep." Booty indicated Charly. "You know, it's going to give me great pleasure to beat his ass Saturday night. I'll grant you Frederick the Great is a good horse and Charly will get the most out of him, but Callaway's Senator is at the top of his game. I'm going to cream Charly."

"What about Larry?" Harry asked.

"Next year—and who knows how many years after that—

Point Guard will rule. But not this year. This is Senator's year. Last class Saturday night, and I'm telling you to put your money on me because I'll ride right over him. Hey, after the show I might just punch out his lights for good measure. Can't stand the bastard. Excuse my French, ladies." He paused, then smiled. "But you've heard worse." He wanted to see if Renata would react, since he figured she and Charly had been lovers. There was too much emotion when Renata quit him, and once he settled down Charly was too nonchalant.

"Charly won't be a pushover Saturday night." Renata betrayed little.

"I'm going to make him eat dirt," Booty promised.

Mrs. Murphy observed the high-spirited man. *"If he hates Charly so much, he didn't act like it early this morning."*

"Hypocrite," Tucker remarked.

"Or a good actor." Mrs. Murphy lifted her silky eyebrows, as Miss Nasty, suddenly silent, listened intently.

"I hate that you two went off without me," Pewter huffed.

"Wake you up in the middle of the night? Not me," Tucker replied.

"Ditto." Mrs. Murphy leaned on the dog.

"I can wake up." Pewter lifted her chin.

"Yes, you can, and you're mean as snakeshit." Mrs. Murphy laughed.

"How crude." Pewter had decided she liked Renata anyway, so she sat in her lap.

All heads turned as they heard a commotion from Barn Five.

"Better see what's going on. Excuse me, ladies. Fair." Booty trotted toward the noise, the monkey on all fours on his shoulder.

Moments later, Larry walked out of Barn Five. Booty turned to fall in step with him.

Pewter jumped off Renata's lap as Larry and Booty strode up.

"Renata." Larry, ashen-faced, stopped to catch his breath. "Did you move Queen Esther?"

Joan, wide-eyed, walked up behind Larry.

"No," Renata replied.

"She's gone."

"How can she be gone? The place is full of people! How can my horse be gone?" Renata was one step from a hissy fit.

Joan, quick to appreciate the potential for a major scene, said, "Renata, the first place we all need to look is Charly Trackwell's. That will upset you, but I wouldn't put it past him to move the mare back in his barn."

"How could he do that? How could he do that and no one saw him?" She was shaking.

"That's just it. They probably did. It's broad daylight. People assumed you'd patched it up and gone back to him." Joan, thinking fast, put her hand under Renata's elbow. "Let's have a look."

The small entourage hurried into Barn Three. Charly, talking to Carlos, his head groom, swiveled his head toward them. "Did you come to your senses, Renata?"

"Do you have Queen Esther?" Renata asked, voice hard.

"See for yourself."

"He's too cool," Tucker mumbled.

"Is, isn't he?" Pewter agreed.

The group looked into each stall. No Queen Esther.

Charly sarcastically directed this to Booty: "Why don't you all troll Booty's barn? Maybe find some hair dye while you're at it. Man can't stand to go gray."

"You'll pay for that," Booty growled.

"Not as much as you will. Saturday night, brother, you'll be dog meat. In the meantime, get out of my barn. All of you!"

Tucker lingered, then followed the others. *"He's enjoying this."*

"Some people need a competitor, a rival, an enemy for their life to have meaning." The tiger cat studied humans.

"And some people like to see others squirm," Pewter, in Harry's arms, called down to the dog.

Larry flipped open his cell to call the sheriff, who was at the bank drive-in window across from the show grounds on the Route 60 side. Within four minutes he met them at Barn Five.

Cody Howlett, young to be a sheriff, paid close attention to everything. His deputies scoured all the barns as he took notes from Larry, Renata, Manuel, Jorge, Booty, Carlos, and other grooms and trainers.

He stopped for a moment when he was questioning Joan. "You all are having some hard luck here with losing things."

Larry, arms folded across his chest, said, "Joan, what's Cody talking about?"

"I lost Grandma's pin."

"Does your mother know?" Larry said the first thing that came into his head.

"Well, no. I'm hoping this will resolve itself before that happens."

While the humans were speaking to Sheriff Howlett, Mrs. Murphy, Pewter, and Tucker investigated the empty stall, door open. All three sneezed.

"Shoe polish." Tucker's eyes watered.

"Or hair dye." Pewter's eyes watered and she sneezed again.

"The humans can't smell it. The stall is clean. No evidence to them," Mrs. Murphy noted.

"Even if they could smell, the scent will dissipate fast as the heat comes up." Tucker inhaled again, sneezing violently, little bits of crushed cedar bedding flying around.

"Someone walked that mare out of here in front of everyone." Pewter appreciated the boldness of the enterprise.

"They did, but he or she knows the Kalarama routine." Tucker was astonished at all this.

Mrs. Murphy closed her eyes as the cedar dust lifted up. Once she opened them, she said, *"He knows the routine, yes. But he stood in here pretending to groom Queen Esther when he was actually dyeing her. That had to be how he got away with it."*

"No way," Pewter disagreed. *"Someone would notice an entire horse changing color."*

"Wasn't the entire horse. Fitted light blankets are on some of the horses. He'd only have to do the neck and legs," Mrs. Murphy replied.

At once all three said, *"The black horse being loaded onto the van."*

"Under everyone's nose." Tucker sneezed again.

5

*W*atching a wind come from the west, one can see trees bend, then calculate how long before the wind arrives. Mrs. Murphy, Pewter, and Tucker watched the news of Queen Esther's kidnapping travel from barn to barn like the wind. People moved quickly from one to another. The noise level rose. Then the owners, trainers, grooms, blacksmiths, and vets emerged from their barns to stand in the sunlight and stare at Barn Five. A few walked over to offer help and sympathy to Renata, Joan, and Larry.

"The good thing about Queen Esther walking off is we're off those damned leashes." Mrs. Murphy sat on a Kalarama tack trunk.

Paul Hamilton drove up in his cream-colored Mercedes E. He got out, appearing calm, and walked into the barn.

Joan, in the aisle talking to Manuel and Jorge, felt relief when her father stepped into the barn.

"Boys." He nodded to the two men. "We've got twenty minutes before the reporters swarm over us from Louisville. Forty-five before they come on from Lexington." He pushed his square-rimmed glasses up on his nose. "And I reckon some of those entertainment reporters will show up, too."

Joan, her father's daughter, which meant she could see the big picture long before others even squinted at a blurry outline, replied, "Daddy, we were just discussing that. I say we take them to the empty stall, let them shoot their footage, then park them in the hospitality room for more questions. Won't hurt for people to see the ribbons and photographs hanging up there."

"Where's Larry?"

"Working horses. If we let this get us off track, we'll lose more than Queen Esther."

He nodded, radiating confidence. "Well, it's a hell of a mess, but I expect the Kalarama name will stick. No such thing as bad publicity."

Joan knew when her father was trying to shore her up. "I hope you're right."

"Where's Renata?" Paul half-expected her to be emoting full force.

"She's walking from barn to barn, checking every stall."

Just then, Harry came around the end stall of the aisle on her hands and knees.

"What you doing there, Shorty?" Paul, despite all, was amused at the sight.

"I wanted to check the stalls and aisles before more people came through. You never know, the thief might have dropped something." She stood up, brushing off her knees.

"Found you have flashlights stuck in tack trunks and on ledges."

"It's not Shelbyville if we don't enjoy at least one big storm and lose power," Paul informed her as he pushed his glasses back up to the bridge of his nose.

Mrs. Murphy gracefully jumped off the tack trunk to return to Queen Esther's stall. Tucker, lying down in front of the trunk, and Pewter, snoozing on a director's chair next to the trunk, roused themselves to follow.

Manuel, tack in hand, baseball cap pushed back on his head, suggested, "Show them Larry working horses." He meant the reporters.

"Good idea." Joan smiled as Manuel kept walking toward a stall, Jorge behind him.

"Jorge, you make sure that every horse in this barn shines like patent leather." Paul put his hands in his pants pockets.

"Sí." Jorge left, calling out some orders to the other men.

"They always do." Joan loved her father, but sometimes when he butted in, it worked on her nerves. "Is Momma upset?"

"She's been on the phone to her sisters." That meant she was upset.

Joan bit her tongue, because Frances would be even more upset when she found out about the pin.

As the humans kept talking in the aisle, Tucker dug a few spots to see if there was anything under the cedar shavings.

"Scent's fading." Pewter curled her upper lip toward her nose, which helped gather what odor there was.

"The cedar shavings are overpowering." Tucker sat on her haunches. *"I should have thought of that!"*

"The cedar shavings are always overpowering. What's the big deal?" Pewter twitched her tail.

"*The big deal,*" Tucker was irritated, "*is that we were minutes behind the deed. The dye smell was still potent.*" Tucker stated what was obvious to her.

"*You're right. But who dyed Queen Esther, who walked her out the back of Barn Five to hand her off to Ward? We know he took the horse.*" Mrs. Murphy swept her whiskers forward.

"*Did he know he was taking stolen goods?*" Pewter wondered.

"*I expect he did, but let's go to Charly's barn first,*" Tucker suggested, and before the last syllable left her mouth, the cats shot out of the stall, bits of cedar shavings hitting the corgi in the face. "*Hey!*" Tucker called after them as she roared out of the stall, soon catching up.

The three animals scooted around trainers, riders, and grooms between barns, only slowing down if the humans were mounted or leading a horse. At only ten-fifteen, August's sultry reputation was well earned.

By the time they reached Barn Three by the practice arena, Tucker's pink tongue hung out. She stuck her head in a water bucket for dogs that was tucked in the corner of the barn, as there's no such thing as a horseman without a dog. The cats, on their hind legs, also drank.

"*Hotter here than in Virginia.*" Pewter panted.

"*It is. At home we're by the mountains, and the ocean's not that far away,*" Tucker thoughtfully replied. "*There's usually a cool breeze.*"

"*From our farm it's one hundred forty miles—well, first you run into the Chesapeake Bay if you draw a straight line, but still, almost the same, to big water,*" Mrs. Murphy stated. She thought of the Atlantic Ocean as big water.

"*How do you know that?*" Pewter doubted the tiger.

"*Because I read the map with Mom. If you draw a straight*

line from Crozet east, you wind up just below Point Lookout, where the Potomac River pours into the Chesapeake Bay. If you crossed the water you'd wind up at Assateague Island, and that's the Atlantic Ocean. Okay, so it's more than one hundred forty miles to the Atlantic, but it's not all that far to where the river meets the bay. Even though we're about the same latitude as here, our weather's different. Anyway, that's what Mom says, and she cares about the weather."

"Will you two shut up? Let's get to work," Tucker commanded.

Neither cat wished to take orders from a dog, but Tucker was right, so they fanned out, alert to any possibility.

Mrs. Murphy, claws like tiny daggers, climbed up the side of a stall to walk along the joists overhead.

Coming in the opposite direction, the large ginger cat in charge of the barn stopped, thrashed his tail vigorously, eyes wide. "What are you doing in my barn!"

Below, Pewter heard the challenge just as the rest of the barn-cat crew emerged from the hospitality room.

Tucker, large enough to scare them, bared her fangs so the cats scattered to encircle Pewter. Tucker was on to that.

Overhead, Mrs. Murphy loudly answered the ginger cat. "We're looking for clues about the stolen horse. We figure Charly had the most incentive."

"Wasn't in my barn." The ginger allowed his fur to settle down, but the tip of his tail swayed.

"No, she wasn't, but we saw her being loaded onto Ward's van. Do you work for Charly?"

"No. I work for the fairgrounds," the fellow replied.

Mrs. Murphy checked where a stall corner was, so she could back down just in case he decided to fight. Looked like he was calming down, so she relaxed a bit.

"Why do you care about the horse?"

"Kalarama. I'm," she told a white lie, *"a Kalarama cat. If anything unusual happens, please tell me. I'm in Barn Five. Doesn't have to be about a horse. Could be anything, you know, sort of strange."*

Tucker walked beside Pewter, the other barn cats eyeing them with suspicion from a distance. The corgi stuck her head in a wastebasket outside a stall. Nothing.

She repeated this, putting her head in a red grooming bucket.

"Tucker, you're just looking for chicken, trying to pretend you're really looking for clues." Pewter taunted the dog.

"In the first bucket I smelled yerba maté tea, health-food-bar wrappers, orange peels, and needles that had contained Banamine." She named a horse tranquilizer. *"In this grooming bucket I smell cocaine in the little green tin marked Bag Balm."*

That shut up Pewter, who became more alert. She even climbed up the stall sides to peer in, then she backed down.

The last garbage bucket did have chicken bones, but Tucker resisted.

"Nothing here," Tucker called up to Mrs. Murphy.

"Try the hospitality room," Mrs. Murphy called down. *"The humans don't use it until showtime."*

Minutes later, Tucker and Pewter emerged from the resplendent navy and red room.

"Big fat zero," Pewter called up.

"Don't talk about yourself that way." Tucker's voice filled with mock concern.

"Bubble butt. Tailless wonder," Pewter shot back, but she was grateful Tucker escorted her, keeping the other cats at bay.

"Thanks for letting us visit your barn. I'm Mrs. Murphy, by the way." The tiger cat watched her two friends below.

"Spike." He smiled, revealing that his left front fang had been knocked out.

Mrs. Murphy hastily backed down a stall corner to drop in front of the cat and dog. *"Come on."*

"We aren't going through every barn, are we?" Pewter, alarmed, raised her voice. *"It's already nasty hot."*

"Yes." Mrs. Murphy ignored her, and they marched over to Ward's barn. His green and white hospitality suite was more modest.

They repeated the process of checking each grooming tray, each wastebasket or open trunk.

Again nothing.

They walked up to Barn One, where Booty Pollard rented one half of the barn. His colors, orange and white, were uncommon in the horse world, but he'd graduated from the University of Texas and proudly used the Longhorn colors. Miss Nasty's empty cage, filled with toys, sported a limp orange pennant with a white "T." The cage sat outside the entrance to the suite, as it needed a good airing out. Miss Nasty was not a good housekeeper, nor was her namesake.

Mrs. Murphy prowled above the horses while Pewter and Tucker worked below.

Although hot, Pewter kept at her task. She was interested since this involved another animal. Usually she and her friends accompanied Harry as she tried to help another human. Pewter loved horses, so she continued to brave the heat. She sauntered into the hospitality tent, where blue ribbons hung from massive longhorns at the top of the canopy. The whole top of the hospitality room was filled with blue ribbons. On the second row, below photos of horses and clients, red ribbons were neatly displayed on clear fish wire strung below the photos. Immediately below that were the yellow ribbons for third place.

Some trainers grouped the ribbons by horse, but Booty grouped by position, another manifestation of his eye for design and color.

Pewter flipped up a tack-trunk hook, but she couldn't lift the lid. She moved to a small bridle box next to the massive trunk, and that was easy to open.

"Bingo." She dashed outside. *"Found it."*

Mrs. Murphy climbed down as Tucker ran into the room. Inside the bridle box were four bottles of hair dye, neatly stacked.

"It's the color of Booty's hair." Mrs. Murphy wondered why people thought other people couldn't tell.

"Four bottles." Pewter was excited. *"Two empty."*

"You've got a point there." Mrs. Murphy was intrigued. *"We've got Booty and Charly supposedly hating each other but best friends at two in the morning. Ward loads Renata's horse. Booty's got the dye."*

"We don't know that was Renata's horse." Tucker watched as Pewter closed the bridle box.

"No, we don't, but the horse that Ward loaded could have been a double for Queen Esther except for color," Mrs. Murphy replied. *"That horse moved like Queen Esther."*

"Charly trained Queen Esther. Don't you think he'd know the horse we saw was her by the way she moved? He wasn't that far behind Ward." Mrs. Murphy pricked her ears forward.

"I'm glad it doesn't have anything to do with us. Not our horses." Tucker could imagine Harry's distress if someone stole one of her beloved horses.

"It will." The tiger heard footsteps approaching. *"Mother won't sit still while Joan and Larry are in trouble."*

"Fair will keep her straight." Tucker recalled the many times before they remarried that Fair tried to rein in Harry's curiosity.

"She's rubbing off on him more than he's rubbing off on her. Mark my words," Pewter observed.

Tucker sighed, eyes riveted on the doorway to the room, but the person walked by. *"Two humans to protect. They can't run fast, they can't smell worth a damn, they can't see very well in the dark, and they always think they know more than they do."*

"Ignorance is bliss." Pewter saucily tossed this off as they walked back to Barn Five.

"Or death." Mrs. Murphy injected that somber note.

6

*I*mpeccably though casually attired in her working riding clothes, Renata DeCarlo answered questions from reporters as she groomed her gray gelding, Shortro. Voodoo stood in the next stall, observing everything. Not that she groomed her horses regularly, but it made good copy. Renata understood good copy. Dreadful as this theft was, she would get something out of it. Shortro initially shied from the minicam, but then he adjusted. He had a good mind.

Joan organized flight control, since media people jammed Barn Five. She answered questions, too. When the media became too great she walked some down to the practice ring. Others shot the grandstand, panning to the show ring, where the fairgrounds crew watered all the flowers in the raised center section used by officials and judges. The organ, a staple of big Saddlebred shows, was covered. The maintenance activity at noon yielded colorful footage. Like so many middle-class people regardless of background and race, the reporters didn't "see" laborers, the result was the same: they missed information by not questioning the barn help, which was mostly Mexican.

Fair, helping another vet who was shorthanded that day in Barn Two, ignored the stream of people traipsing through the aisle, notebooks or minicams in hand. What no one could ignore was that none of these people had a clue about how to behave around horses. The nervousness of grooms and trainers was translated by the media as anxiety over the theft of Queen Esther. It never occurred to them that their presence fed anxiety. Much as a sweating, hard-pressed groom might secretly wish for a horse to kick one of these intrusive twits out of the barn, the ensuing lawsuit would make the happiness short-lived. Now, a little nip on an arm or shoulder probably wouldn't provoke a lawsuit, and that would please both horse and groom.

Renata left Shortro. The reporters followed like ducklings behind momma duck.

"You all need to ask your last questions. The next group is ready to come on in." Joan, back from the grounds tour for the first group, smiled when she said this. Of course, what she wanted to say was, "Get your sorry selves out of here. You're troubling my horses and tiring me out." However, she kept smiling.

A pretty woman from the ABC affiliate in Louisville stepped outside into the light as Renata stood in the barn doorway, which was quite wide. The actress was framed, a prudent choice by one who lived in front of the camera, and the reporter knew this shot would be picked up all over the country. Her cameraman knew it, too, obviously.

"Miss DeCarlo, would you like to make a film about a Saddlebred someday, a Saddlebred *Seabiscuit*?"

"Wouldn't that be wonderful? Yes, I'd love to." Renata beamed into the camera. "Screenwriters, you heard it here first."

The reporter, raven-haired, then asked, "Have you been happy with your most recent roles?"

Renata's face set for a split second, because her last two films had been high-budget stinkers, then relaxed. "No," she honestly replied.

"Bad scripts?" The reporter kept fishing.

Renata looked down at her paddock boots, specially made for her by Dehner in a peanut-brittle color rarely seen these days. Then she looked up, thoughtfulness on her face. "You can always find a reason why something doesn't work. You can always point the finger at someone else. The real reason my last two movies haven't been box-office hits," she paused for effect, "is I'm getting away from what's really important."

The reporter was sucked right in, giving Renata her forum. "Would you tell us what that is?"

"I want to make films about real people facing real problems. You'd be surprised at how difficult that is. No one wants to make those kind of films." She paused again, then complimented the reporter. "That's why your idea for a film about Saddlebreds is, forgive the expression, on the money."

Renata stepped back into the aisle, into the shadows, and Joan stepped into the light. "Thank you all." She beckoned for the next group to come in, determining that this would be the last. Commotion takes its toll on horses, many of whom would show tonight.

Joan was a horsewoman: horses first, people second.

Harry retreated to the last stall Kalarama rented. If Joan needed her, she'd tell her, so she stayed out of the way. Astonished at how Renata had manipulated the media, how polished and poised she'd been in the face of boring questions, Harry realized how shrewd Renata was. She also thanked the good Lord that she wasn't a public figure.

Mrs. Murphy, Pewter, and Tucker tagged along.

At the south side of Barn Five, Harry started to step outside, when she noticed all the hands of Kalarama in heated discussion with the Mexican grooms of Barn Four. They stood in a clot between the two barns.

Her Spanish was the high-school variety, but she knew horseman's Spanish. She listened intently.

Manuel, arms folded across his chest, shook his head; Jorge, towel thrown over his shoulder, seconded the stable manager.

Harry couldn't pick up all of it, but what she did hear was a slender young man from Barn Four repeat that he saw nothing. Then Jorge reminded Manuel that the watches were over by nine in the morning. No one was on watch duty when the horse was stolen.

Manuel again challenged the others by demanding to know who walked Queen Esther out of the stall. The horse didn't open the door and walk herself.

The men's voices grew higher in pitch; they spoke faster. All she could figure was accusations had been made, but she did hear loud and clear an older, gray-haired man say to

Manuel that whoever walked out Queen Esther worked for Kalarama. No other explanation.

Manuel threw up his hands, stalking off toward the practice arena.

Harry took a deep breath. She checked her watch. One-thirty, and the night show was five and a half hours away. If people watched the five o'clock news before driving to Shelbyville, they'd see Renata, the empty stall, Joan, Larry, Charly Trackwell, Booty Pollard, Ward Findley, other trainers, owners, and riders, and this place would be pandemonium.

"Pandemonium," she whispered, her animals looking up when she spoke. "You all know about Pan."

"I don't." Pewter wanted to get in the shade.

"The satyr—half god, half goat. He plays the double pipes." Mrs. Murphy usually read whatever Harry was reading by draping over her neck or on the pillow behind her.

As if understanding them, Harry knelt down to pet her friends. "When Pan plays his pipes, all creatures forget their tasks; they play and frolic the way goats play and frolic. Cut a caper. 'Caper' means 'goat.' Well, anyway, so far so good, but sometimes Pan plays a different tune and all creatures become frightened, rumors fly, they run around and bump into one another, and no good comes of it. That's pandemonium."

Harry was prescient, but even Harry couldn't have imagined the events of that Thursday night.

7

*B*y six that evening, large cumulus clouds began piling up in the western sky. White though those clouds were, the oppressive heat and the odd stillness of the air hinted at a later thunderstorm.

The flurry of reporters and camera crews had left for long languid lunches. A few decided to stay for the evening show, since the footage might be exciting and they could string out the story for two days. Fans were filling up the grassy parking lots; junior riders preparing for their first class betrayed a mixture of nervousness, arrogance, and bad makeup.

Although Springfield was only forty-five minutes away from Shelbyville thanks to improved roads, Joan and Larry kept a room at the Best Western in case they couldn't get back to the farm in time to change for the evening.

People dressed up at night, Saturday evening culminating

in their finest outfits. Given the heat, women wore linen dresses or even shorts, but color coordination mattered, as did hair, nails, and jewelry. As for the men, some wore jackets and ties, others fought the heat with Ralph Lauren Polo shirts, light pants, loafers without socks. If a man wore jeans in the evening it usually signified he was a groom. The trainers dressed up; it was an indication of success.

Renata understood this, just like she understood that less is more. Her makeup, so perfect as to be nearly undetectable, especially to the male eye, accentuated her cheekbones, her high coloring. Attention was heaped on her with expressions of sympathy and concern. Despite her hardship, this was not entirely unwelcome.

A stream of well-wishers, like ants at a picnic, trudged to Barn Five. A few tacky ones asked for autographs, but most were horse people, so asking for an autograph from another horse person would cast doubt on one's seriousness as a horse person. However, horsemen did bring on their coattails family, friends, and almost friends, all of whom were dying to meet the beautiful movie star. In having to choose whether to try Renata's patience or land on the bad side of relatives and people one sees every day, most people elected to please their friends.

Renata exuded graciousness.

Joan marveled at it as she checked the horses and conferred with Larry, Manuel, and Jorge. There were bits to be discussed. What if a horse had a lackluster workout? Tack was inspected for spotless sheen. Kalarama horses had to be perfect. Any horse could have a fabulous night or an off night, but a Kalarama horse looked incredible regardless of the result in the ring. The horses were full-blown personalities, often more vivid than the humans on their backs. They knew it was an important show. They wanted to look their best.

The cats and dogs—for Cookie had returned for a night of socializing—kept out of everyone's way. Tucker informed Cookie of what they'd learned in the other barns as well as what they'd smelled in Queen Esther's stall.

"If only Joan knew." Cookie cocked her head, watching Joan deal with yet another gawker. *"Can't smell a thing, poor woman."* Cookie sighed. *"Well, she could smell a skunk, but not the hair dye. And to think you found the hair dye!"*

"I found it." Pewter puffed out her chest.

"We don't know for certain that Booty Pollard is in on this." Mrs. Murphy avoided jumping to conclusions. After all, someone could have used his hair-dye stash. Someone who knew him very well. Or he could have used it on his own hair. The horse thief could have bought a bottle of hair dye as easily as someone else.

"Piffle." Pewter, irritated, half-closed her lustrous chartreuse eyes.

The crush of people drove the animals outside between barns. Horses walked to the practice ring, riders raced into changing rooms, but still, it was better than the masses trooping through Barn Five. There was nothing Joan and Larry could do about it. Renata was a client—if only for twenty-four hours. Her horse had been stolen, big news at any show.

As the half hour before the first class at seven P.M. approached, people filtered out to find good seats. The class, ladies five-gaited, was usually hotly contested. No one wished to miss it, especially since mastering the rack and slow rack demanded even more skill than walk, trot, canter. The horses sighed gratefully in the relative quiet. They'd be fired up enough when they walked into the ring, for the winners, like all performers, came to life in front of a crowd.

"God." Joan rolled her eyes as the last of the visitors waddled out.

"I hope He's watching over Shelbyville," Harry laconically noted as they stepped outside.

Fair looked west, the direction in which Harry was looking. "Dark."

Joan, too, glanced westward. "Sure is. I expect when it hits it will rattle the fillings in your teeth."

As they talked at the end of the barn, Manuel led out Zip, the horse whose stage name was Flight Instructor. The gelding was a little girthy; Manuel couldn't tighten the girth all at once. He would walk a few paces, then stop and hike it up a notch. He handed Zip over to Larry, who held the gelding as Darla Finestein, a client, mounted up.

A red grooming rag flapped from Jorge's jeans' hip pocket as he slipped between the barns, heading toward the practice arena while the others trooped to the show ring.

"Let's go." Tucker followed Jorge.

"Too many people. I'm repairing to the hospitality room," Pewter announced.

Cookie stuck to Tucker. Mrs. Murphy watched as Pewter disappeared into the barn entrance, then the tiger hurried after the dogs.

Jorge heard the organ play and the announcer begin his patter for this evening's events. He ducked behind Barn Three. Moving faster, Jorge entered the parking lot, then hopped into the green and white horse van parked in the lot closest to the practice arena.

The animals dashed under the van.

Ward Findley's voice could be heard. "Good work."

"Gracias," Jorge replied, then lightly leapt out of the open side door of the van, ignoring the ramp. As he quickly walked away, Mrs. Murphy, first out from under the van, saw Jorge jam a white envelope into his hip pocket after pulling out the grooming rag. He slung that over his shoulder.

The two dogs came out as Ward casually walked down the ramp.

"Like walking a gangplank," Cookie said, her Jack Russell voice a trifle loud.

Ward, halfway down the ramp, heard Cookie. "What are you doing here? And you, forgot your name." He noted Tucker, then laughed. "You two spying on me?"

Mrs. Murphy kept after Jorge. She turned to see Ward bending over, petting both the dogs. Since they knew their way around, she didn't return but continued to stalk Jorge, who was kind to animals. She liked him. Whatever was in his hip pocket bulged a little. He walked to the south side of Barn Five, then sauntered up the aisle. He opened a stall door, walked inside, and began preparing a dark bay for the second class, show pleasure driving open, whistling as he worked.

By the time the dogs returned to Barn Five, both Pewter and Mrs. Murphy had been put back in their collars and were being carried to the Kalarama box. Neither cat looked thrilled.

The dogs followed Joan when she called them.

Once at the box, Cookie declared, *"Ward's nice. He scratched our ears and told us to go home."*

"He may be nice, but he's up to no good." Mrs. Murphy sat in Harry's lap as the first horse, a pale chestnut, stepped into the ring. The middle-aged lady astride looked grim until Charly, her trainer, yelled, "Smile."

Paul and Frances slipped into the box.

"Perfect timing." Paul laughed as he held the chair for Frances.

Fair entered the box; he'd been sewing up a cut for a horse in Barn One. The trainer found Fair since he couldn't get his vet there on time. The horse was bleeding profusely, even though the cut wasn't serious. However, it was serious enough that the deep-liver chestnut, a gorgeous color, wouldn't be competing this week.

"You've got blood all over you. Are you all right?" Frances opened her purse for a handkerchief, which she handed to Fair.

Frances's purse contained a host of ameliorative pills, handkerchiefs, plus a small bottle of her perfume.

"Thank you, Mrs. Hamilton. Eddie Falco's gelding sliced a deep 'V' right in front of his hoof. He somehow managed this feat between the practice ring and the barn." Fair half-smiled.

Paul folded his arms across his chest. "You never know, do you?"

"Not with horses." Fair put his arm around his wife.

"Not with people." Joan laughed.

"Well, let's hope someone finds Renata's horse so we can have some peace." Frances popped a mint in her mouth. "And that the horse is safe."

"I'm surprised she hasn't received a ransom note," Harry said.

The others stared at her, then Paul spoke. "That's an interesting thought."

No one said much after that, for the class held everyone's attention.

One by one the contestants trotted through the in-gate and circled the ring at a flashy trot. The class was filled except for one contestant, Renata DeCarlo. Out of the corner of her eye, Joan saw Larry on one side, Manuel on the other, running alongside Renata, who wore her new Le Cheval navy coat. She sat on Shortro for the three-year-old three-gaited stake. The stake was three hundred dollars, but the real incentive was for a young horse to show well.

When the two entered the ring, a roar rose that shook the roof of the grandstand. Shortro thought it was for him and gave the performance of his young life.

Frances, enthralled by the crowd's enthusiasm as well as the drama, clasped her hands together. She turned for an instant to study Joan. "Where's Grandmother's lucky pin? You usually wear it for this class."

Joan flinched. Another roar from the crowd distracted her mother.

A rumble distracted them for a moment, too.

Every trainer on the rail with a client in this class turned westward. Neither Charly nor Booty had a rider up, but Ward did—a nervous rider, too.

Pewter wailed, *"I hate thunderstorms."*

"Weenie." Mrs. Murphy watched the horses fly by—chestnuts of all hues, seal browns, patent-leather blacks, one paint, gray Shortro with Renata aboard—their tails flowing, their manes and forelocks unfurling.

A flash of lightning caused Paul to twist around and glance upward. "Won't be long."

Fortunately, the judge didn't want to be struck by lightning, either, so he began pinning the class. Two horses remained. The red ribbon fluttered in the hand of the judge's assistant.

When the announcer called out the second-place horse, the judge then signified Renata for first, and the crowd exploded. Shortro trotted to the judge, and the sponsor of the class held up an impressive silver plate. Manuel hustled into the ring to collect the plate as the sponsor then pinned the ribbon on Shortro's bridle. He stood still for it, rare in itself.

Then the muscular fellow gave a victory lap in which his happiness exceeded Renata's. He'd won at Shelbyville.

As they exited the arena, a tremendous thunderclap sent horses and humans scurrying. Shortro held it together, calmly walking into Barn Five. Harry noticed Shortro's un-flappable attitude and thought to herself, "He has the mind for hunting."

Renata slid off and hugged her steady gelding, tears running down her face as photographers snapped away.

The party was just beginning. Manuel took Shortro back to his stall. Renata followed. The second his bridle was off, she gave him the little sweet carrots he adored.

After answering questions, including ones from yet another TV reporter, lights in her eyes, Renata left the stall. She figured Shortro deserved to be left alone.

As Renata walked to the changing room, Pewter, puffed up like a blowfish, zoomed by her in the opposite direction.

"Afraid of thunder?" Renata laughed.

"It's horrible! Murphy, where are you?" Pewter called for her friend, who had turned the corner to go into a stall to answer nature's call.

"What's the matter with you?" Mrs. Murphy asked.

Before the wild-eyed gray cat could answer, a barn-shaking blast of thunder hit overhead; the lightning was so bright it hurt the eyes, and the rain fell so heavily one couldn't see through it. But even the tremendous noise of the thunder and the rain couldn't drown out the bloodcurdling scream that came from the changing room.

8

*T*he searing lightning was followed by another bolt, which hit a transformer nearby. People, huddled in the barns away from the lashing rain, heard the sizzle, then pop, followed by another tremendous clap of thunder. Pink and yellow sparks from the transformer flew up in the darkness.

Another scream ripped through Barn Five.

Mrs. Murphy, who could see well enough, called to Pewter, *"Come with me."*

"No."

"What did you see?"

"Go see for yourself. The changing room." Pewter climbed up the side of the stall, backing down to be with one of the Kalarama fine harness horses. Each needed the other's company.

Tucker and Cookie, at the other end of Barn Five, ran

like mad upon hearing the first scream. They reached the crowded hospitality room. Just entering the hospitality room they could smell fresh blood. They threaded their way through many feet. To make matters worse, people couldn't see. They bumped into one another. They were scared.

Joan called out, "We'll have a light in just a minute, folks. Keep calm."

The buzz of worry filled the air.

Harry kept a little pocket light on her truck key chain. She pressed it. A bright blue beam, tiny and narrow, guided Joan to the Kalarama tack trunks outside the hospitality room. Harry flipped up the heavy lid while Joan pulled out a large yellow nine-volt flashlight.

Larry called in the darkness, "Joan, are you all right?"

"Yes. I'm getting a flashlight."

Fair, who was with Larry, then called, "Harry?"

"I'm with Joan. Where are you?"

"Shortro's stall. Checking him over," Fair replied. "What's wrong down there?"

"We don't know."

Outside, the rain pounded. One could barely make out headlights as cars pulled out of the parking lot before it became too muddy. No one wanted to get stuck. In the distance, the flickering lights were eerie, like white bug eyes that then switched to tiny nasty red dots.

A fire-engine siren split the air as the truck hurried in the opposite direction.

Mrs. Murphy slithered through the people. *"Tucker, can you bump your way through?"*

Cookie, smaller, worked her way toward the tiger cat. *"Here I come."*

Mrs. Murphy thought to herself, *"Jack Russells,"* but said nothing.

Tucker, tempted to nip a heel like the wonderful herder she was, resisted because there would have been more screams. Tucker saw better in darkness than the humans, but Mrs. Murphy had the best night vision.

The three managed to reach the changing room just as Renata threw aside the heavy curtain, pushing her way through the crowd, blindly knocking people over. The animals dashed in as she bolted out, still screaming, tears flooding her face although no one could see them.

"Oh" was all Mrs. Murphy said.

Tucker approached the corpse, which sat upright on the floor. The heavy, slightly metallic scent of blood filled her nostrils. Blood spilled over the front of his checkered cotton shirt. *"Throat slit, and neatly done, too."*

Cookie used her nose, while Mrs. Murphy observed everything in the room, not just the body.

A tack trunk had been knocked sideways; some clothes were off the hangers. Two slight indentations, like skid marks, were on the sisal rug thrown on the dirt floor.

"He didn't have time to put up much of a fight, but he tried," Mrs. Murphy noted. *"His killer dragged him backward, see."*

Tucker walked over to Mrs. Murphy. *"His boot heels dug in."*

The changing room was twelve feet by twelve feet, the size of a nice stall.

Mrs. Murphy, pupils as wide as they could get, also noticed the tack trunk askew. *"A human could hide behind that. It's a huge tack trunk."*

"Maybe he didn't have to hide," Cookie replied.

"True enough," Tucker, now sniffing every surface, agreed.

Apart from her formidable kitty curiosity, Mrs. Murphy possessed sangfroid. She walked onto the man's lap, stood on her hind legs, and peered at the wound, a little blood still seeping; the huge squirts from when the throat was first severed had shot out onto the sisal rug. As the heartbeat had slowed, the blood ran over his shirtfront and jeans.

Mrs. Murphy didn't like getting sticky blood on her paws, but there was no time to waste. Who knew when a human would barge in, screwing up everything? She sniffed the wound, noticing the edges of it.

"Whoever did this used a razor-sharp blade or even a big hand razor like professional barbers use. It's neat. Not ragged."

"Professional job?" Tucker wondered.

"That or someone accustomed to sharp tools," Murphy answered.

"A doctor, a vet, a butcher, a barber." Cookie was fascinated, as this was her first exposure to human killing.

"The cut is left to right," the keenly observant tiger informed the others. *"If he grabbed him from behind, hand over mouth, and pulled his head back to really expose the neck, he'd slice left to right if he was right-handed."*

As the cat scrutinized the wound, Tucker touched her nose to his opened right palm. His temperature hadn't dropped; the blood hadn't started to dry or clot. This murder was just minutes old.

"Hey." Tucker stepped back, blinking.

Cookie, who had touched her nose to his left hand, walked over to Tucker. *"That's weird."*

Mrs. Murphy dropped back on all fours and looked at his opened palm from the vantage point of sitting on his thigh. *"Two crosses."* Tucker wondered, *"Two? Maybe he was extra religious."*

"It's cut into his palm but more scratched than cut real deep." Cookie turned her head to view the palm from another angle.

Just then the curtain was pulled back and Harry and Joan stepped inside, flashlights in hand, quickly pulling the curtain behind them.

"Oh, my God," Joan gasped, but she held steady.

"Jorge!" Harry exclaimed.

Larry, having grabbed one of the many stashed flashlights, pushed his way into the changing room. Fair, right behind, guarded the curtained entrance once inside.

Meanwhile, Renata had collapsed in the aisle right outside the hospitality room. Frances, mother of eight children, was equal to any crisis. She propped up the beautiful actress, called for a bottle of water. In the darkness, people fumbled about; a few slipped out, knowing the authorities would show up sooner or later and they'd be questioned, held for who knew how long.

Manuel, another flashlight in hand, fetched water and knelt beside Renata.

As Renata's eyelids fluttered, Frances fanned her with a lace handkerchief. "You need a little water, Renata."

When Renata opened her eyes, she let out another bone-chilling scream that was so loud, Frances dropped the bottle of water she'd just taken from Manuel. The water spurted out, but Frances quickly picked it up, wiping off the mouthpiece.

Manuel held Renata steady, for she was prepared to scream more. Finally the two got her under some control.

Paul Hamilton, soaked to the skin, hurried over from the

large grandstand. Despite the thunder and rain, the piercing scream had reached the hundreds of people huddled there. All he could think about when he heard the screams was the safety of his wife and daughter. He didn't know, initially, that the terror was coming from Barn Five.

Joan, always fast-thinking, called her father on his cell as he hurried through the downpour.

Larry had stepped back out of the changing room to see if he could find an umbrella for Paul. He found none. Larry walked outside into the storm just as Paul ran toward him, oblivious to the trees bending over, the rain slashing sideways. Joan's call had given him a few minutes to compose himself.

Larry led Paul through the people in the hospitality room. As Larry threw open the changing-room curtain, people tried to see, but there wasn't enough light for them. Paul stepped in.

Dead bodies didn't rattle him—he'd seen enough in the war—but murder upset him. He felt a sudden chill as water dripped over his face, his shirt stuck to his body.

"Dad," Joan simply said.

Fair knelt down to touch Jorge's wrist, confirming again that the murder was but minutes old. He stood back up. "Mr. Hamilton, this happened under everyone's noses. He's been dead ten minutes at the most."

Paul noticed the clean cut, the severed jugular. "Someone knew what they were doing."

"And had the tools to do it," Fair corroborated.

Manuel, still on the other side of the curtain, did not yet know his second-in-command and friend had been sliced from ear to ear.

Paul, arms folded across his chest, ticked off orders in a

low and calm voice. "Larry, go outside and keep everyone here. If you can find a bigger flashlight or anything, set it up so they aren't standing around in the dark. Joan, is anything missing?"

"I don't know."

"Count every piece of tack, every coat and vest." His voice imparted strength. "Fair, is there any way you can better examine the body without disturbing evidence? It would be good if we knew before Sheriff Cody arrives. Given the circumstances, it would be easy for even the best forensics team to miss something."

"Fair, if you go back outside, the tack trunk with vet supplies is in the center aisle. It's the one that stands upright like a cupboard. There are rubber gloves there," Joan said.

Fair borrowed Joan's flashlight, stepped out, and groped his way uneasily through the talking people.

Fair soon returned with his own flashlight, as there'd been one in the Kalarama vet trunk, and he returned Joan's to her. As he carefully checked Jorge, Joan inspected all the clothes. Larry, following Paul's orders, now returned with another flashlight, which he tied to the side of the door using baling twine.

Joan held her breath. She was going to have to tell Manuel but not right this minute. She called out to him as Harry told her he was still inside the hospitality room. "Manuel, will you go count the saddles and bridles in the tack room, then come back here and call for me?"

"Sí."

The two cats, not even twitching their whiskers, crouched on a tack trunk as they watched Fair. Pewter hadn't been able to stand it any longer, so she'd come into the changing room. Tucker and Cookie sat in the corner, also watching.

Outside, the storm moved east. Although the rains continued to lash, the lightning and thunder mercifully grew fainter.

A siren in the distance gave hope that the sheriff was on his way.

Fair, turning over Jorge's right hand, noticed the two crosses. "Look at this."

Joan swung the flashlight onto Jorge's palm. "Two crosses."

Harry, bending on one knee, whispered, "Double cross."

9

*I*t was still pitch black, but the rain had slowed to a drizzle. Although it was only eight-thirty P.M., Harry felt like it was one in the morning. The sticky hot days tired her, but being in semidarkness made her want to go to sleep. She struggled to keep alert.

"Does anyone mind if I walk outside? I feel like I'm going to fall asleep," Harry asked the small group in the changing room.

"Go ahead, honey. When the sheriff arrives, you'll know. If he needs you, I'll find you." Fair then quickly added, "Don't go far. There's a killer out there."

"Oh, Fair, he isn't interested in me." Harry, a logical soul, knew the double cross carved in Jorge's palm had a special meaning to someone. She felt perfectly safe.

Mrs. Murphy, Pewter, and Tucker felt otherwise. Harry

might not be in immediate danger, but her curiosity coupled with practical intelligence landed her in trouble too many times and made the animals want to stick close.

As Harry pushed open the curtain, picking her way through the now-hushed crowd, Mrs. Murphy and Tucker followed. Pewter pleaded that one of them should stay in the changing room in case of developments. She fooled no one. The gray cat hated getting her paws wet. Cookie stayed there, too, to protect Joan.

Leaning outside the barn, tucked just under the overhang, Renata smoked a cigarette. In the darkness no one could see her until right upon her. She was grateful for that, since her hands trembled.

Harry leaned next to her. "Feeling better?"

"A little. Would you like one?" Renata offered Harry a Dunhill menthol.

"You know, I don't smoke, but under the circumstances, I believe I would."

Renata plucked one out of the green pack and handed it to Harry, who lit it off Renata's half-smoked cigarette.

"The trick is not to let a raindrop hit the end." Renata inhaled deeply.

Tucker looked upward, blinking. *"Smells so awful."*

Mrs. Murphy, standing next to her friend so as not to get her bottom wet, replied, *"Some of them mind the smoke, others don't, but it burns my nostrils."*

"Supposed to calm the nerves." Tucker thought a moment. *"Must be like chewing a bone. Calms my nerves."*

"Chewing a bone won't give you lung cancer." Mrs. Murphy didn't much like chewing bones herself, although if they were quite fresh she could be persuaded to do it.

"Murphy, you have to die of something," the corgi stated.

"That's the truth. What is it that Harry says?"

"When the good Lord jerks your chain, you're going."

"Someone sure jerked Jorge's chain. One clean slice." Mrs. Murphy shuddered.

"Seemed like a nice man. I never smelled fear on him, or drugs. Boy, I can always smell drugs, can't you?"

"Yeah, they sweat them out, whether prescribed by the doctor or bought on the street. Hard to believe the humans can't pick up those chemical odors. But you're right, Jorge smelled clean enough."

As the two animals talked, the women smoked quietly.

Finally Renata spoke. "All the movies I've done, all those murders and killings and blood on the bodies, it's different when it's real. I can't believe I fell apart. I'm sorry. I didn't help the situation one bit."

"Renata, a six-foot-eight-inch linebacker would scream, too, if he'd never seen someone with their throat slit."

"You didn't."

"I'm a farm girl. See a lot."

"Dead bodies? Humans, I mean?"

"A couple." A big drop fell on Harry's head. "Thank God, that wind has died down. Kind of brings a chill, though, doesn't it?"

"Does." Renata looked out over the darkness. Her eyes were adjusting and she could see movement in the closer barns. "Were you really a postmistress?"

"Was. But I always farmed. What did you do before becoming a movie star?"

Renata shrugged. "The usual—waited on tables. I even delivered messages by bicycle when I lived in New York. That was death-defying." She smiled. "If the buses and cabs didn't run you down, the potholes wiped you out."

"You must have quick reflexes."

"I do."

"Most stars have their own production companies. Do you?"

"No. I can't run a company."

"You could hire someone to do it." Harry thought it wise to get away from the murder. She wanted to keep Renata calm.

Renata waved her cigarette in the air and immediately regretted it, for a fat raindrop landed on the end, the sizzle and smoke signaling the demise of that Dunhill. "Dammit."

Harry said, "Bet you couldn't do that again if you tried."

"You're right about that." Renata flicked the extinguished fag into a puddle. "Sayonara, my little tranquilizer." She paused. "Hire someone. Right. Then I just pay his or her salary, and they have to justify it, which means meetings, scripts they think I should read, along with what my agent shoves down my throat. And then I need to rent a decent office, maybe in Twentieth Century City or downtown Wilshire Boulevard. It adds up. Until I think I can really do it right, I'm not wasting my money, and like I said, I don't think I can do it right."

"You weren't born with money, were you?" Harry asked as Mrs. Murphy and Tucker observed Renata stiffen, then quickly relax.

"No."

"Takes one to know one."

"What else do you know?" Renata tossed this off lightly, but an edge crept into her voice.

"Nothing." This wasn't exactly true, because Harry knew Renata wasn't a happy woman. She'd thought the rupture of her relationship with her trainer, upon whom she depended to help her improve, would cause unease. She wondered if there wasn't more to that relationship. But underneath all, Harry felt a sadness. She didn't know why, but does anybody know why anyone else is unhappy, really?

"I haven't heard that expression since I was little, 'Takes one to know one.' Funny."

"In Virginia we use a lot of old expressions you don't hear much. Virginia is a world unto itself."

"So is Kentucky."

"Used to be part of Virginia." Harry couldn't help this tiny moment of bragging.

"I know." Renata reached into her thin jacket to fetch another cigarette. "Learned it in school. I wanted to get out of Kentucky so bad when I was a teenager, I would die for it. Nearly did, too—like I said, being a messenger I came close."

"Did you sing 'Nearer, My God, to Thee'?"

Renata laughed. "Did not." She lit her cigarette, dragged on it, then said, "Thanks, Harry."

"For what?"

"Taking my mind off this."

"It was his time."

"You believe that?"

"I do."

"But he was murdered."

"It was still his time. That doesn't mean we don't try to find the murderer, that we don't demand justice, but I still believe in the three fates, spinning and snipping."

Renata shuddered. "That's a potent image."

"The myths are powerful."

"I wasn't the best student, but acting teaches you things.

I remember the three fates; kinda think the Three Witches in *Macbeth* are the Renaissance remake."

"I'm sure you know a lot else." Harry paused. "Taking the sheriff a long time to get here. There must be trees down and wires across the roads and, for all we know, car crashes. A bad night."

"Yes." Renata closed her eyes a moment. "And when he does get here, along with the forensics team and God knows who else in an official capacity no matter how trivial, Queen Esther will be long forgotten. How am I ever going to find my horse?" She stopped abruptly. "You must think I'm awful. A man is dead and I want my horse."

"It's natural. There's nothing you can do for Jorge. After all, she is your horse and extremely valuable. Who would steal her?"

"The only person I can think of is Charly Trackwell, that slimy bastard. But Charly is too smart to do something like that. God, I hate him."

Harry ignored the personal connection lest Renata let fly another stream of invective. "Charly ever steal other people's horses?"

"Not that I know of. He confined himself to money."

"For real?"

"Well, no. He didn't rob a bank, but he padded his board bills. I know he did, the schmuck. He'd charge me for supplements that weren't given, tack I didn't buy. Stuff. Not thousands on one month's bill. Little bits here and there. Adds up."

"You confronted him?"

"Did. He denied it, of course, but I put every bill in front of him with an inventory of my tack. I also—and he didn't know this—had blood drawn so if supplements were in my horses' systems, I'd know. If he'd given them anything, including glucosamine, stuff like that, you know. Anyway, the tests proved they had some supplements perhaps, but not all that he claimed." She paused. "Hard to pin that on him."

"How'd you get blood drawn?"

"Paid off a groom. Charly always has Mexicans in and out. Carlos is different. That's his right-hand man. Obviously, I did this behind Carlos's back, too."

"Ah." Harry's sense of Renata's intelligence, cunning even, was deepening.

"We had a knock-down, drag-out. He swore he didn't know anything about it. Someone in his stable wasn't doing the job properly." She stopped to inhale again. "The kind of bullshit you hear when people try to cover their asses. Enron. Hey, fill in the blank. It's always the same. But he groveled and we patched it up and he even gave me back what I claimed had been pilfered."

"That's good."

"I thought so. But underneath, I didn't trust him. I always felt he was trolling for another rich client through me, you know, or a very rich wife." She waved her right hand, cigarette glowing in front of her face, a gesture indicating something had flown away. "I'm over it." She wasn't.

"You think he'll get even?"

"He already has. He has my horse, or he knows where Queen Esther is."

"He wouldn't kill her? You know, like Shergar." She named the famous racehorse who disappeared in the twentieth century, presumably kidnapped for money. No trace of the horse had ever been found.

"No. Charly loves horses, even if sometimes he's too

harsh for my taste. But then he says to me, 'A horse that's woman-broke is no good.' Pissed me off."

"Actually, Renata, there is a scrap of truth to that, whether it's horses or dogs. Women have a tendency to be too lenient—not every woman but most women. An animal must have consistent discipline, good nutrition, and love, but you can't leave off the discipline."

"You train your horses?"

"Do. If you ever can, please come visit us. If you come in the fall you can foxhunt."

"God, I'd love that." She brightened considerably. "Think I could do it? All I really know is saddle seat."

"Ride with the Hilltoppers. They don't jump, and if there's one thing I know about saddle seat, most of all you need good hands. The horse I would put you on, Tomahawk, would be most grateful."

"I will do it. You think I'm just shooting my mouth off, but I will."

"Shortro has the right attitude for the hunt field," Harry said.

"Three years plus a few months and he really does have a good mind, doesn't he?" Renata smiled.

"I'll introduce you to Alicia Palmer."

At this Renata straightened up. "Alicia Palmer, the movie star?"

"Renata, you're a movie star."

Renata laughed. "Harry, Alicia is a real movie star. No one is like that today."

"She's a wonderful woman and a pretty good horse-woman, too. In fact, one of the reasons Fair and I are here, apart from our honeymoon, is to find a horse for Alicia that I can make into a hunter. She has a lot of youngsters, but many of those go on to the steeplechase circuit or to the Keeneland sales."

"I bet she's still beautiful."

"Unbelievable." Harry finished her cigarette, dropping it on the wet ground, grinding it to bits. "When you worked with Charly, did you ever see drugs? Human drugs, I mean?"

Renata shrugged. "Horse world is full of it. So is every other industry, but have you ever noticed Hollywood and the horse biz are the scapegoats for everyone else?"

"But those big corporations drug-test. Don't employees sign a paper for those jobs stating they will allow random drug-testing?"

"I don't know, but I know it doesn't mean much. Any test can be beaten. But I don't care. It's not the drugs that bother me, it's the hypocrisy about it all. Does Charly take drugs? Well, I think if he wants to celebrate he might drink some champagne while inhaling an illicit substance. Is he an addict? No."

"Might he be a drop-off station?"

"No. I can't stand him, but I'm not going to accuse him of being a dealer."

"Someone in the barn?"

She waited. "I couldn't say."

Tucker remarked, *"She can say well enough. She just won't say."*

Harry, either visited by divine inspiration or having a crazy moment, blurted out, "If I find your horse, will you do something for me?"

"Yes," Renata replied without hesitation.

"Will you advertise my wine? You know, say it's good?"

"If it's fit to pour on a dog. If it's not fit to pour on a dog you'll make a laughingstock out of me. Look, if it's awful, I'll give twenty thousand dollars to you, cashier's check."

Harry gulped hard. "Renata, I don't want your money for doing something that's right. The horse comes first."

"Take the money and run." Tucker let out a little yelp.

"No, Tucker, Renata as a spokeswoman is worth a hell of a lot more than twenty thousand dollars."

"I thought you farmed."

Energized by this exchange, Harry answered, "I put in a quarter of an acre of grapes, Petit Manseng. I won't get a true harvest—a mature one—for three years, so you're off the hook until then. I wish I could do more, but it costs about fourteen thousand dollars an acre to establish a vineyard."

"Fourteen thousand dollars," Renata echoed in amazement.

Harry held out her hand. "Is it a deal? You advertise my wine so long as it's fit to pour on a dog." She smiled.

Renata gave her her hand. "If you find Queen Esther, I will live up to the bargain—as long as you throw in an introduction to Alicia Palmer."

"Deal." Harry grinned.

"Deal." Renata suddenly felt happy, even though it seemed absurd under the circumstances.

They leaned back against Barn Five.

"Sometimes I wonder if our beloved Harry is one brick shy of a load." Tucker found this deal amusing.

"Tucker, sometimes I think that about you," the tiger teased.

Renata said, almost languidly, "If you find Queen Esther, maybe you'll find whoever killed that poor man in there."

"Might could." Harry used the old Southern expression

against which English teachers had fought for over a century.

Whatever Harry would find was as cloudy as a night's sky. The one certain thing was that out of the moist, dark soil of fear, rumors would multiply like mushrooms.

10

Mrs. Murphy and Pewter curled up on the bed pillows. After wiping Tucker's paws, Fair spread an old blanket at the end of the bed, lifting Tucker onto it.

The animals listened as the humans showered, washing for warmth as much as cleanliness, for both were clammy and cold from the night air, the temperature having dropped after the monumental thunderstorm. They could hear Harry and Fair talking as they scrubbed each other's backs.

"Ever notice how all animals like to groom one another?" Tucker lifted her head off her sparkling paws.

"Cleans those hard-to-reach spots," Pewter, fond of her toilette, replied.

"Makes us feel closer." Mrs. Murphy felt drowsy.

"You're right," Pewter agreed. *"I'd never let anyone I didn't*

like groom me." She wrinkled her nose. *"Can you imagine grooming Miss Nasty? Even another monkey wouldn't do it."*

"Booty gives her baths. I heard Joan telling Mother that he lavishes attention on her. Joan says it's a surrogate child or maybe he does it as penance. Don't know for what, but Joan was laughing about it." Tucker rolled onto her side, stretched her legs fore and aft.

"Men are descended from apes," Pewter declared with authority. *"Booty's grooming a family member, sort of."*

"If men are descended from apes, then what are women descended from?" Tucker smiled mischievously.

"Angels," Mrs. Murphy answered, her eyes half closed.

The three laughed at that, then Tucker thoughtfully wondered, *"Is that why men behave as they do—you know, can't face reality, dream a lot—because they're imperfect monkeys?"*

"Apes," Pewter corrected her.

"Same difference. Size—" Tucker didn't finish, because Mrs. Murphy interrupted.

"They're a mess because their senses aren't good, and they are even more eroded because of pollution—noise pollution, too."

"But so are we." Tucker wasn't argumentative as much as curious.

"Yes, but our noses and ears are so much better that even with some damage we remain vastly superior to the human animal." Mrs. Murphy did not say this with a conceited air.

"That's a thought." The day's excitement and upset caught up with Pewter. She felt tired all at once. *"I do hate to think of Harry and Fair being related to Miss Nasty."* With that statement she closed her eyes, let out a tiny little puff of air, and was asleep.

"I'm tuckered out, too, forgive the pun," Mrs. Murphy said to the dog.

"Me, too. Who would have thought our visit to Kentucky would be so"—Tucker searched for the right word—*"depleting."*

Mrs. Murphy replied, *"One murder, one stolen pin, and one horrible monkey, all in two days' time. Oh, one stolen horse, too."*

Harry and Fair emerged from the shower, dashed for the bed, and bounced under the covers. They snuggled to keep warm. The bounce disturbed the cats on the pillows but only for a second, as the cats resettled to curl by the humans' heads. Pewter went right back to sleep.

"Chilled to the bone. You don't think about getting chilled in August." Harry pulled the blanket under her chin. "Good for me you're big. You warm me faster than I warm you."

"I wouldn't say that." He sighed with contentment as she rested her head on his shoulder. He looked at the alarm clock. "It's two in the morning."

"I lost track of time," Harry murmured. "I feel like we're inside a washing machine on spin cycle."

"My mind feels like that."

"What? I mean, what's whirling around?"

"Jorge's body temperature." He exhaled. "Given that his temperature was pretty close to ninety-eight point six—didn't have a thermometer, but he felt normal to the touch—what keeps going round in my head is, was this a planned execution or a crime of opportunity?"

"The storm and loss of power sure were convenient," Harry said.

"Help me place everyone. Joan and her folks were with

us. Larry, Manuel, and Jorge were getting horses ready, I assume."

"Larry and Manuel were on the rail when Renata rode Shortro."

"Right. Where were the other trainers?"

"Don't know. Ward was on the rail. He had someone in the class. Charly wasn't there. Guess he didn't want to see Renata ride, or maybe he had someone in the next class, junior exhibition three-gaited show pleasure. I know Booty had a kid in the class, because we saw him in the practice ring with her when we first came to the show grounds yesterday. If he was there we missed him, but, Fair, the place had so many people it was like ants at a picnic."

She sounded sleepy. "I'll read my program in the morning to double-check clients, though. Seems to me what matters is the double cross. Noticed Sheriff Howlett questioning the Mexican workers."

"Sure are a lot of them," Fair idly commented. "Seems like the number doubled since the first day."

"Big show. All hands on deck."

"Big show. Workers shipped in." Mrs. Murphy opened one eye. *"Big profit, too, I bet."*

"What are you fussing about, pussycat?" Harry, warm now, pulled her arm from underneath the covers to stroke the cat's silky forehead.

"Doesn't matter." Mrs. Murphy closed her eyes again.

"Pretty much everyone was on the rail, except for the grooms and trainers getting horses and clients ready for the next class." Harry returned to who was where partly because she was losing steam and losing track of the conversation. "Watching Renata and Shortro. Great guy, Shortro."

"Whoever killed Jorge had ice water in his veins. Cut it close." He stopped. "Bad pun, sorry."

"Mmm."

"You falling asleep?"

"I'm resting my eyes," she fibbed.

Fair glanced at the animals and his wife. "I'm wide-awake."

"Drink milk." Mrs. Murphy opened her eyes again, offering good advice.

He smiled at the cat. "You're listening to me."

"I'm trying, but I'm pretty sleepy, too."

"This is my point: if Queen Esther was stolen in the open, Joan's pin, as well, and Jorge was killed in the blink of an eye—if these things were in the open, what's hidden?"

"Fair, you're starting to think like Harry." Mrs. Murphy sighed.

*B*loodlines have signatures, right?"

"Right." Joan made a pot of coffee and a pot of tea while Harry cut into a big coffee cake as they sat in Joan's kitchen.

"Certain animals breed true. You can spot their get." Harry used the word meaning "offspring." "In the past the credit usually went to the stallion, but the mare is as important, if not more so."

"Actually, the latest research is leaning more toward the mare, but who knows? I've bred horses all my life, and if it were a matter of brains," Joan tapped her head, "I'd be right one hundred percent of the time."

"Know what you mean. Your foundation sire, Denmark, foaled in 1839, consolidated the look and the action of the Saddlebred, you think?" Harry enjoyed the soft light flooding through the kitchen window.

"Harrison Chief, too; he was foaled in 1872." Joan listened to the coffeepot burble. "But like the Thoroughbred, there's so much we'll never know. You figure horses started coming over sometime after 1607. Not everyone kept good records."

"Not everyone could read and write." Harry paused a moment. "Although I read somewhere that our literacy rate was higher at the time of the American Revolution than it is now. Boy, that's a smack in the face."

"Doesn't surprise me." Joan shrugged. "But what we do know is that Thoroughbred blood, Morgan blood, and even Old Narragansett blood is in the Saddlebred."

Narragansett blood is the blood of pacers, a type of racehorse that pulls a sulky. A pacer's legs, unlike a trotter's, move in parallel, so the right side—fore and hind—will move in unison, as will the left. The movement of the legs for a trotter—in fact, for the trotting gait in any horse—is diagonal.

"Who were the great foundation mares?" Harry asked as she watched a robin swoop down on a wriggling worm.

"Uh, Stevenson mare, Saltram mare, Betsey Harrison, Pekina, Lute Boyd, Lucy Mack, Daisy the Second, Queen Forty-eight, and Annie C."

"You could teach a class."

Joan smiled as she poured tea for Harry, coffee for herself. "You know your Thoroughbred lines, I know Saddlebred. The American Saddlebred Association, ASHA, started in 1891, helped concentrate breeding information." She paused a second. "But when you close the books the problems arise."

"Meaning you run out of blood?"

"Yes. Horses, dogs, whatever, can become inbred. I linebreed. I'm not saying you shouldn't, but you shouldn't even dream of it if you haven't studied and looked at a lot of horses—a *lot* of horses."

In linebreeding, one dips back into the same bloodlines, the theory being it reinforces the strong points of that blood. Do it too close and one can breed weak animals or idiotic humans. It takes an incredibly intelligent human to successfully linebreed horses.

"Right." Harry gratefully drank her tea once Joan sat down. "I shy away from it, but I lack your gift."

Joan waved off this compliment as they both attacked the coffee cake.

"I should make you a real breakfast, but you know me." Joan wanly smiled since she never had time nor much inclination to cook.

"I'm the same way. Fair usually brings something home after his last call, and he likes to grill."

"Don't they all. I mean, have you ever seen anything like men hovering over their barbecue? They're even competitive about the sauces, and if they marinate the meat—" She rolled her eyes heavenward.

"Didn't you say they were just as bad in Australia and even South Africa when you visited there?"

"Honey, they're probably attacking one another with tongs in China. Show a man a grill and a piece of steak and he loses his mind."

"True, but we get to eat it." Harry winked.

"Ever notice how we're cooks but they're chefs?"

Both women laughed at that.

"You've got a couple of Thoroughbreds." Harry noticed how moist the crumbs were on top of the coffee cake.

"I do, but I don't breed them. Paula Cline and I run a

couple. My older brother Jimmy's usually got a few on the track, too."

"If you hear of a good youngster, good mind, a little too slow, and the owners want out, let me know."

"I will. For you?"

"Make it into a foxhunter for Alicia Palmer."

Because Joan knew Harry's friends, she needed no biography of Alicia. "Still hot and heavy with BoomBoom?"

" 'Tis."

"I'd never thought that of BoomBoom, not that I care. She just mowed men down like a scythe."

"Both did. That may be why they found each other. They got bored." Harry laughed.

"Or maybe it's truly love." Joan hoped it was, because underneath she was a romantic.

"Funny, isn't it? All those years I hated BoomBoom. Hell, we even fought in grade school, and then when I divorced Fair I could avoid my own failings by being angry at her."

Fair had had an affair with BoomBoom.

"The Lord works in mysterious ways, His wonders to perform."

"Miranda says that all the time."

Miranda had worked with Harry for years at Crozet's post office.

Joan looked up at the round kitchen wall clock. "What time do you have?"

"Nine." Harry checked her wristwatch, which had been her father's.

"Forgot the power was out." She pulled her chair underneath the clock, stepped on it, and moved the hands forward. "What a storm. I'm surprised there wasn't more damage. We must be okay, because Larry hasn't called on his cell."

Larry and Fair, both on ATVs, were checking the entire farm. While Manuel could have assigned someone to this task, the men really wanted to drive around on the ATVs, plus Fair would be there if any horse had sustained an injury. Poor Manuel had been devastated by Jorge's murder. The first thing he did this morning was to go to Mass and say a prayer for Jorge's soul.

"That's some good news."

Joan pulled the chair back, sitting down with a thump, which made Cookie bark. The animals had flopped on the couch in the living room. "Oh, Cookie, it's just me."

"Never know," the Jack Russell called back.

"You know, I'm kind of all right, my mind is clear, and then all this hits me again, and I feel my heart beat faster, I go back over every little thing, and I can't figure it out. Then I get kind of obsessed and I go over and over where we were, what we were doing, and everyone else and who's mad at whom, and I get dizzy."

"At two last night, Fair and I tried to remember who was on the rail for Renata's class and who wasn't. I finally fell asleep." Harry put both hands on her teacup. "This morning I read the program to see who had horses in the class and who didn't. I thought anyone not on the rail could be a potential murderer, but the storm put an end to that theory. Folks starting running in all directions at the first thunderclap."

A car drove into the driveway. The door to the garage, which was under the house, was open.

"Grandma's here," Cookie announced.

"Yoo-hoo," Frances called up.

Paul and Frances lived at the corner of Kalarama Farm in

a lovely, unpretentious two-story brick house that went back to the time of the great Kalarama Rex, foaled in 1922.

Harry whispered, "She know?"

"Not yet." Joan stood up as her mother opened the door into the kitchen.

"Good morning." Frances kissed Joan on the cheek, then kissed Harry. "How are you girls this morning?"

"All things considered, as good as we can be," Joan replied.

Like most mother-daughter relationships, this one was mostly good, with a few spots of strain.

"I hope they find who did this terrible thing." Frances didn't sit down when Joan pointed to a chair. "But he wasn't killed here, and that's a good thing."

Joan stared at her mother, who was not an unfeeling woman. "Mother."

"No, no, I didn't mean that the way it sounded, but I was thinking, if Jorge did something or crossed someone, why didn't they kill him here? So I think whatever happened happened because of the show."

"Or maybe that's where it all came together." Harry followed Frances's line of thought.

"Well, I'm not a policeman." Frances flattened her lips together for an instant as she wrinkled her brow. "That coffee does smell good." She accepted the proffered chair.

Joan walked over to the stove, and Cookie breezed in to sit by the older woman.

"Coffee cake?" Harry had the knife poised over the cake.

"No, thank you. I eat so many sweets at these horse shows. I'm determined to be good."

"You've kept your figure." Harry complimented her.

"Why, thank you." Frances beamed, then turned to Joan

as her coffee was poured. "Joan, I don't like to meddle in business. After all, I don't know horses like you, Larry, and Paul do, but," she picked up her silver spoon as Joan put the pot back on the burner, "Renata will cause trouble."

"She already has." Joan sat back down.

"Trouble with men."

"Oh." Joan blinked as both she and Harry turned to look at Frances.

"Women like that stir up men. Charly's behavior proves that. I heard how he acted when Renata took her horses from him."

"Has Charly been vengeful in the past?" Harry asked.

"Well, one time he and Booty got crossways. Booty accused Charly of making a pass at his wife." Frances lifted her left shoulder, then let it drop. "Why, I don't know. Well, we don't look at women the way men do, but Charly swore he didn't, which then insulted Annie Pollard, who wants to think of herself as universally attractive. Booty got loose with his mouth, Charly didn't take kindly to it, then it seemed like things were patched up. At the next big horse show, Charly stuck ginger up the tails of Booty's horses when he wasn't in the barn."

Joan laughed. "You should have seen Booty trying to show the horses. 'Course, Charly soaked the ginger in turpentine. Made them wild."

"He was an explosive guy in the first Iraq war." Frances nodded.

"Explosions, Mom."

"And explosive."

They chatted a bit more, then Frances finished her coffee and carefully placed the cup on the saucer. "Joan, do you think we're safe?"

"I don't know," Joan honestly answered.

"Well, your father is worried, although he says the double cross means something and it doesn't have anything to do with us or we'd know what it means. Jorge was such a nice man, I can't imagine what he could have done to— well, you know."

"If we knew that we'd be halfway to the killer." Harry picked up a square of crystallized brown sugar out of the bowl, placing it on the tip of her tongue.

Frances folded her hands together in her lap. "He didn't gamble, drank a little beer on the weekends, didn't run after women. He always said he was putting his money in the bank so he could buy his own farm. He kept his trailer pretty clean." She mentioned this because Jorge lived on the farm, behind a palisade to give the workers privacy. A few were married. Occasionally Frances, Paul, Joan, or Larry would visit their living quarters, but they respected their need to be away from the bosses. "He did have a girlfriend for a while."

"What happened?"

"She got a scholarship to go to William Woods University in Fulton, Missouri, part of an equine program. I don't know the details, but anyway, she left Kentucky and I think the romance just faded away," Joan told Harry.

"No bad blood?" Harry inquired.

"Don't think so," Joan replied.

"All the no-counts in the world and Jorge gets murdered." Joan, exasperated, put her chin on her fist, elbow on the table.

"Well, girls, I've got errands to run. I went to Mass this morning and lit a candle for Jorge, came here, and now I'm off to the dry cleaner's, the supermarket, and who knows what I'll find along the way." Frances turned to Joan. "If you give me your beige linen jacket I'll take it to the cleaner. Remember to take off my mother's pin. And Joan, didn't I raise you not to put your elbows on the table?"

Joan gulped. "Give me a minute."

Harry made small talk with Frances. Joan returned with her jacket.

Frances stood up, draped the jacket over her arm. "Remember, we need luck tonight, three-year-old fine harness class. It's pin night." She smiled.

"I was going to rest it tonight and save it for the five-gaited." Joan really was a bad liar, but Frances didn't notice at that moment.

"Luck won't run out as long as the points of the horse-shoe are up." Frances opened the door to the basement and descended, each wooden step reverberating until she reached bottom.

Neither Harry nor Joan spoke until they heard the motor turn over.

"I'm cooked. I'm such a coward. I can't tell her."

"There's still time. I don't think you're a coward. We might find it."

"Here I am, fussed up over a pin. Jorge is dead and Renata's horse is missing." She shook her head. "Sometimes I can't believe myself."

"Joan, it's human nature. We can't fix the big problems so we concentrate on the small ones."

"Well, I've got some whopping big problems."

"Would you recognize Queen Esther if you saw her?" Harry asked.

"I would."

"I think I would, too, even though I haven't seen her as

much as you have. But she's regal, she truly is a queen. Why don't Fair and I cruise around and look, say, at Charly's back pastures? You're on overload. We might come up with something."

"I'll draw you a little map where the different trainers have their farms." She reached for a pad and pencil, always on the counter. "But I'll tell you this, you won't find Queen Esther at Charly's."

"Why?"

"He knows people think he's behind this because he's so angry with Renata. If he did take the horse, he'd put her with someone else."

"Out of state?"

"Maybe, but I bet when all this quiets down, Renata will get a phone call or e-mail. Could be wrong, but I think he's trying to rattle her cage. If the horse were truly stolen, she would have received a ransom note, like you said."

"Charly is rattling her cage."

"In all respects."

Harry leaned forward as Joan drew county lines and made arrows to where the farms were. "Sex thing."

"Charly is a snob—I mean, he hides it, but he wants good things, the best, and if he could marry Renata, wouldn't he be on top of the world? He wouldn't be the first good horseman to marry a rich wife."

"Ah, what about her?" Harry's eyebrows raised quizzically.

"I don't know. I expect she has stronger feelings for him than she's admitting. Would she marry him? Who knows? Look at all the actresses who marry men who become their managers, or they marry their directors. It's not such a far jump to marrying their trainer. I mean, an actress is told what to do. They look for leadership."

"I never thought of that."

"Because you don't. Maybe not every actress or actor is looking for someone to pick up the reins, but a lot are. Her career is sagging. She's looking for something."

"Wouldn't a good script make more sense?"

Joan laughed. "When have people used sense?"

"You've got a point there. What about Booty? Maybe she'll go over to him."

"On the one hand, I'd like her here. The publicity is good for us, and Larry could make her a better rider. She's not bad now. But she'll need a lot of attention. Larry doesn't have it to give and neither do I, although I doubt she'd need it as much from me as from him." She smiled slyly. "Booty's good. Big rep, but she doesn't like him, I can tell, and one of the reasons is Miss Nasty."

"She is pretty awful."

"She is, but it's the humiliation aspect: he's telling the world his ex-wife is a monkey. The duplicate wardrobe is screamingly funny. I can't help it, I laugh, but Renata gets it, you know. She'd never fall for Booty."

"Another actor?"

"Could be, but she loves the horse world. She'll land here ultimately one way or the other. And who knows, Charly might be a good husband, although at this exact moment it is hard to picture."

"Monkey business." Harry smiled.

12

*T*he deep-green pastures of central Kentucky reminded Harry of Virginia. Missing were the dense oak and hickory forests of the Appalachian states, as well as the allure of the Blue Ridge Mountains.

However, the picturesque towns testified to the fact that, with few exceptions, Kentucky had emerged from the War Between the States relatively intact.

Whether Paris, Versailles, or Harrodsburg, the towns evidenced a tidiness, a coziness, that could beguile even the snottiest Virginian.

Neither Harry nor Fair was particularly arrogant about their old bloodlines, back to the first quarter of the seventeenth century, so central Kentucky charmed them without recourse to reciting Virginia's many virtues.

At this moment, lack of virtue was on their minds. Fair,

upon hearing of Harry's plan to sneak around Ward Findley's, figured he'd better go with her. No telling what hornet's nest she'd stir up. He didn't say that.

What he said was how much he'd like to cruise the countryside, no particular destination or timetable in mind.

As the two cats, the dog, and two humans were pulling away from the main Kalarama barn, Cody Howlett and two deputies arrived to go through Jorge's effects.

In the rearview mirror, Fair saw Larry leading the law-enforcement officials to Jorge's trailer.

No sooner had Fair and Harry turned onto Route 55 than they passed the sheriff of Washington County, the one in which Springfield was located, two counties south of Shelby.

"Turf war," Fair remarked.

"You think?" Harry watched the cruiser slide by.

"Oh, someone from Washington County will have to supervise. The newspapers will call it interdepartmental cooperation."

"The murder took place in Shelby County. What's there to fight over?"

"Publicity."

Harry smiled. "Ah."

"Humans like getting their picture taken." Pewter figured the Washington County sheriff wanted to be seen on TV, too.

"Unless it's a mug shot." Tucker settled on Harry's lap.

Fair turned off the highway in a half hour, and soon they cruised on blacktop two-lane roads. They passed through Versailles, the impressive public buildings evoking admiration.

Within another fifteen minutes they drove by the new Thoroughbred lay-up facility.

"Spent the bucks," Fair laconically noted.

"Did." Harry observed what she could. "I really like Paula Cline's place, Rose Haven—the right balance between high-tech and a real farm."

Breeding establishments such as the august and success-ful Lane's End Farm would send some horses to Paula for rest, rehab, and relaxation. As Paula was a longtime friend of Joan's, the two pushed each other along, each seeking to know more about the latest medical advancements than the other.

Joan, knowing Harry's active mind and Fair's profession, had introduced them to Paula years ago.

Somehow, good horse people always found one another and never ran out of things to talk about.

"Must be the aquatic building." Fair slowed. "My God, they've got an outdoor pool, too."

"Fair, every horseman in North America, maybe the world, owes a great deal to the Thoroughbred industry and to Kentucky."

"We do." He slowed again as a hay truck coming from the opposite direction swayed toward his truck. "Honey, in-tersection coming up. Left? Right? Straight?"

She checked Joan's notes on her map. "Straight. Then the next left."

The left appeared so fast, it was more of a dogleg turn. Fair braked.

Pewter, aroused from her snooze, stretched. *"Are we there yet?"*

"Just about." Mrs. Murphy, ears forward, had her hind paws on Harry's knees, her front paws on the long dash.

"Huh." Fair grunted.

"More four-board fencing. Ward may not be in the big bucks like Larry, Charly, and Booty, but he's not on food stamps."

"Not by a long shot." Fair whistled. Four-board fencing cost more than three-board fencing.

A dirt farm road snaked between two pastures. Fair turned in and cut the motor. "Wonder if anyone can see us."

"If we can't see them or a building, I reckon we're okay." Harry had already opened the door.

Mrs. Murphy and Pewter shot out of the truck.

"Hey, you two." Fair lifted Tucker down. "Tucker, herd those cats, will you?"

"Fat chance." Pewter, running quickly for an overweight girl, blasted into a verdant pasture.

"If anyone does come after us, we can say we had to let the cats go potty and they ran away." Harry put her boot on the bottom rail of the fence, throwing her leg over the top.

"I'm not saying 'go potty,' " Fair growled.

"Not manly enough?" she teased him.

He smiled. "Need to keep up my butch credentials."

The little family walked toward three mares. The sweetness of the clover mix, the humming of the bees, exalted their senses.

Mrs. Murphy reached the three mares first. *"Hello, girls."*

"Hello, pussycat. Who are you?" an older bay mare inquired, her soft eyes beautiful.

"Mrs. Murphy from Crozet, Virginia."

The other two mares looked at each other, then down at the pretty tiger.

Pewter, clover buds rubbing against her fur, arrived. *"Hi."*

"Hi," the mares responded.

Tucker came next. *"I hope we aren't disturbing you."*

"Not at all. We like company," the older mare replied. *"I'm Brown Bess, this is Amanda, and that's Lucy Lu. Those are our barn names. We're retired now from showing."*

"Miss it?" Pewter asked.

"Sometimes," Lucy Lu, who'd had a good career, replied.

"Not me." Amanda thought this was the perfect life.

"Girls, any new horses come on the farm in the last two days?" Tucker asked.

"Oh, during show season the vans are in and out every day," Brown Bess said.

"This would be an elegant mare wearing Ward's green and white summer fly sheet. She'd be black where her fur showed, but really she's chestnut." Mrs. Murphy filled them in.

Harry and Fair walked up to the mares.

"They belong to us," Pewter announced.

"That's the first time I've heard you say anything like that." Tucker, surprised, lifted her nose to touch Brown Bess's downturned nose.

"They do belong to us. They can't do anything right without us." Pewter puffed out her gray chest, quite fluffy.

Lucy Lu laughed. Fair patted her neck. "Happy horses."

"If nothing else we know Ward takes good care of them." Harry scratched Amanda's ears, then reached over to Brown Bess.

"He does," Lucy Lu confirmed.

"Come to think of it, last night, a mare in Ward's colors did come in. A real beauty. Black. But I haven't seen her since she stepped off the van. She'd be on the other side of the farm if not in a stall," Brown Bess told them.

"Where were you when you saw her?" Mrs. Murphy inquired.

"By the barns. Two barns. This pasture's almost fifteen acres. Goes right down to the barns," Brown Bess informed the cat.

"Lot of people there now?" Tucker wanted to keep looking without being conspicuous.

"Hard to say. Shelbyville show is always busy," Amanda volunteered. *"But it's lunchtime."*

"It's been so nice meeting you." Mrs. Murphy thanked the mares, then scooted over the rise. She could now see the two barns.

"Murphy, come here," Harry called, walking toward the cat.

Mrs. Murphy kept a few steps ahead of Harry as she angled toward the barns.

"I'm not going to miss this." Pewter hurried up to Mrs. Murphy.

"Damn!" Harry hated the thought of being caught trespassing.

"If we turn and leave, she'll come 'round," Fair predicted.

"No, I won't!" Mrs. Murphy moved at a more determined pace.

At six feet five inches, Fair's legs could cover more distance in one stride than Harry's. He began trotting. "Miss Pussycat, stop."

"Never." Mrs. Murphy kept in front to tantalize him.

He started running, and she took off like a shot, Pewter a little behind.

Tucker, sensibly, stayed with the humans. *"You'll get in trouble."*

"Where's your grit?" Mrs. Murphy called over her shoulder.

Fair stopped. "Dammit, I know better than to chase a cat."

"She's got something on the brain." Harry watched as the tiger cat and her gray sidekick, tails to the vertical, bounded toward the green barns with the white trim. "Now what are we going to do?"

"Let's stand here for a minute to see what they do. So far there's no sign of life down there at the barns." Fair saw the two cats circumvent the barns to dash into the adjoining pasture. "What's gotten into those two?"

"They're on a mission." Harry couldn't help but laugh, even as she was concocting what to say if they were caught.

"Guess we are, too." He jammed his hands in his jeans pockets. "I don't know about you, but I'm going after them. I'm not running, though."

"Too hot." Harry walked alongside Fair.

Tucker didn't go all the way to the barns. She darted across the main drive to the barns, then under the fence into the pasture where Mrs. Murphy and Pewter walked.

"Good idea." Harry followed.

Within a minute all were in the large pasture, which mirrored the retired mares' pasture.

If someone came out of the barns looking in their direction, they would see them, but if they left by the other side, they'd miss the small convocation.

"That's her!" Mrs. Murphy cried jubilantly when she saw Queen Esther, whose neck and legs, although washed, were still a tad darker than her chestnut body.

Pewter dashed up to the sleek mare, who chatted with five other ladies at the peak of their show year. *"Queen Esther."*

Bemused, the chestnut laughed at the rotund cat. *"I am."*

"We've been looking for you," Mrs. Murphy piped up.

"Well, I'm right here. Food's good. I'm glad I'm not at the fairgrounds. Where's Renata?"

"Esther, you've been stolen!" Pewter blurted out.

Tucker, now with them, asked, *"Sure you're all right?"*

"Of course I am. I didn't like that awful dye, but Ward washed it off the minute I arrived here. I'm not stolen."

"You didn't think it odd that you were painted?" Mrs. Murphy noticed how hard and healthy Queen Esther's hooves were.

"Of course not. They put hair shine on our manes, tail sets when we're in the stalls, dye those little white spots or scars on the forelegs should we have any. No, I didn't think it strange at all. Seemed like one more human peculiarity to me."

At this, the other horses laughed along with Esther.

"Who led you out of the Kalarama stall?" Tucker smiled at Queen Esther.

"Jorge. Dyed my legs, face, and neck, too."

"And you weren't scared? No one treated you badly?" Pewter felt something was strange beyond the theft.

"I've been treated like a queen!"

The other horses laughed again.

Finally, Harry and Fair reached the gorgeous mare.

"That's her! I swear that's her." Harry was excited.

"I think so, too." Fair looked all around. "Ward's farm is in the back of the beyond, but she's out in a pasture."

"If she goes over the hill there, one wouldn't notice her." Harry was confused. "It is bold, though."

"Hide in plain sight." Fair slapped his thigh. "'Course, we could be wrong. No one knows these horses better than Joan and Larry or the other trainers, but I'm pretty sure this is the mare."

"I am Queen Esther," she affirmed.

"She is," came the three-voiced chorus.

"How did you all know?" Harry knelt down to the "kids."

Fair had flipped open his cell phone. "Larry, I think we've found Queen Esther." He filled in the details, then asked

Larry to call the sheriff of Woodford County, as well as Renata. "We'll wait here."

They didn't wait long. The sheriff arrived within ten minutes.

What was peculiar was that no one came out of the barns when the sheriff showed up.

13

*W*hile one of the Woodford County deputies searched the barns, Harry, Fair, Mrs. Murphy, Pewter, and Tucker remained in the pasture.

The animals chatted with the horses.

Sheriff Ayscough, portly and in his early fifties, appreciated that Fair was a vet.

"She's in good condition?"

"Sheriff, she's in excellent condition. Her legs are sound, no hoof damage. I don't think she has a temperature, but if you'd like me to be absolutely sure I can go back to my truck and get a thermometer."

"No," Sheriff Ayscough replied.

"Someone's coming." Tucker sounded the alarm.

Two someones. Ward turned down the main drive, truck motor thumping.

Immediately behind him was Renata in her new Dodge truck.

Each pulled off the road behind the sheriff's squad car.

Ward hurried up the rise.

Renata walked briskly.

"Sheriff Ayscough, where did you find her?" Ward breathlessly asked.

"I didn't. These folks here did."

Ward beamed at Harry and Fair just as Renata reached them. She saw Queen Esther.

"Esther." She put her arms around the mare's neck.

"What's the matter with everyone?" Esther blew air out of her widened nostrils.

On the other side of the drive, Brown Bess, Amanda, and Lucy Lu stretched their heads over the fence. Given the lay of the land they couldn't see the assemblage, but their curiosity ran high.

Ward walked over to Queen Esther and felt her legs. He picked up each hoof.

Fair watched. "She's fine."

"How'd she get here?" Ward asked.

"That's what I want to know." Sheriff Ayscough's thick eyebrows rose upward.

"I don't know," Ward said.

"He's lying through his teeth." Pewter sat back on her haunches.

"He is. He brought me here," Queen Esther volunteered, but the humans missed it, of course.

Harry asked, "This is the first you've seen her?"

"It is," Ward solemnly replied.

"Mr. Findley, where is everyone?" Sheriff Ayscough thought an empty farm mighty peculiar.

Ward checked his watch. "Lunch, but Benny should be here."

"Who's Benny?" This was no sooner out of Sheriff Ayscough's mouth than the deputy emerged from the second barn with an older fellow, grizzled, unshaven, walking beside him.

"That's him." Ward nodded as the two men drew closer.

"Boss, I fell asleep in the feed room. I swear I did. I didn't touch a drop." Benny hit verbal third gear without coasting into first, his words rushing out of his mouth.

Ward's eyes narrowed. "Benny, I hope you're telling me the truth."

"I am. I swear I am. Shelbyville wears me out. I fell asleep on a chair in the feed room."

"You didn't hear a van or trailer come down the road?" Ward persisted as everyone watched.

"No."

"How'd this mare get in this pasture?"

"Dunno," Benny, contrite, replied.

Renata, overcome at her good fortune, tears in her eyes, kept petting the spectacular mare. "Thank God she's unharmed."

Sheriff Ayscough removed his hat to reveal thinning sandy hair. The slight rustle of wind cooled his head. "Ma'am, would you like to press charges against Mr. Findley?"

Disconcerted for a moment, Renata stared at Ward, then back at Harry and Fair. "No charges."

"You don't want to know how she got here?" Harry blurted out.

"Of course I do, but all that really matters is she's fine. And I don't want to jump to conclusions."

"It will all come out in the wash," Ward predicted, obviously grateful that he'd been spared legal proceedings.

"Well, if you folks don't need me, I'll be on my way." The sheriff crooked his finger for an instant at his deputy and then both started for the squad car.

"Benny," Renata asked the fellow, eyes a little red-rimmed, "do you think she could have jumped the fence, you know, from another farm?"

"Like the rehab center," Ward volunteered. "Backs up to my land. She could have easily sailed over a fence."

"Saddlebreds can jump." Benny shrugged.

"Ward, will you take Queen Esther to Kalarama?" Renata asked.

"You don't want her at Shelbyville?"

"No." Renata was firm.

"I'd be glad to." Ward smiled, patting Queen Esther.

Renata finally focused on Harry; a big smile crossed her face. "We both came out ahead." She paused. "How did you find her?"

"I found her." Mrs. Murphy cast a jaundiced eye up at Renata.

"Mrs. Murphy found her," Harry truthfully replied.

"I was there! I was right behind her." Pewter quickly plumped her own contribution.

"Don't start," Tucker warned them.

"The cats ran off and they discovered Queen Esther."

"But why did you come here?" Renata asked, Ward's eyes darting from Renata to Harry and Fair.

Before Fair uttered word one, Harry glibly said, "Fair wanted to drive by the new rehab center. He'd heard so much about it. Joan told me your establishment was behind it, Ward, so we cruised by. Tucker had to go to the bathroom, and when we pulled off, the cats jumped out of the truck and kept going." She paused. "Why did you come here?"

Renata, not missing a beat, replied, "Ward wanted to show me a horse for sale."

Ward knelt down, not exactly eye level with the cats and Tucker. "Thank you."

"You're welcome," Tucker replied.

"Yeah, you liar." Pewter giggled.

He stood up. "Benny, bring me a lead rope, will you?"

Benny ambled off.

Queen Esther touched noses with Mrs. Murphy. *"Why is he lying?"*

"I don't know, but it can't be good." The tiger purred, for she loved horses.

"Do you all need a hand?" Fair inquired.

"No, thanks," Ward replied.

"We apologize for trespassing," Harry said.

"Now she's lying!" Pewter exploded.

"Don't be an ass, Pewter. Mother knows something's off. She's trying to protect all of us," Mrs. Murphy sharply rebuked her friend.

"You've got a point there." Tucker frowned.

"We'll be on our way, then." Harry headed for the fence line.

"Harry, I really am thrilled." Renata ran after her, gave her a big embrace, and then hugged Fair, too. "I'll see you all back at Kalarama."

Neither Harry nor Fair spoke as they climbed over one fence, walked across the main farm drive, and climbed over the other fence.

Brown Bess walked after the humans, then Amanda and

Lucy Lu thought that was a good idea, too. It would have made a lovely photograph, two humans, three retired mares, two cats, and one smiling corgi treading over summer's green pastures.

"What's going on?" Bess flicked a fly off her hindquarters with her luxurious tail.

"Yeah," Amanda and Lucy Lu sang in chorus. *"The sheriff was here."*

"The flashy chestnut who came in—well, she was stolen." Pewter liked giving out important information.

"She didn't look stolen. 'Course, we didn't get a good look until this morning." Lucy Lu thought Queen Esther's coloring a bit off, since her face, neck, and legs were darker than her flaming chestnut coat.

Of course, "the girls" couldn't have known how many shampooings Queen Esther received until the worst of the dye washed off.

"Well, it's all worked out." Tucker didn't quite believe this.

As they ducked under the fence while Fair and Harry climbed over, Mrs. Murphy, Pewter, and Tucker bid good-bye to the nice mares.

"Why does Renata believe Ward? I wouldn't." Tucker waited for Fair to lift her into the cab of the truck.

"Maybe she doesn't. Maybe she just wanted her horse back." Pewter let Harry lift her up. *"There's been enough fuss."*

Mrs. Murphy jumped up into the foot well, then onto the seat. *"Glad he left the windows open."*

"Yeah." Tucker wedged between Harry and Fair.

"We know he's lying. Queen Esther knows he's lying. I think Renata knows he's lying." Pewter sounded definitive.

Mrs. Murphy, whiskers forward then back, asked, *"How do you know Renata's not lying?"*

14

"hat's going on?" Harry blinked, then added, "Locusts."

The main barn, white, greeted a person as soon as he or she turned into Kalarama, passing the grave of the great Kalarama Rex as they did so. In line behind the old main barn was another barn housing horses in competition.

The white vans, TV call letters on their sides, were parked on the drive to the right next to the outdoor practice track.

The small mobile TV crews shot footage of the barn, of the whole layout, of Paul and Frances's brick home, trimmed shrubs, weeded flower beds, Rose of Sharon and crepe myrtle in full regalia.

Fair parked by the round pen.

Once out of the truck, the little band stayed still.

"I don't want to get in the middle of all this." Fair folded his muscled arms over his forty-two-inch chest. Fair had about nine percent body fat, which meant his muscles were well defined.

"Honey, Joan and Larry might need us."

He exhaled from his nostrils. "You're right."

They trudged up the hill, heat waves shimmering. They entered the barn from the open north end. Fortunately a light breeze swept across the long main aisle, and both doors were fully open at each end.

The office and gathering room, both well appointed, were crammed with clients, newspeople.

Krista, blond and efficient, had her hands full answering questions and giving directions. Being the office manager at Kalarama, busy consistently, was overwhelming at this moment. Krista possessed a sunny personality, so she handled the pressure better than most.

Joan organized tours of the other barns, but she kept everyone out of the enclosed concrete arena.

Reporters or not, Larry and Manuel had to work horses. At that moment Larry was riding Point Guard.

A five-gaited horse learned two artificial gaits, a slow rack and a fast rack. The high-stepping gaits—with the horse in a frame not quite like dressage but a frame nonetheless—required concentration and conditioning from both horse and rider.

Larry, fabulous hands, lightly jigged the bit so Point Guard would begin his slow rack. Today would be a light workout. No point running a young horse through the bridle, risking his future.

The horse's mind was probably more important than his conformation. Point Guard had a good mind.

Fair knew Larry's schedule, as they had discussed it that morning. As he pushed open the glass door from the main aisle into the crowded room, out of the corner of his eye he saw Manuel walk toward the arena.

"Good," Fair thought to himself. "They can get Point Guard out of here before the reporters realize who was working."

Fair assumed the reporters knew the young horse's promising reputation and that the last class Saturday night would be a shoot-out between Larry, Charly, and Booty. He assumed too much.

What they wanted was a shot of Queen Esther disembarking from the van, of Renata's rapture.

It occurred to Fair that Renata had probably called the media. Who else would do it?

As if reading his thoughts, Harry whispered, "This won't hurt Renata's career."

Joan pushed through the people, hugged Harry and Fair, then turned to the reporters after giving her friends a wink. "These are the people who found Queen Esther."

Like lampreys, the reporters sucked onto anything that might provide copy, the cameras clicked on, one camerawoman stood on the sofa to shoot from a different angle.

Before they could all ask the same question—"How did you find the horse?"—Harry, shrewdly, smiled. "We'd love to take credit for the discovery, but"—she bent over to pick up Mrs. Murphy as Fair lifted up Pewter—"the cats were the real detectives."

Mrs. Murphy, eyes wide, stared at the closest reporter. *"We recognized her immediately."*

"We ran away from our humans. We knew because the old mares told us!" Pewter added.

The cameras rolled.

Tucker, the picture of obedience, sat in front of Harry.

"My corgi was right there, too." Harry smiled, and the cameras panned down to Tucker.

The questions flew fast and furious. Pewter answered each one, although both Mrs. Murphy and Tucker told her to save her breath.

Harry and Fair told the same story they had told Sheriff Ayscough, that a doggie bathroom stop was in order.

The reporters ate it up.

They'd no sooner finished when Ward turned in. His white and green van was forced to park at the entrance since the TV trucks hogged the drive as well as the large area behind the main barn, where a secondary barn for horses that were showing stood.

The lower barns housed mares and yearlings, plus there was the well-fortified and farther distant stallion barn. Both were down the hill where Fair had parked.

The reporters and cameramen ran out of the office and gathering room.

Joan, hands on hips, swiveled to face Harry and Fair. "Do you believe it?"

"It's their bread and butter," Fair evenly answered.

Joan frowned, then suddenly laughed. "Guess it's mine today, too. Well, let's go bow at Queen Esther's hooves."

Cookie bounded up from the enclosed arena as Manuel, obviously down since the loss of Jorge, opened the doors. Cookie bolted out, turned right at the main aisle, little legs churning, and she came out into the sun. Seeing the other animals, she joined them in a flash.

"Wow. Wow. Wow."

"Cookie, if only you'd been with us." Tucker then told the Jack Russell everything.

Just then, Ward rolled out the gangplank, and who should come out, horse in hand, but Renata, tears streaming down her cheeks as she led the mare out of the van.

"Guess she left her truck at Ward's." Harry tended to focus on and remember practical details.

"This makes a better entrance," Joan said out of the corner of her mouth and then, in a shrewd move of her own, walked up to the other side of Queen Esther. Both women led the mare to a stall specially prepared for her.

The reporters and cameramen followed, some walking backward.

Renata, face wet, kept repeating, "I'm so happy. I'm just so happy."

"We hear you owe it to two cats," the raven-haired female reporter from Louisville said, voice filled with humor.

"Mrs. Murphy and Pewter are the real heroes." Renata let go of the lead shank as Manuel, now at her side, led the mare into her stall.

On cue, Mrs. Murphy, Pewter, and Tucker sat in the sunshine at the barn's entrance. Cookie started in, then joined her friends.

Made a great shot.

This continued for an hour, until Renata excused herself and got back in the van—the cab this time—with Ward, who had also been peppered with questions.

Once they left, the reporters withdrew like low tide.

Joan walked down to the arena. Larry was in the center on foot, watching a client drive her hackney pony, an elegant gelding with high knee action. The wheels of the practice sulky kicked up the arena loam. "The last one left."

"Jesus." Larry whistled low. "Be more tonight."

"Won't be as bad, I hope."

"Where're Mom and Dad?" Larry inquired.

"Lexington. Dad had business. Mom went shopping. I called, gave them the news, and told them to take their time getting home."

After a few more words, Joan rejoined Harry and Fair. They told her all they knew.

"This is a strange situation." Joan sat down gratefully on the leather couch. "The horse reappears. Renata doesn't believe Ward stole her, and Jorge has been murdered."

"For today anyway, this story will overshadow the murder," Harry said.

Joan dropped her head back on the couch. "What if that's the point?"

"God, Joan." Harry's voice dropped.

"We were caught up in the horse, Renata's reaction, Ward's protestations of innocence." Fair slid his palm along his cheek.

"Right. Jorge fades away and maybe some evidence fades, too." Joan sat upright. "If only I knew what this was about!"

"If you knew you might be the next victim." Mrs. Murphy swept along Joan's legs.

"Don't say that!" Cookie yelped.

"It's true. Cookie, we need to find out what all this is about before they do." Tucker indicated the humans.

Cookie bared her long fangs. *"No one is hurting Joan. My bite is worse than my bark."*

15

*N*o sooner had Joan walked back into the small office than the phone rang.

"Kalarama." Krista's feminine voice pronounced the name with a lilt. She listened, put her hand over the mouthpiece, and whispered to Joan, "Renata."

Harry watched with amusement as Joan sighed loudly, then took the phone from Krista. Harry knew just how Joan felt, since the phone, useful though it may be, was also an infernal device for interruption.

"Renata, Queen Esther is a happy girl." Joan sounded as though she was as happy as the horse.

On the other end Renata said, "Don't take her to Shelbyville. I know our class is tomorrow night, but I want to ride her in your arena. Well, actually, I don't want her at Shelbyville in her stall. Don't trust it."

Joan paused. "Queen Esther is very sensitive, I wonder if traveling to a big show before she has to compete might affect her negatively."

"What I was thinking—and I have to give Ward credit for this—is that she likes to be on a trailer or van. He noticed driving her to Kalarama. Don't ask me why, but she's pretty relaxed. Why don't we trailer her to the show and let her stay on the trailer? She has her hay bag and we can put down a big water bucket and the crowds won't know where she is."

"We can try it, but I'm not allowing her to travel alone and be there alone. We'll have to put another horse in the trailer with her, and, Renata, given all that has gone on, one of my men needs to stay on that trailer, too. I'm not taking any chances."

"I'll pay for the extra horse's travel and for the guard. I know the bills run up."

"That's not necessary, Renata. My request is you ride the best you ever have." Joan was impressed that Renata offered, since most clients rarely factor in extra costs such as these.

"I will, although I confess I'm considering not riding Saturday night. She's been through a lot and so have I."

"We all have," Joan agreed.

Joan kept a sharp eye on the money. She'd be out of business in a heartbeat if she didn't. But she was wise about people and knew that not toting up every penny for Renata would help cement the relationship. Renata could and would, over time, buy a lot of horses. Joan devoutly hoped some would be bred by Kalarama. Renata might also use Joan to find horses suitable for her from other breeders. Joan had an incredible eye for a horse, as did Larry.

The worry was that Renata would become needy.

Amazing how many women clients became needy the longer they worked with handsome Larry. Joan kept a good perspective about it, but it could be wearing.

Fortunately, Renata carried no bad reputation on that score, nor did she suffer from the jumping-bean disease—jumping from barn to barn and trainer to trainer. Whatever had happened between Renata and Charly happened after a fruitful and relatively long association.

Once Joan handed the phone back to Krista to hang up, she filled Harry and Fair in, then asked Harry, "Do you think Renata's going to be a pain in the ass?" Joan liked to double-check her own feelings.

"How do you mean, apart from her horse being stolen?" Harry countered as Tucker walked behind the desk to visit Krista.

"Needy."

"No, I don't get that sense of her, but," Harry paused, "I don't believe her even though I like her." Joan and Krista sharply looked at the slender Virginian. "I don't believe her concerning her split with Charly, and I have even deeper doubt concerning Ward Findley. He had to have known and she let him off the hook. She called you from the van?" Joan nodded in the affirmative. "Joan, they're in cahoots."

"Ward and Renata?" Astonishment shone on Joan's face.

Even Krista blurted out, "He's such a small-fry. Why?"

"Maybe because he's a small-fry."

"What on earth could she gain by this? And it's a hell of a risk to the mare." Joan thought a minute. "Maybe not. She did say Queen Esther likes to ride in vans."

Krista, who had known Ward from childhood, added, "He's not exactly a liar and not exactly a cheat, but if you left one hundred dollars on the table and walked away, he just might pick it up and say the dog ate it."

"That's a recommendation." Joan laughed as she crossed her arms over her chest. "Harry, get to the point."

They were dear friends and Harry took no offense at Joan being direct. Besides, Joan was under tremendous pressure. "What if Renata stole her own horse?"

"What!" both women loudly replied.

"What if she knew Queen Esther would be in good hands? Ward runs a tidy little barn, but he needs money, he needs big horses. He's young, on the way up. She makes a deal with him and off goes the Queen. My cats and Tucker demolished the deal."

"Publicity. Her career needs a lift." Joan put two and two together.

"Maybe a juicy role will come of this. Someone in Hollywood will send her agent a better script than she's been receiving in the past. Or . . . ?" Harry held up the palms of her hands, pleading ignorance, but she felt she was on the right track.

"Maybe Ward was going to find Queen Esther. He'd look like a hero. Well, there are a lot of ways to slice the baloney, but, Harry, you might be on to something. I wonder if she promised to send her horse to Ward eventually," Joan said.

"Time will tell," Krista succinctly replied.

"Sure will." Harry seconded Krista's evaluation. "And maybe that is too obvious. But maybe she promised him rich clients, friends from the business who want to get into Saddlebreds. If she goes over to Ward herself it's a bit obvious."

"Like William Shatner." Krista cited the *Star Trek* star who also made some very funny commercials. "Bring Ward big clients like Mr. Shatner?"

"He can really ride." Harry had witnessed him many times at shows, and the man wasn't a passenger.

"The perfect client for Ward would be someone young, rich, and needing heavy-duty training, as well." Joan's brain whirred. "Damn."

"It's a theory."

"And a good one, but," Joan uncrossed her arms to hold up her right forefinger, "Jorge."

"His death may have nothing to do with this." Harry felt a heavy kitty run right across her sneakers as Pewter hurtled in from the gathering room for clients. Harry looked down to behold a tasty piece of chicken, thin sliced, in the cat's mouth. "Uh-oh."

Joan saw it, too. "There goes someone's lunch."

"I can help you with that," Tucker volunteered.

Pewter growled ferociously, then gobbled the prize.

"If someone pounds in here cursing a cat, we'll know where it came from." Joan giggled.

Harry returned to Jorge. "But we don't know. Joan, did the sheriff take anything from Jorge's trailer?"

"No."

"We should have a look. Going to have to clean it out, anyway."

"I hate to think of that." Every now and then the loss of Jorge hit Joan anew, but one thing that prevented her from fully mourning was the nagging feeling that she wouldn't truly grieve until she understood why he was killed. Was he in the wrong? Did she do anything to inadvertently hasten his end?

Krista offered, "Why don't I call Trudy and see if she can come out Monday?"

Trudy ran a high-powered cleaning service.

"All right, Harry, let's go."

The two walked out the front door of the main barn, turned right, then turned right again, dipping down behind the main barn and the indoor arena. Within a few minutes they walked through a privacy fence where a trim trailer sat along with other outbuildings and trailers. One could walk by the privacy fence, a palisade, and have no idea people lived back there. The married men usually lived in rentals Joan found for them, since she thought it unwise to have little children running all about the horses. They might be in the trailers for months, but eventually she'd find them other quarters. No mother can be on duty twenty-four hours a day, and a child's piercing voice could set off a yearling.

Currently no one else was living back there. Manuel rented a tidy house in Springfield.

Joan opened the door; a blast of air-conditioning hit her. Mrs. Murphy, Pewter, Tucker, and Cookie followed. "I didn't even think to turn the air-conditioning off."

"Joan, in a way it hasn't sunk in yet."

"I know. Well, where do we start?"

The two women glanced around the Spartan surroundings. Harry spoke up. "I'll check the refrigerator, you open the cabinets."

This took five minutes. The refrigerator had half a carton of milk, three Cokes, one beer, and one pizza slice. The cabinets reflected Jorge's bachelor status, coupled with a genuine lack of culinary concern. Harry poured out the milk.

"Trudy sure isn't going to have much to do in the kitchen." Harry shrugged.

The living room contained nice furniture that Joan had bought years ago but it remained in decent condition, all sturdy stuff, and one TV. No books or magazines dotted the coffee table.

His bedroom yielded girlie magazines, though. His closet contained a few shirts, one nice coat for church, a few ties. Socks, boxer shorts, and T's filled one drawer, jeans another, and the bottom drawer carried but two sweaters, one sweat-shirt.

The bathroom—surprisingly clean, as the women thought the shower and sink would be filthy—also offered nothing by way of explanation for Jorge's demise.

"Nothing." Joan slapped her hands on her hips. "Nothing. One bottle of Motrin." She paused. "Is there a rider who doesn't use Motrin or Advil? You know, he made a good wage. We pay better than most farms."

"Didn't spend it."

"He didn't spend it on himself," Joan shrewdly observed.

16

Friday, August 4, began to feel like the longest Friday of Harry's life. Back at the Best Western by four-thirty, she took a shower to rouse herself.

Fair, already showered, handed her a steaming cup of tea when she stepped out of the shower. They'd brought a traveling teapot, since one could never get a truly hot cup of tea in even the best hotels in America. An even greater sin was a coffeepot in the room, teabags in a bowl. Who could possibly drink tea from a pot that made coffee? Terrible.

"Honey, I love you." She gratefully took a sip while he toweled off her back.

Harry had told him about Jorge's trailer while they drove back from Kalarama to the hotel. He was as mystified as Harry and Joan about Jorge's whistle-clean trailer and, by extension, life. No one could be found to utter a disparaging word about the hardworking man.

Once dry, her hair tousled, Harry leaned against the headboard of the bed and stretched her legs out.

Fair joined her. The day had proved full for him, too. After the Queen Esther drama he'd delivered a foal, a long and difficult birth, at a small quarter-horse establishment. In a panic, the owners, new to Springfield, called Larry, not knowing it was Shelbyville week. Their vet was out of town and they thought Kalarama might know of a reputable equine vet.

Fair drove over, saving them much time. Like most veterinarians or medical people in general, he did not shy away from a crisis regardless of when it appeared. The middle-aged couple tried to overpay him, they were so grateful. He refused it, but when he climbed into his truck he found an envelope with four hundred dollars cash, which really was over the top. No point giving it back, they wouldn't take it, so he decided to put it toward the lovely diamond and ruby horseshoe ring Harry had admired at the jewelry booth at the show.

As a vet, Fair paid special attention to horseshoes. Each type of equine activity called for a specialized shoe. Racing shoes made of aluminum with no grabs or caulks cost a bloody fortune and lasted all of three weeks. Titanium shoes, of any stripe, cost even more, but they could be reset, sometimes twice, which actually offset the cost. Fair carefully examined hooves, shoes, proper shoe size, because a good farrier—and there were but so many—could save an owner thousands of dollars in vet bills. Most lameness problems in horses involved the hooves and the foot; a good farrier would stop a problem before it started, as well as correctly shoe the horse for balance, angle, and size of the hoof.

The horseshoe that people saw in pins, pictures, and good-luck charms was usually a keg shoe, a common shoe, like sneakers for humans. The ring Harry kept returning to admire was a keg shoe in miniature.

"More tea?"

"No, I'm slowly coming back to life." She had commiserated with him on the drive to the hotel about the delivery. "Don't you wonder why some foals or babies won't come out headfirst? You turn them, they turn back around."

He smiled. "I turned that little bugger three times. The last time I held on and pulled him out. He could have torn the mare to pieces if he came out feet first. He was determined. Loud, too." By "loud," Fair meant brightly colored, a paint. "People pay for color."

"Seems silly to me. Always has."

"Me, too. The right horse is the right color, but I am partial to blood bay."

"Let me know when you see one." Harry knew the spectacular coloring described as mahogany or oxblood showed up rarely. The mane, tail, and usually the lower part of the leg, by contrast, were black.

"I love a flaming chestnut." She noted all three animals fast asleep on their sides at the end of the bed. "The television interviews exhausted them. I'll bet your shoulders are sore."

"Hands, too."

"Let me slide behind you and I'll rub your shoulders."

"Ah" was all Fair could say as Harry's strong fingers worked his knotted muscles.

"Thought about drugs—maybe Jorge was selling. I mean,

most of the noncorporate crime in America is drug-related somehow. But he wasn't doing that. His little place was clean as a whistle, too."

"If he'd been on drugs, Larry and Joan would have known. I figure users often turn into sellers."

"I know." She quickly added, "Not if they're smart."

"You'd think he'd have flashed a little bit of the money if he was doing anything illegal to make money."

"Yeah." Harry dug her thumbs into his rhomboids, then bumped them down over his vertebrae all the way to his waist. "I keep coming back to selling even though I know that's not it, because the murder wasn't passionate. It was swift and brutal, efficient but not passionate. It wasn't about a woman. And he wouldn't have a double cross carved in his palms, now, would he?"

"I doubt it." Fair groaned when she came back to rub the big knot under his right shoulder blade.

"Sorry."

"No, it will unkink if you keep at it."

"How much did the foal weigh?"

"Quarter horses are supposed to be small," Fair humorously replied, "but not this one. I swear he was three hundred pounds. I'm exaggerating, but he was thick-built. If I were a team-roping man, I'd snap him right up. You should see the momma. Built like a freight train. All she needs to do is set her haunches and slide."

"So you're the guy who throws the calf, is that what you're thinking?" She smiled, because Fair was imagining himself riding Western, an odd transition for a hunt-seat rider accustomed to close contact with the horse due to the small, light saddle. The bulky Western saddle removed "feel" from the hunt-seat rider, and the longer stirrups made them think they were almost standing up on the horse. The reverse was equally true: a Western rider switching to an English saddle would figure they might as well ride bareback.

Fair closed his eyes because the darned knot hurt. "Being that Jorge was Mexican, what kind of things could he do or be involved in where that would be an advantage?"

"Silver."

"What?"

"Silver jewelry. The Mexicans create gorgeous stuff, and for a lot less than we or anyone else does, I suppose."

"I never knew that."

"Honey, you're a man. Men don't care about jewelry."

He smiled to himself, because he did at least care about his wife's jewelry. "We care about watches. And every man needs one ring besides his wedding ring."

"Cuff links."

"Nah. Too much trouble. But, yeah, you need 'em for the monkey-suit nights."

"You're awful."

"I don't like getting trussed up."

"You look better in a tuxedo than anyone, and in tails or morning suit, sweetheart, you could have any woman in the world."

"Just you." He breathed deeply as she finally worked out the knot. "You're being very, very good to me. What's cooking?"

"Nothing."

"Honey."

"Really." She was a rotten liar; her voice or eyes gave her away.

Fair couldn't see her eyes, but he could hear well enough.

So, being a highly intelligent man, he dropped it. Sooner or later she'd come 'round with what she wanted.

And being a smart man, he also knew there would be no delight for a Virginian to ask her husband flat out for what she wanted or needed. No, this had to be a sport, like fishing. The woman picked her spot, sat down under the trees or perhaps on a nice little craft. She baited her hook depending on the size and type of fish, maybe a little crank bait, then she cast it lazily over the river to drift. For a Virginian and Southerner in general, sure, the result was important, but the means of obtaining it should be worthy of the result. The bobbing down the river proved as much fun as catching the fish. Engagement was everything to a Virginian, even if you were only with them for two minutes. Well, he was in it for life.

"You got it." He rotated his shoulders.

"Good. I'll keep rubbing because I don't want to stop on the one side. Have to balance the muscles."

"You could have been a masseuse."

"I would have hated it. I don't like touching people, but I like touching you."

"Whew." He exhaled. "Had me worried there for a minute."

The phone rang.

Fair reached over for it, since his arms were a lot longer than Harry's. "Hello."

"Fair, how are you? It's Paula Cline."

"Paula, good to hear your voice. Will you be at the show tonight?"

"Overload." She said by way of explanation.

"I bet you want to speak to my bride."

"I do."

"Honey." Fair twisted to hand Harry the phone and sighed because his upper back didn't ache when he did.

"Paula, I hope you haven't been too virtuous."

"Oh, Harry, if only. I'm working so hard I don't have time to get into trouble. It's depressing."

"I'm sorry."

"Thanks. Of course, that's nothing compared to what's happened to Joan and Larry.

"And Jorge. And then I caught the early-afternoon news and there you were with the cats and dog. You all are stars for finding Queen Esther."

Harry laughed. "It's gone to Pewter's head. She wants an agent."

"Hey, Lassie had one." Paula laughed, too. "Renata looked divine; maybe she needs a new agent. She and Pewter could share one."

"Movie stars are supposed to look divine. What is she, thirty-two?"

"She's an eyelash away from forty. Girl's thirty-eight. One of my girlfriends went to high school with her."

"Then she really looks divine." Harry was impressed.

"They have to. It's their job. If you had the facials, manicures, and three-hundred-dollar haircuts, to say nothing of the color jobs, the massages, personal trainers, and clothes designed just for you, hell, you'd look better than Renata."

At this Harry burst out laughing, really laughing. "Liar."

"True. Hey, the reason I called, apart from complimenting you on the industry of Mrs. Murphy and Pewter, is to tell you I think I have the right horse for Alicia."

"Really." Harry was intrigued.

"He's a spectacular gelding by Sir Cherokee and he's here for a low bow. He's been here six months, healed up, but

Fair can make that judgment. If given time to heal, low bows usually don't cause future problems. But you know how some people are, they won't ride a horse with jewelry." Paula used the term that meant a horse who carried scars on its legs, wind puffs or low bows, a bowed tendon, or a variety of other blemishes caused by use or silliness in the paddock.

"Good mind?"

"Wonderful. This fellow has the best disposition and he's smart. Really smart. Sixteen one hands. Gorgeous head. Typical Thoroughbred bay, a little chrome on his legs"—by this she meant one white sock or more—"and a blaze."

A hand was four inches, the standard measurement for height of a horse.

"How much does the owner or owners want?"

"That's just it. The economy has tanked, and you know what happens to racehorses that don't win or are laid up. They want out from under the board bill."

Harry grimaced. "God only knows how many will wind up at the killers' like Ferdinand." She named a winner of the Kentucky Derby, shipped to Japan; he didn't pan out as a stud so the owners sold him for meat.

Because Ferdinand had won the Kentucky Derby, this murder sent shock waves throughout the horse world, but in truth, many good, useful horses were destroyed daily.

"This is a good horse. Swing by tomorrow? I'll be at the farm all day."

"We'll come by, won't we, Fair?"

Although he hadn't heard Paula's end of the conversation, he replied, "Yes."

"I do have a request. Even though the owners want out from under, I work with the Thoroughbred Retirement

Foundation, and I would like a donation of two thousand dollars. He sold as a yearling at auction for three hundred fifty-seven thousand."

"If we take him it will be done."

"What if Alicia doesn't like him?"

"If she doesn't, I will." Harry meant it, for she could usually get along with most any kind of horse, as long as it wasn't mean.

After saying good-bye, she gave Fair Paula's side of the conversation.

"Worth a look."

"I was thinking, the first class goes off at seven tonight. If we dress, grab a sandwich on the run, we could swing by Charly Trackwell's barn, because he'll be at the show. He knows something. I just feel it."

"No."

"Why?" She didn't expect such a firm no.

"Because there will be a watchman, for starters, my darling. Why would we be there when Charly's at Shelbyville? To snoop." She started to protest. He held up his hand. "Let's go tomorrow, after we leave Paula's. She's in Lexington, he's here, so we'd get to his place, what, maybe twelve? We should ask him if we can drop by."

"But, Fair, he'll have time to hide whatever he, well, whatever he has to hide."

"I don't think so. He knows we're best friends with Joan and Larry. His first thought might be that we're coming to see Frederick the Great, spy on the horse. Is he in good condition? Is he lame? Are there drug bottles in his stall? Which I doubt. Charly is too smart to leave Banamine or whatever around. But I can say, truthfully enough, that I'd like to see his setup, and if there's a vet on the premises, I'd like to meet him or her."

"He'll still know we're coming with the searching eye." She used the old Southern expression.

"He will, but it won't be as sneaky as coming when he's showing horses. If you think about it, how mad would it make you if someone trolled through our barn and you were out hunting or at a show?"

"Yeah."

"And furthermore, you beautiful girl, if we were to go now, we'd make an enemy. If we're aboveboard, we probably haven't made a friend, but we haven't burned our bridges. And you never know when you might need someone's cooperation."

"I never thought of that." She sighed. "Between you and Miranda, I get set straight."

"That's why we need people. All of us are smarter than one of us." He leaned back on her, she put her arms around his chest. "Let's get dressed, eat at the grandstand."

She concurred. "The food is fabulous."

"It is. If we get there early, we'll have a nice place to sit, enjoy the meal, and then we can go down to the barns or the box. But I need a little R and R."

"Me, too. We'll have to put the critters in the hospitality suite, because they won't be allowed in the grandstand."

When Mrs. Murphy, Pewter, and Tucker walked into the hospitality room, the sight of Cookie softened the blow of not going to the grandstand. Pewter in particular believed she needed to sample the food and provide her expert opinion to the humans. Being an obligate carnivore, Pewter knew she could taste meats and fishes better than any human.

"I could save them from mercury poisoning," Pewter declared as she was plopped in the burgundy, white, and black room.

Harry suffered a twinge of passing guilt.

She and Fair enjoyed a lovely meal while watching the first three classes: hackney pony pleasure driving, five-gaited pony, and junior three-gaited stake.

When they finished, Fair escorted Harry to the box. Paul and Frances sat up front on the rail. Conversation started immediately.

"Joan will be here in a minute. She's been down at the practice arena. Trying to get Looky Lous out of Barn Five," Paul informed them.

"Folks, I'll be back in one minute." Fair smiled. "You take care of my girl, now." He nodded at Paul.

"With pleasure."

To some women, this might have sounded like an insult. After all, women had been taking care of themselves and others for thousands of years without getting much credit for it—politically, anyway. But among these people, the sentiment was one of both form and affection. It would have been a careless husband who didn't, in some fashion, draw attention to how much he loved his wife.

Fair zipped around the back of the western grandstand, the one open to the skies, now rich with twilight's many-hued soft pinks and blues. He waited patiently as customers preceded him at the jewelry booth across from the grandstand's back.

Finally he smiled at the lady behind the counter and pointed to the desired ring. "Size seven."

"You're a decisive man." She unlocked the glass, her gray hair blueing with the light. "Would you like this wrapped?"

"I would."

"Do you need a card?"

"Yes, please."

This transaction lightened his wallet by three thousand dollars, but he wanted to do it. The parting with money caused no pain, because he knew how happy it would make Harry. He'd give it to her Monday, August 7. They'd be back home in Crozet.

Harry, pretty tight with the buck, spent money reluctantly even on needed items. She wouldn't buy herself jewelry. She might buy him something quite special for Christmas, his birthday, or their anniversary, but she wasn't a consumer in the typical American sense.

Fair, while not profligate, enjoyed treating himself and Harry. His philosophy was "You can't take it with you."

He slipped the dark green box, the thin white ribbon tied in a bow, into the inside pocket of his blue-and-white seersucker jacket.

Just as he rejoined his wife, Joan walked into the box. Harried, tired, she'd been dealing with more reporters, plus Charly, who was on the warpath, accusing her of stealing the horse for Kalarama's publicity. That was an unanticipated twist.

She sat down, smiled weakly, leaned forward to kiss her father then mother on the cheek.

Frances beamed. She liked attention from anyone but especially from her children. She checked the program. "Amateur roadster pony, one of your favorites." Frances swiveled around. "Where's Mother's pin? You always wear it for this class."

Harry and Fair swallowed, having the presence of mind not to look at each other, but the swallowing told the tale.

Joan, utterly miserable, confessed, "Mother, it was stolen the first night of the show."

Frances burst into tears, rose, and left the box.

Paul stood and put his hand on his daughter's shoulder. He didn't say anything but walked in a hurry after his wife.

Tears welled up in Joan's eyes. "What next?"

17

The answer to Joan's plaintive question wasn't long in coming, but first she watched the roadster class, followed by a junior-exhibitor class. Then Joan and everyone at Shelbyville gripped the railing as a tremendous class unfurled before them, the three-year-old fine harness.

All the great trainers drove the light four-wheeled buggies. The chromed wire wheels flashed as the open-topped vehicles passed by. The subdued but handsome turnout of the male drivers focused one's attention on the elegant, refined harness horses. Even at the park trot, a mid-speed gait, the horses' full manes and tails flowed. The lady drivers might wear a colorful dress that complemented the horse's color. The visual impact of the fine-harness class was potent. The class, large at fifteen, filled the expansive show ring. The sky darkened, and the lights flooding the ring danced off the bits, the wire wheels. The heat finally abated with a slight drop in temperature. Men slipped arms through their jackets; women threw jackets or sweaters over their shoulders.

The drivers sweated in their handsome attire. Rivulets poured down Charly's face under his three-hundred-dollar navy Borsalino hat. Booty favored a two-tone straw porkpie. Ward wore an expensive dove-gray fedora pulled rakishly toward his left eye.

After a long look at the class, the judges selected three horses for further inspection, Charly, Ward, and Larry. Charly cut off Larry, who was too smart to flash the anger he felt. Larry simply pulled back without breaking the trot and then moved to the edge of the rail, where he was silhouetted. Charly basically shot himself in the foot with that maneuver, because the mare he was driving, Panchetta, broke her gait, which the judges observed. Ward also observed it and made certain to glide right by the judges as he drove a compact but quite lovely seal-brown mare. Her trot wasn't as high nor her reach terribly long, but she was fluid and exhibited that charisma so desired in the ring. Without a doubt, Ward moved ahead of Charly in the judges' estimation and that of the knowledgeable audience. The crowd, cheering lustily, further animated Ward's mare, Om Setty. Booty drove wisely, but his mare just wasn't on form tonight.

The judges spoke to the announcer, who asked the contestants to line up. They drove in a clockwise direction.

When the judges walked by to carefully look over the Kalarama mare, Golden Parachute lifted her head, flicked her ears forward, and struck her pose. The crowd cheered.

The judges moved down the line. Each horse had an

attendant, his or her groom, standing two paces from her head, because the driver stayed in the buggy.

Ward, clever, placed himself at the end of the line, away from the bigger horses. Americans foolishly believed bigger was better. Om Setty, just pushing fifteen point one and a half hands, gleamed. She believed everyone was there to see her. Her conformation was superb. Her deep chest gave much room for her heart. Her nostrils had the delicate shape that Saddlebred breeders desire but were not so small that they hindered her intake of oxygen, which all athletes needed plenty of to perform at the highest levels. Her neck, long, drew attention to her perfect head, as classic a Saddlebred head as one would wish to see. Her one slight flaw was that she was a tiny bit wider behind than most people like, but she wasn't cow-hocked or bowlegged or anything like that.

The judges then left the lineup to mark their cards, without fiddle-faddle. The crowd, spellbound, didn't notice a pea-green school bus followed by two black cars lumber into the parking lot by the practice arena. The officer directing traffic at that entrance quickly moved out of the way.

Frances Hamilton might have seen it, but she was still crying as she sat in the second story of the big grandstand. Paul had brought her a light drink, but she didn't want it, so he sat with his arm around her and let her cry. After all those years of marriage he'd learned there were some things a man couldn't fix, so it was best to let his wife get it out of her system. From that height and angle, one could see a bit of the parking lot. He noticed the little caravan, but it didn't register that something unprecedented was taking place, something the officer on duty felt was beyond his jurisdiction.

The announcer called out the order of ribbons from eight forward. Charly received a fifth, which disgusted him but he disguised it. Booty was fourth. A newcomer was third, which was good for the sport, so the crowd cheered. Then it was between Om Setty and Kalarama's Golden Parachute. Everyone held their breath.

When second place was given to Golden Parachute, the crowd erupted, for as wonderful as the big light chestnut mare was, this was Om Setty's night. The little mare radiated quality, energy, and that elusive star quality. When Ward, sweat still dripping from his brow, had the ribbon pinned on Om Setty's brow band, the tricolor fluttered a bit as the crowd cheered with pleasure. Benny loped on foot to pick up the handsome and expensive silver bowl.

As was the custom, Om Setty was expected to give a victory lap, but an uproar in the barns cut it short. A young Mexican groom tore through the middle of the show ring and vaulted over the eastern fence to disappear into the night. Om Setty didn't shy, but Ward thought it prudent to drive out. Benny ran alongside and Ward slowed Om to a walk.

Neither horse nor human could believe the chaos. Grooms were running everywhere. Men and women in dark suits along with armed men fanned through the barns.

On hearing the commotion, Joan left her seat to hurry back to the barns. Fair ran ahead of his wife and Joan, in case Larry needed someone who could use his fists as well as his mind. He saw Larry step out of the buggy before the entrance to Barn Five. No sooner had Larry put a foot on the ground than a man in a dark suit came up to him.

The Immigration and Naturalization Service, INS, wanted to see documentation that his non-American-born employees were legal. Any nondocumented immigrant worker would be seized for deportation. Over the years INS had

descended upon horse shows for the various types of horses—
Tennessee walkers, hunter–jumpers, racehorses, etc. Ap-
parently disrupting a show in progress brought them deep
satisfaction.

The day had been long, the competition fierce, and
Charly Trackwell's display had tested Larry's patience. It
was all he could do not to blow up. He handed Golden
Parachute to Manuel.

"Does he have his green card?"

"He does." Larry spoke evenly to the man. "But if you'll
just give us a minute, we have to unhitch and wipe down the
horse. She's been in the ring a long time."

"How do I know your workers won't bolt?"

Offensive as this response was, Larry had observed the
track meet when he rode back to Barn Five. It was a fair
question. Luckily, he also saw Fair.

"Fair, will you help me out?"

"Of course."

"Will you wipe down Golden Parachute?" Then Larry
turned to Manuel. "Bring the boys into the hospitality suite."

"Done." Fair walked on the right side of Golden
Parachute.

"Who's that?" The INS man clearly felt he was entitled to
interrogate everyone and to suspect everyone.

"My veterinarian."

Larry walked into the hospitality tent and drew back the
curtains to the changing room. A long clothes rack stood at
the back; some tack trunks were inside, as well as a full-
length mirror, boots lined up neatly alongside it. A bridle
case on the wall served as a makeshift paper holder, filled
with registration forms, Coggins information, and so forth.
He unlocked it just as Joan and Harry came in. He was

tempted to hand the humorless official all the Coggins papers, which proved via blood tests that each horse tested negative for the disease.

Mrs. Murphy, Pewter, and Tucker, released from their quarters, ran through the hospitality suite.

Pewter skidded to a halt. *"There's ham up there again."* She gazed up at the table, glorious to her.

"Fatty," Tucker yelled as she reached the aisle.

"Come on, Pews, we'll get some later." Mrs. Murphy, curious as ever, wanted to see what was going on.

Cookie joined the three other animals as they stepped outside. *"Looks like mice, running in every direction,"* Pewter said.

"The guys hauling after them aren't dressed for it." Cookie giggled. *"And look at that lady: can't run in a skirt like that."*

Six workers had jammed into a car, but they no sooner reached the exit than a police barricade turned them back. Caught.

The ones on foot, though, would get away if they were patient and kept quiet all night once out the back of the fairgrounds. Heavy bushes and foliage at the grounds' western edge provided enough cover for them to slip out, making their way behind homes if they headed north, or businesses, now closed, if they headed west.

Larry showed the official their paperwork, copies of the originals kept in a file cabinet at the farm.

Harry remarked to Joan, "I'll go back and work with Fair so Manuel can have everyone lined up for the INS man."

"Thank you." Joan's anger masked her exhaustion.

Damn them for pulling a stunt like this at one of the crown-jewel shows. And damn them for driving in before the three-gaited pony class, thereby spoiling this for the kids riding.

Manuel brought three men into the hospitality tent, the official peered intently at their green cards. Since everything was in order, with a light air of disappointment he left the room, walked the aisle, and looked over the stall door at Fair.

"May I see your license?" He had already been told that Fair was a vet so he did this to irritate since illegal workers are rarely veterinarians.

Fair pulled out his wallet, flipped it open to his photo. "Honey, do you have yours?" he asked Harry, now in the stall helping to wipe down Golden Parachute.

"In my purse in the truck."

The official handed Fair back his wallet, then said to Harry, "Won't be necessary." He turned to leave the barn, then double-checked his list. He came up to Larry again.

Larry had hung up his coat and grabbed a tonic water from the bar just as the man walked in. "Would you like a drink?"

"No thank you. I have a Jorge Gravina on my list. Thirty-two."

Larry pulled a moleskin notebook from his hip pocket, bent over the table, and wrote the name of the undertaker in Springfield. "He died unexpectedly yesterday. You can view the body if you like. I do have a copy of his green card."

"Oh, uh, I'm sorry. Will you send me a copy of his death certificate?" The official handed Larry his card. Obviously he hadn't read the newspapers, but he was a single-minded person. He was here to bag illegal workers. If one was dead it was no skin off his nose. He actually liked raiding the horse shows, upsetting people he viewed as rich. Little men make the most of little power.

"I will." Larry compressed his lips lest the wrong words fly out.

The fellow left Barn Five to assist another INS person.

Mrs. Murphy, Pewter, Tucker, and Cookie scampered through legs to Charly's barn, since that's where most of the noise was coming from now.

Four hapless young men, neatly dressed in jeans and pressed cowboy shirts, were lined up, backs to the stalls.

The animals quietly walked in. Mrs. Murphy climbed up onto a stall beam. Pewter followed with effort, as Spike, like a skyscraper steelworker, sauntered toward them from the other direction.

"What a fuss," Mrs. Murphy greeted the tough guy.

"You missed the knockdown." Spike grinned, his three good fangs yellowed a bit.

The two visiting cats glanced down, noticing a roly-poly INS official with sawdust on his back and backside.

"Did Charly do that?" Pewter enjoyed the evolving spectacle.

"No, that guy walked right into a stall and asked one of the boys for his green card. The Mexican pushed the chub in the chest, the chub fell flat on his back, and the Mexican ran like hell. Then Charly showed up, foul as a bad storm; guess he didn't do what he wanted to do in the class. He rode right toward the fatty, now out of the stall, stopping on a dime in front of him. Gave the boys in the back of the barn time to get out, because the official's attention was on Charly, then Carlos, who was right behind him."

"Did the INS man—"

"What's INS?" Spike inquired.

Murphy answered. *"Immigration and Naturalization Service."*

"Oh." Spike sat down. *"Humans have hunting territories like us. These fellows are in our territory."*

"Who, INS?" Pewter asked.

"No, the Mexicans. I listen to the barn radio, you know. Illegal immigrants, all in the news." He opened his mouth wider; his missing left fang gave him a sinister appearance, but at heart, Spike was a good cat.

Down below, the two dogs sat on their haunches as Charly excoriated the INS official. Carlos took Panchetta.

"I want to see his papers."

"And you will, but I can't have the mare standing here in harness. If you want this to go faster, help us." Charly put the man on the spot.

The fellow stepped back. "I'm kinda afraid of horses."

"Then wait, because I'm not going to risk my mare for you or anybody. I wouldn't give a good goddamn if the President of the United States walked in here. I wish he would." Charly overflowed with hostility, but he did add, "So he could see what idiots you people are."

"Politics isn't my department."

Charly and his groom rapidly unhitched Panchetta, then walked her back to her stall for a rubdown. "Bullshit. Politics is everyone's department," he yelled from inside the stall. "Don't stand there like a bump on a log and tell me you're just doing your job."

The official, cowed by Charly, stood up for himself on this one. "I am just doing my job."

"Sure. You raid us at one of the biggest shows of the year.

You tell me that isn't political?" Before the man could answer, Charly turned to his groom. "Carlos, show him your card, will you?"

"Yes." The skinny, good-looking man fished in his hip pocket, retrieving a worn leather wallet, the hand tooling nearly smooth. He stepped outside the stall.

The roly-poly man brought it close to his eyes. "Hmm, fine." He handed it back to Carlos as Charly stepped out of the stall.

"I could have you arrested, you know," the official declared but without belligerence. "You've been using illegal workers."

"Prove it." Charly was calming down. "You go ahead and prove it. I don't know who those men are." He pointed to the four hapless illegal workers.

The INS official knew that one man knocking him down didn't prove that Charly had hired the worker. The evidence was circumstantial, and the illegal had fled. But circumstantial was better than nothing.

"I'll have to cite you."

"Go ahead. And when you get back to your dreary little desk in your dreary little office, remember this: I will fight you, I will fight the INS tooth and nail. You have to prove I hired illegal workers. My employee has shown you his green card. He is the only non-American working for me." This was a bald-faced lie. "And furthermore, you find me white people who will shovel shit and clean out water buckets. Americans don't want to get their hands dirty. They'd rather sit on their sorry asses and collect welfare."

"He's getting ugly," Tucker laconically said.

"And you know what," Charly's voice rose again, "you find me some blacks who will shovel shit or some Koreans or Chinese or, hey, whatever you got. And even if they'll shovel, they ain't horsemen, brother."

"Those questions aren't my concern."

"I guess not. If we solve this problem, you'll be out of a job, won't you?"

Tilting his many chins upward, the official asked, "Who are these men?"

"Never saw them in my life."

"He's good." Spike chuckled.

"Lies without batting an eye," Pewter agreed.

"I found them at the end of your barn just outside. One was pushing a wheelbarrow."

"So?"

"They don't work for you?" His voice carried doubt.

"They don't work for me. But you do. My taxes pay your salary. If you want to stand here," he handed him a pitchfork, which the INS man handed back with disdain, "work."

On that note, the roly-poly man left, glad to be out of the barn unharmed.

The dogs moved closer to the stall as the cats nimbly walked overhead in time to hear with their incredible ears Charly, under his breath, hiss to Carlos, "Double cross."

18

The disruption caused by the INS agents delayed the ensuing classes, many of them junior classes, which outraged many people, not just Joan. They could have come in the daytime or after the last class. Some of the young competitors were crying.

Larry, arms crossed over his chest, said, "I'm going over to Ward's to congratulate him. Nothing I can do about this damned mess."

"I'll stay here." Joan sank into a director's chair. "This feels like the longest day of my life." She waited a moment. "Told Mom about the pin and, well, it's been a long day."

Larry leaned over to kiss her on the cheek. "Some days you get the bear, some days the bear gets you."

Harry said, "Joan, do you mind if I tag along with Larry?"

"No, go ahead."

"In that case, I'll keep this beautiful lady company." Fair smiled as he walked to the bar to fix Joan a gin rickey.

As Harry and Larry left the barn, Joan glanced up. "Are you plying me with alcohol?"

"Made it light. I know you're not a drinker, but, Joan, a little relaxation at this moment is good for you." He handed her the tall glass, the bubbles rising upward promising to pop on her tongue. "I'm fixing you a sandwich and one for me. How about turkey? High protein, low fat, not that you need to worry."

She took a sip, feeling better instantly, part of that being psychological. "I ruin the low-cal benefit by smearing mayo over everything."

He beamed. "You will always be beautiful, so if you want mayo, mayo it is."

"Fair, you're so sweet. I'm glad Harry saw the light."

"I had to see it first." He put crisp lettuce on the dark bread. "When I slipped out of the box, I managed to get to the jeweler without her knowing, and I bought the horse-shoe ring she liked. She'll be forty in a heartbeat. She should have a big present." He grinned.

"That is a gorgeous ring. You know, I had a bad moment when I turned forty, and then it vanished. I really don't care, do you?"

"Yes and no." He held the knife aloft for a moment, the large mayo jar below. "I fear not being able to pull out foals if they need it or not being able to lift sixty-pound bales of rich alfalfa. I do worry about that. But you know, you do what you can, and if I can't physically perform, I hope I can still serve. As long as the brain works."

"Mine has shut off." She laughed.

"Been a hell of a couple of days." He handed her a plate,

then sat next to her. "At least it's quiet right now. No one's here, they're back on the rail or running away from INS."

Joan bit into the succulent turkey sandwich, then put it on the plate. "Mmm." She swallowed. "Hey, where's Cookie and the gang?"

"I don't know, but if they're not back by the time we finish our sandwiches, I'll go look. They're Americats. Don't need a green card." He winked.

"Cookie will jump in any open car. She loves her rides. One time a customer came to the barn, called a half hour after he left. Cookie was asleep in the backseat of his car and he didn't know it until she woke up. Had to drive to the Louisville airport to pick her up from Hertz since he was in a rented car."

They both laughed.

As they visited, relishing the bit of peace they had, Harry and Larry walked into Ward's barn, where a congregation had gathered to congratulate him.

Ward easily saw Larry, since Larry was tall. "Hey, drinks on the tack trunk."

"Great ride, Ward. Om wanted it tonight. She's a terrific mare. Hope you breed her someday." Larry pushed through and shook Ward's hand.

Harry, in his wake, also offered her congratulations.

"I guess all this commotion stole some of my thunder." Ward smiled. "Glad all I have is Benny, and he's red, white, and blue." Ward made it a special point to note he hired no Mexicans. No one much thought about it at the time.

Benny, leaning against a stall, raised his beer. "Sometimes I'm Confederate gray."

They laughed, since Benny would whip out his Confederate Zippo lighter if he thought someone was touchy, which meant Yankee.

Charly Trackwell came into the barn. Mrs. Murphy, Pewter, Tucker, and Cookie followed. Given what they'd witnessed, they thought they'd tail Charly. He was so wrapped up in things he didn't notice the posse behind him.

Harry exclaimed, "Where have you been?"

Charly thought she spoke to him. "In the barn dealing with a goddamned idiot INS agent."

Harry smiled at him. "I'm sorry." She figured it better not to say she was greeting the animals, all of whom ran to her.

"I'm tired. Pick me up," Pewter whined.

"Pewter." Harry sighed but bent over to pick up the solid cat. Pewter was overweight, but she had a lot of muscle, too.

"Oh, I love seeing from this height." Pewter purred.

Mrs. Murphy climbed a stall post. *"I've got a better angle."*

"Who cares." Pewter put her paws around Harry's neck.

The dogs decided to keep out of it.

"Let's see if Ward has Bag Balm," Tucker whispered to Cookie. *"Seems to be the standard for rubbing on little cuts and irritated skin."* They had observed a young rider surreptitiously open her little green Bag Balm tin. The small tin was a good place to hide things once the heavy balm had been washed from it. Fortunately, most folks kept their drinking and other treats in check—at least until after the last class of the night.

Cookie, being a Jack Russell, scooted to the grooming bucket, since she'd heard all about this stuff.

However, the dogs couldn't get their noses in because Benny shooed them away.

Charly paid his compliments to Ward, then edged away from the small crowd. Larry, too, turned to go.

"Larry, you son of a bitch, you called INS, didn't you?"

Startled at this off-the-wall accusation, Larry laughed it off. "Have another drink, Charly."

Harry kept a few steps back. She didn't trust Charly's temper.

"I'd say it's damned convenient for you, Hodge," Charly snarled. "Your men have their green cards on them, too. And by the way, where's Renata? You kept her out of this because of the bad publicity?"

"Charly, you're out of your mind. She doesn't have a class tonight."

"Oh, bullshit. With that massive ego, you think she'd pass on everyone fawning on her tonight because Queen Esther showed up? You bet she showed up. You took her in the first place."

Larry's face, beet red, betrayed his own rising anger. "You know what it is, Trackwell? You can't stand losing. You cut me off in the ring tonight to make Golden Parachute break. Didn't work. And you aren't going to win the five-gaited stake, either, so who are you going to blame Saturday night? Think ahead. Has to be someone else's fault."

"I'll win and I'll win big. Panchetta was off. Happens." He pulled in his horns somewhat, thinking about the horses and also because he knew Larry could throw a hard right.

"We'll see." Then Larry taunted him: "How many Mexicans did you have running out the back of the barn? You don't think I've noticed Little Tijuana at your barn? Come on, Charly. You got what you deserved."

Charly leaned forward, hissing through clenched teeth.

"And you got a dead one. Why is that? What are you covering up?"

Larry, deeply upset over Jorge's death although he had kept it in check, let fly. "Too bad it wasn't you, you sorry—"

"You'll die before I do." Charly stepped back, digging his heels in the loam. "Maybe they came for you and killed Jorge instead."

"Is that a threat?"

"Take it any way you want, but I'll see you dead."

19

*A*fter the last class, the show organizers shut down the selling booths, encouraging the spectators to leave. They shut the gates when the crowd vacated but left two men there for the trainers, riders, and the few other spectators who would be late in leaving. If the reporters from Louisville and Lexington came out upon being notified of the INS raid, they would find the gates closed. This gave the horse people an opportunity to prepare for tomorrow's grilling. Not that any of them had anything to do with the illegal workers or tonight's debacle, but they needed to formulate a clear statement. This show was turning into a media hot spot.

The trainers, grooms, and owners trickled out. A few, overburdened by chores without their workers, stayed behind. The men at the gates knew who they were. One walked to each trainer, asking for a sense of how long they would be.

Booty Pollard, whose junior had won the last class of the night, the junior five-gaited stake, walked across the paths to Ward's barn. The lights glowed overhead in the aisle as Ward and Benny put blankets over the two horses to return to the farm. No one else was in the barn.

"Congratulations, Ward. Had a kid in the next class, so I didn't have a chance to tell you what a great ride you put in."

"Thanks." Ward leaned over the back of Om Setty, her green and white blanket crisp and clean. "Heard you won the last class."

"Did."

"Congratulations to you."

Booty moved closer, then spoke freely in front of Benny. "Any idea who made the call?"

"Charly accused Larry Hodge."

Booty snorted. "Jesus."

"Threatened to kill him, too."

Om Setty, a good girl, didn't even twitch when Booty put his arms on her back. The two men spoke with perhaps eight inches between their faces as they leaned over the very special mare.

"Time to jerk Charly's chain."

"Shit, Booty, he's off the chain. Don't know what he's going to do or say next." The handsome younger man wiped his brow with a handkerchief; the humidity remained oppressive. "Who does he think he's fooling?"

Booty smirked. "Started when Renata left him. I always thought there was more going on there than Charly let on."

Ward's eyebrows shot upward. "If Charly Trackwell was

nailing a movie star, he'd put a full-page ad in the *Lexington Herald-Leader*."

Booty considered this. "You've got a point there." Then he asked, "What is it? The money? She's a dream client."

"That she is," Ward agreed, a crooked smile on his boyish face. "But women like Renata aren't easy keepers." He used a term meaning a horse you had to feed extra, making owning it more expensive.

"Some stunt, Queen Esther in your pasture." Booty laughed as he probed for an incriminating response. "Anyone believe you?"

Ward smiled, shrugged, but admitted nothing.

"Don't make the mistake that Charly did, Ward. Don't assume because Renata is beautiful she's dumb. When you think about it, Larry's a tough competitor, he'll go all-out to win, but it's not like him to pull something like this. Just not."

"Maybe so." Ward thought about it.

"And it doesn't really benefit Kalarama to have this show turned inside out any more than it does us. Upsets the organizers, makes the fans wonder, and everyone loses time to the federal government. Won't keep the fans away, though, thank God."

Benny, hands behind his rear end, leaned against the stall, taking in every word. With two days' growth of beard—he hadn't time to shave—he resembled a desperado.

"Yeah, but who would call? Can't see what someone would gain by this." Ward knew something was out of kilter, but he couldn't pinpoint the source.

"Well now, if you want publicity, if you want cameras at this show all the time, that seems to be right up Renata's alley." Booty stepped away from Om Setty, crossing his arms over his chest.

"Ah, Booty, think she went around and toted up Mexicans?"

"I do. This show is all about Renata DeCarlo. Won't break her heart to set Charly down on his ass, neither."

"We got to do something about Charly," Ward again advised.

"Ward, if you're that worried about his mood, talk to him."

"We both need to talk to him." Ward walked out of the barn to look down toward the practice arena and the parking lot. "Looks like he's gone."

"Tell you what. Let's meet him for breakfast tomorrow. The Nook just outside of town. If he doesn't have time to go, we'll go to him. I expect he'll be more settled tomorrow. I'll call him. Call you in the morning."

"Let you know. Where's Miss Nasty?"

"Changing her clothes." Booty smiled. "Gotta go."

As Ward and Benny walked the two horses to the van down in the lot, Ward asked, "What do you think?"

"I don't trust either one."

"Don't like 'em or don't trust 'em?"

"Both."

Ward kept quiet, because Booty's comment about Queen Esther meant Booty didn't trust him any more than he trusted Booty. He took the lead shank from the gelding Benny was leading, while Benny dropped the heavy ramp to the back of the van, walked up the rubber-coated ramp, and flipped up the heavy door bolts. He swung open the door to behold fifteen illegal workers. Wordlessly, he motioned for them to flatten against the side of the van.

He walked down, took the gelding. "Boss, we got precious cargo."

"Inchworm." Ward named one of the men he knew as highly intelligent.

Inchworm had probably led those he could through the bushes, waited until they could slither into the lot, and jammed up into the van using the small side gangplank to get in, as it would be much easier to pull up from inside.

Benny led the gelding right by the men. The horse planted his hooves for a second, but Benny sweetly coaxed him to his spot and tied him by the feed net.

Inchworm, who humped up his back when he worked a horse, silently pointed for some of the men to get behind the gelding and flatten themselves at the bulkhead.

Om Setty walked on, looked around, and reached for her feed bag.

The men stood or sat around the horses.

Benny and Ward slid into the cab of the old van and fired her up. She sputtered and stopped.

"Not now, baby, not now." Ward sweated.

"Gotta rebuild this engine." Benny crossed his fingers.

"If I win a couple more classes, I can." He pulled the choke, pushed it in a bit, cranked her. She belched black oily smoke from her exhaust, coughed again, rumbled a little, then started to hum. "Sweet Jesus, I adore Thee." Ward then eased off the brake, pushed in the choke completely, and rolled out of the lot.

They just had to get past the fellow at the gate. He waved at them as he unlocked it. What he saw were two immaculately groomed horses reaching up for their feed bags, their windows open to let in the night air.

They turned left onto Route 60, Ward thinking it better to avoid I-64, the corridor from Virginia to where the

Mississippi River creates a border between Illinois and Missouri.

"What if INS comes to the farm?"

"Won't. Just you and me. We're golden."

"Where you gonna put these guys?"

"They'll sleep in the outbuildings. Can't risk them in the barns, just in case. Guess they're hungry." He thought. "Gonna be cereal tonight. Nothing in the fridge."

"I'll make a food run in the morning," Benny said. "Then we can call folks to come pick up their grooms." He exhaled. "Whooeee. Gonna be busy." He paused a second. "You're smart not to have Mexican grooms in your barn. 'Course with me, I do the work of two men." Benny cackled.

"Right, Laurel and Hardy." Ward smiled, then asked, "You think Renata called INS?"

Benny shrugged. "Booty's right about publicity."

"Wouldn't she want the publicity about her?" Ward concentrated on the road.

"Still, brings the reporters around and keeps them around. They'll be there for her class."

"See, that's what I mean. She's got it all set up with Queen Esther so when she rides tomorrow night it doesn't matter if she wins or loses, she wins."

"Yeah. She should win the three-gaited open stake. Helluva mare."

"She doesn't come out ahead by what happened tonight. Can't see it." Ward frowned.

"You falling for her?"

"No." A long, long pause followed. "Wouldn't mind taking her to bed, though."

"That's when your troubles really begin," said the man with three ex-wives and children to boot.

20

*H*orse people tend to be tough. They work hard physically, keep long hours during shows, sleep little. The compelling passion, obsession perhaps, for horses drives them ever onward, to the astonishment of those who like differing pastimes such as golf or tennis. It's not that those sports lack committed competitors. Yachting creates an equivalent passion, but these other escapes from daily drudgery don't have another living creature for a partner, except for dog shows. Dog shows are more sedentary, though. Horsemen are a breed apart from other sportsmen. It strikes horsemen as perfectly normal to build their barn before their house; to go without when money is tight so long as the horses are well fed, well shod; to run into a burning barn to save one's horses without considering the danger to one's self.

Different as Charly Trackwell, Booty Pollard, and Ward

Findley were, they shared this iron bond. They also shared a deep appreciation of profit: being horsemen did not deter them from dipping into dishonesty.

They sat in a secluded booth in a white clapboard house west of Shelbyville that served the best breakfasts and lunches between the Kentucky and Ohio rivers. The place was packed at seven in the morning.

Booty wanted them to be seen by others but not heard. Let people wonder what they were doing.

Ward eagerly cut into his three sunny-side-up eggs. He'd burn off his huge breakfast by eleven. Charly and Booty kept fit, as well, although being slightly older than Ward they had learned to keep an eye on it.

Each time the waitress, Miss Lou, red lipstick freshly applied, swept by to pour fresh coffee or drop off condiments and side orders for unvanquished appetites, they spoke of horses, classes, competitors.

"Boys, the coffee cake defies description."

Longing passed over Charly's face, but he waved off the suggestion.

"I'll try it." Ward smiled. "Be finished with the eggs and sausage by the time you hit the counter."

"Just so's the counter doesn't hit back." Miss Lou winked. "Booty, you'll like it. 'Course, I have giant cinnamon buns, too, vanilla icing dripping all over. I know how you boys like your buns." She sighed.

Booty caved. "Oh, what the hell. Buns!"

Smiling triumphantly, she spun in her special shoes, needed since Miss Lou worked on her feet all day, her starched apron flaring slightly with the quick turn.

"I swear Miss Lou is as happy selling us a piece of coffee

cake and a cinnamon bun as we are selling a three-hundred-thousand-dollar fine harness horse." Booty laughed.

"All relative, brother, all relative." Charly reached for nonfattening creamer.

The delicious concoctions appeared. Miss Lou, pencil behind her ear, didn't write up a ticket, just in case they needed something else.

When she moved to the next booth, the men paused a moment. The noise level in the restaurant rose upward; a line snaked out the front door.

"Who killed Jorge?" Charly asked, voice low.

"Not me," Booty said as a joke.

"Booty, get serious. It just might be one of the reasons INS swooped down like carrion crows." Charly enjoyed a vivid turn of phrase. "The double cross on his palm points to someone or something. I can't figure it out."

"Well, it doesn't make much sense to think Larry called them." Ward spoke cautiously since he was very much the junior partner in this trinity. "Jorge was his employee. Why bring on more badges?" He used "badges" as a general term for anyone enforcing the law, a relatively hopeless job when he considered it.

"Why give him credit for thinking it through?" Charly, irritated for a second partly because he did want a piece of coffee cake, snapped. "He wants to wreck me for Saturday night's five-gaited. The man is a ruthless competitor."

"That could be said of you, too, Charly." Booty's tone was even. "Larry isn't the problem. The problem is if any of the, um—the desired term these days is 'undocumented workers'—squawks."

"They won't," Charly firmly said.

"You're sure?" Booty tapped the side of his coffee cup with his forefinger.

"Sure, I'm sure." Charly leaned back, tilting his chin upward. "They'll drop 'em off across the border. Big deal." He threw up his hands. "The guys wait a couple of days and come back over. We need workers, and we really need people who can work around horses. So if we don't bring back the same batch, they'll go to other horsemen. Those guys aren't stupid. They want these jobs. They'll keep their mouths shut."

Booty squished the crumbs from the buns between the tines of his fork. "Might be."

"And remember," Charly leaned forward, voice low, "the INS can't prove we employed any of these men. They ran out of those barns like rats off a sinking ship."

"That doesn't bother me." As Miss Lou passed, Booty smiled and raised his forefinger.

They waited quietly, and she returned and refilled everyone's coffee cup. "Hope you boys aren't far from a bathroom today." She laughed, then added, " 'Course, you do have the advantage there, don't you?"

They all laughed as she sashayed away.

"What troubles me is Jorge's murder. We don't want it to come back on us." Booty finished his thought.

"Why would it come back on us?" Charly shrugged.

"Don't want anyone to find out we're importing the Mexicans." Ward perceived Booty's direction.

"Jorge's dead. He won't tell." Charly seemed unconcerned.

"Until we know who killed him and why, we'd better have long antennae." Ward gulped his coffee. "Jorge ratted on someone."

"It could have been a woman problem," Charly said. "He

knocked up a girl and her brothers knock him off. Who knows? Those folks still do things that way."

"I don't know. He could have done any number of things, but I sleep lightly now." Booty folded his arms across his chest.

"What can we do?" Ward asked.

"Nothing. Except listen. Keep a sharp eye," Booty replied.

"And win. 'Course, I'll win in the classes we're in together." Charly puffed out his chest.

They laughed, then Booty smiled. "Gotta beat me first."

"I'll put up a fight," Ward added.

"That's the trouble with you making money." Charly shook his head. "You'll buy better horses, get better clients. Steer clear of Renata."

"She's at Kalarama," Ward replied, dabbing his mouth with the paper napkin.

"She'll come to you after a suitable interval."

Booty raised his eyebrows but said nothing.

As there was no point in denying it, Ward kept his mouth shut. They had taught him a lesson—a couple. If Charly and Booty had figured out that he "removed" Queen Esther at Renata's bidding, presumably being well paid with promises of a future with a celebrity or other well-heeled clients, they were smart enough. But it also meant each of them was capable of doing it. He trusted his two senior partners as far as he could see them.

"I don't fault any man for getting ahead. Horse was unharmed. Renata got her publicity fix." Booty looked at Ward. "You'll come out ahead."

"I know you two don't think Larry is stirring the pot," Charly said, "but tell me how it was that those friends of theirs, the Haristeens, wound up at Ward's? I don't like it."

"Nothing we can do about it. And for all we know, Charly, it was a lucky shot on the part of the Virginia folks."

"Virginians are so damned snotty." Ward wrinkled his nose. "Those two seem all right, though."

"Yeah, well, those two are sticking their noses in other people's business. The wife—not bad-looking, actually—asked me if I'd seen Joan's pin." Booty was incredulous. "What the hell do I know about Joan's pin? She's nosy."

"Nosy is one thing," Charly lowered his voice again, "but even a blind pig can find an acorn sometimes. We don't want her snooping around."

"Well, what do you propose, we bind and gag her?" Ward laughed; he couldn't help it.

"No." Charly wasn't finding it funny. "I propose we keep an eye on that woman and we keep our mouths shut."

Easier said than done.

"By the by, fifteen undocumented workers at my farm," Ward whispered. "They were in the van when Benny and I drove out."

"Inchworm there?" Charly asked, his voice even quieter than Ward's.

"Yep. Some are yours."

"Keep 'em until after the show." Charly sat up taller.

"Great. If the feds come by, I'm holding the bag." Ward's eyes hardened for a moment.

Booty soothingly said, "Won't happen. What you'll be holding is a bag of money." He leaned back, hands on his stomach. "Hey, I bought a coral snake yesterday. You guys should come see her. She's beautiful."

Charly flinched slightly. "I saw you milk a rattlesnake once. That was enough."

"Chicken." Booty laughed. "You know snake venom has a lot of medical uses. That's why I did that."

"How do you do it?" Ward asked.

"Catch them with a thin pole, kind of like an old-fashioned buttonhook. Then you grab them by the neck; they can't twist. A rattlesnake's fangs are hinged. He's mad now, so he flips those fangs out and you put him over a little cup with plastic wrap over it, stick his fangs in it, and the venom just drips out. Easy." The other two men listened with no comment. "What's interesting about a coral snake is the fangs don't retract. You should see her."

"I see Miss Nasty. That's enough," Charly said.

21

*B*efore Ward reached the entrance to I-64 to head east, his cell rang.

Charly, on the other end, growled, "Ward, do you know where Renata was last night?"

"No."

"She rode back with you in the van."

Ward replied, "She left her truck at my place. When we got back, she drove off."

"She tell you where she was going?"

"No. Why would she?"

"You tell me." Charly, peeved, disconnected the call.

His call did convince Ward that Charly's relationship with Renata went deeper than being her trainer. Ward kicked himself for being blind, or maybe he just didn't want Renata to have had an affair with the likes of Charly.

Within ten minutes Charly turned down the long, winding, tree-lined drive to his immaculately manicured establishment.

His house, with the white Ionic pillars standing out from the weathered red brick, the boxwoods and magnolias dotted about, the freshly painted barns, fence lines trimmed neatly, looked like David Selznick's version of Tara.

As someone who sold at the high end of the market, Charly understood that rich folks might not know too much about horses, but they wanted the dream, "the look."

Some folks with big bucks did know horses, but they, too, succumbed to being doted upon in Charly's vast front room in the main barn. Sofas, chairs, a fireplace, a kitchen, and a huge plasma TV flat on the wall shouted money, money, money. The indoor arena, larger than the one at Kalarama, had two viewing areas, one enclosed with glass in case the client didn't wish to inhale the dust. There were small refrigerators in the viewing areas should a body desire to drink but not wish to walk the few steps back to the sumptuous lounge.

Charly, vain about his dress, proved equally vain concerning his surroundings. No surprise then that the women in his life fit into the perfect picture. The affairs were ornamental. He did love his ex-wife, but she, too, had to meet a standard of beauty reflected in fashion magazines, television, and film. One day she'd had enough of being eye candy, walked out, matriculated at the University of Kentucky to study physical therapy, and she never looked back. She didn't tell tales out of school, which Charly appreciated, especially after witnessing Booty's sulfurous divorce.

Charly tired of affairs and one-night stands. They took too much energy. Chasing women distracted him from his main purpose: making and selling spectacular Saddlebreds. He wanted, needed, a wife who could be spectacular herself but who could ride, too. His first wife, whom he had married when he returned from the first Gulf War—a first lieutenant glad to be home—possessed all the necessary graces, but she wasn't a horsewoman. It seems superficial to non-horse people, since many couples enjoy differing sports, pastimes, but it just doesn't work that way too readily with horse people.

Charly made money. He made even more bringing in the undocumented workers. The profit for each worker was two thousand dollars in cash, no checks. Still, he was forever scrambling. A rich wife would help. If he had to pick between money and beauty, money would win. A man could find beauty on the side.

Standing in front of his main barn, hands on hips, pouted a woman who radiated both beauty and money. Renata DeCarlo, fresh at nine-thirty in the morning, wore white Bermuda shorts and a magenta belt; a pair of white espadrilles on her size-8 feet completed the ensemble.

Curious how sometimes friends, lovers, husbands, and wives will select the same colors to wear that day without consulting each other. Charly wore white jeans and an aqua shirt.

He parked by his house and walked the two hundred yards to the barn.

"Where have you been?" she asked, then smiled irresistibly.

"Breakfast with the boys. I could ask the same of you. Why weren't you at the show last night?"

"I wasn't riding in a class and I had a script to read."

"Renata, how fortuitous." He was in front of her now.

"Heard. I'm very glad I missed it."

"When I find out who called, I'll break their neck." He checked himself, because no one except his two partners knew of his lucrative sideline supplying workers to horse farms. "Disrupted the show. I wasn't riding that well anyway, but this," he shrugged, "a bolt out of the blue."

"I can't believe you're admitting you had an off night."

"Once a decade." He smiled down at her, intoxicated by her beauty, her closeness, her scent—Creed's Green Irish Tweed, also once favored by Cary Grant and Marlene Dietrich.

"Come on up to the house?" he politely asked.

"Carry me to the back pastures where the yearlings are."

"Sure."

They walked up to the house, climbed into his truck, and bounced along the interior farm roads to the back where the yearlings grazed. Most horse breeders put the yearlings farther away from the main barns and drive to them, because they go through a gawky, ugly stage, just like human teenagers. By the time they're two, Saddlebreds usually begin to look like real horses.

Charly pulled alongside a white fence, painted every two years at a hideous expense. He cut the motor and Renata hopped out.

Charly, soon beside her, glanced down at her white espadrilles. "Ruin your shoes."

"Bought four pair. Have another in the truck. They're so cool in the summer but they still give some support. Too bad men don't wear them."

"Maybe the ones who carry purses do."

She shrugged. "To each his own." She looked at his feet. "Top-Siders."

"Summer." He nodded. "I love summer."

"I do, too. But I miss fall, winter, and real spring when I'm in California. When I'm out of California I don't miss it at all, except for the smell of eucalyptus trees in Montecito."

"I like that, too." Charly had showed often in California, plus he'd visited Renata there. "Let me whistle them over. There's still a lot of dew on the grass; you might have three other pair of espadrilles, but these will be green and your feet will be wet." He put his fingers in his lips and let out a piercing whistle.

The yearlings—geldings in one pasture on one side of the road, fillies on the other—lifted their heads. They stared, then slowly trotted toward the figures at the fence. Halfway there, they decided to make a race of it, youthful high spirits abundant.

At the gate they skidded to a halt. Charly turned back to his truck and pulled out a big bag of carrots, which he always kept with him. He then handed some to Renata and she fed the boys. He walked across the dirt road to feed the girls, a fair amount of ear-flattening and nasty looks between them, since each girl wanted more than one carrot. The lower fillies on the totem pole skittered away, and Charly threw them carrots while hand-feeding the more dominant fillies. He made note each time he visited the yearlings as to pecking order. He wanted his workers to handle the animals daily. It made working with them so much easier when training really started.

An animal could not be dominant in the herd yet be amazing in the ring. You never knew until you worked with them. He made note of that, too.

Renata fed the boys one by one, shooing off the pushy

ones after they'd received their carrot. "Who's the almost-black fellow with the star on his forehead and a thin white stripe coming out of it, kinda like a fairy wand?"

"Captain Hook." He called the fellow by his barn name.

"I think it looks like a star wand."

"Well, it does, but I couldn't call him Tinker Bell."

"This is the foal I liked. Took me a minute. He's grown. He'll be sixteen hands." She studied him. "He's flashy. What do you want for him?"

"Hadn't thought about it."

"Liar."

"No, I really hadn't."

"Start thinking." She turned to the fillies. "The bright chestnut has quality."

"It's a good crop, but she is the standout, isn't she?"

Renata said nothing but climbed back in the truck. They returned to the house. Charly, although full of coffee, made another pot. They sat on the back porch with their cups.

"How much?"

"No less than one hundred thousand."

"For a yearling? We're not talking about Thoroughbreds here."

"I meant one hundred thousand for the colt and the filly." He grinned, always the horse dealer.

"Hmm." She drank her coffee.

"Ward hopes you'll leave Kalarama and board with him," Charly fished.

"I never said that."

"What did you say?"

"Exactly what you and I discussed. I'd bring him a few big clients, and I will. He's decent enough."

"He's a good trainer and will get better." The cut grass

glistened with dew; the white crepe myrtles at the end of the lawn by the fence line bloomed. Soon enough the zinnias would reach full height, too. "Think he has any idea?"

"He knows I did it for the publicity. He doesn't know we're together."

"What about Joan and Larry?"

"They say nothing but they aren't dumb. They may not know we've cooked this up, but I don't think either one will be shocked when I return to you, citing we've mended our fences, et cetera, et cetera." She smiled languidly. "It worked. God, I got fabulous publicity out of this. Scripts poured in within twenty-four hours. My agent FedExed a few, and he says the others are waiting for me."

"How'd he pick?"

"By reputation. Doesn't mean they're good. Every now and then a rookie hits a home run. Hard, though. Hard to be a screenwriter. It's never yours—the work, I mean."

"No, but the check is."

"That's true." She laughed. "And the writer gets paid first. I have to wait but not too long. And I do receive goodies no writer can dream of—you know, jewelry, signing bonuses, trailers with everything in them for my comfort between scenes. It's a good life that way. The rest of it stinks." Her voice dropped.

"Make hay while the sun shines."

"Charly, I bet I hear that every other day." She sipped more coffee. "I know it, but I also know there will be a day, sunny or not, when I can't take it anymore. It's not my passion, acting. I can do it. I'm good. I'm not great. I'm not Meryl Streep. But I'm good. Still, I don't want to spend too much more time not doing what I love. I don't want to be eighty and think that all I ever did in my life was look into a camera."

"Horses."

"They're all I've really cared about since I came into the world."

"Me, too." He frowned for an instant. "But at this level, it takes millions."

"You make that."

"The best year I ever had I made three million. I pretty much average about a million and a half, which you know. I've been honest with you." And he had, except for his sideline. "This place eats that up, buying and breeding new stock. And don't forget farm maintenance, either. It takes money to make money."

"It does. That's why I live in a small but adorable house in the Valley." She meant she lived on the other side of the low mountains dividing Los Angeles from the Valley, on the east side of Mulholland Drive. "I keep expenses low. I'm up off Ventura in the hills, which you know, but I watch every penny and I sock it in the bank or in stocks. When I walk I want my money to make money."

"Smart, but I've always said you were smart." He hadn't always said that, but he was learning now that he had to pay more attention to her mind, dazzling though her physical attributes were. "Of course, I never realized how creative you are until you came up with the idea for us to have a big scene."

"You've got a little talent there, Charly." She laughed at him.

"Studying you," he flattered her.

"One thing eats away at me."

"Which is?"

"I wonder if Ward killed Jorge."

"What?" Charly sat up in his chair.

"Well, Ward used Jorge to dye Queen Esther's legs and neck. He told me when I asked how he got Queen Esther out from under everyone's nose. He paid Jorge five hundred dollars cash, which was a lot for Jorge, and then I think he gave him a little more for odds and ends, whatever they were. Jorge—apart from you and me and, well, Benny, who says nothing—was the only one who knew."

"You didn't tell me about Jorge."

"Charly, I haven't seen you. There's been no time."

"Could have called on the cell."

"Never. Do you have any idea how easy it is to pull a conversation out of the sky? I mean it. I never say anything on the cell I'm not willing for the whole damned world to hear, and you shouldn't, either."

"Now, Renata, don't do the conspiracy-theory thing."

"Charly, I know my business, and technology in the film business is very sophisticated and changes quickly. Didn't used to, but there's so much downtime on the set that I learned about cameras, editing equipment, iPods, downloading, and cell phones. I've soaked up everything I can about electronics and computers. Nothing that is electronic or in your computer is secure. Nothing."

"Even the CIA and Pentagon stuff?" He felt an odd flutter at the thought.

"A genius hack could get into anything they have. We really have painted ourselves into a corner. You and I will be the last generation to know privacy."

It frightened Charly that she had so much power: physical power, financial power, and mental power.

"I hope you're wrong." He meant that.

"I wish I were." She dropped the subject, as it was deeply depressing the more she thought about it. "Thought I'd leave Kalarama at the end of the show. I'll pay them extra for the time and trouble, all the media stuff, but I'll tell the truth. I'm going back to you. I just won't say why I left."

"Joan isn't going to take extra money."

"Then I'll give it to her favorite charity in Kalarama's name. I've put them through a fair amount, and they have Jorge's murder to deal with, as well." She shuddered. "That sight will haunt me forever."

"Ward didn't kill him."

"How can you be so sure?" She responded to the conviction in his voice.

"He's not the type."

"That's what neighbors say about serial killers when they're discovered."

"Ward isn't some psychopath who can fool the neighbors. He wouldn't kill Jorge. If nothing else, the stakes aren't high enough. He agrees to hide Queen Esther. He's part of a harmless ruse. No one's hurt. No one loses money, except ostensibly me. Yes, Joan and Larry juggle a media circus, but, hey, it throws a great big klieg light on Kalarama, and that's good for them and good for Saddlebreds. They run a good barn. They're at the top of the food chain. No, Ward couldn't."

"I suppose." Her voice trailed off. "But it's unsettling."

"It's some kind of personal vendetta. Doesn't have anything to do with our world." Charly believed this, especially after breakfast with the boys.

Four grackles landed on the luxurious grass, walking with their bird waddle. A large bird feeder lured them, but they had landed a few feet away just in case anything juicy appeared in the emerald grass.

After a long silence, Renata asked, "How much?"

"For what?"

"Captain Hook and the yearling filly. Really how much. Your bottom line."

He turned to her, put his coffee cup on the rattan coffee table. "Free. If you marry me, they will be your wedding present."

"Charly, don't tease me." She rolled her eyes upward.

He rose from the chair, then knelt before her. "Marry me. Do me the honor of being my wife. I am dead serious."

$$\boxed{22}$$

*T*hankful for a quiet morning, Fair was reading *Equine Disease Quarterly,* published by the Department of Veterinary Science at the University of Kentucky. The research carried out at the Maxwell H. Gluck Equine Research Center at the university benefited horsemen the world over. Since he specialized in equine reproduction, his office filled up with reports, technical papers, as well as more general publications aimed at horsemen. However, he particularly enjoyed *Equine Disease Quarterly* for its concise reportage of projects.

At just the time that Charly went down on bended knee, Fair removed his reading glasses, his first concession at forty-one to encroaching middle age. The concession irritated him.

Harry returned from the ladies' room. "Ready."

"I am, too."

They'd driven into Lexington for breakfast at the country

club, which had been arranged by Alicia Palmer. She knew everybody and everybody knew her, thanks to her Olympian career in film. When she'd called the night before, they caught up about everything on the farm—hers and theirs, since BoomBoom, Susan Tucker, and Alicia were taking turns managing it until their return.

Once in the truck, the animals happy to see them, Fair drove out toward Iron Works Pike.

Since many of the three hundred plus Thoroughbred farms fell into a half circle from the little town of Paris in Bourbon County to the town of Versailles in Woodford County, they thought they'd start out by going to Paris, northeast of Lexington, and work their way back toward Versailles, which was due west.

Harry marked the farms she wanted to see, starting with Claiborne. Not that she knew anyone there, but she wanted to peek at the back pastures.

Each farm displayed a distinct personality. Some, such as Calumet Farms, were covered in glory for decades, only to fall from grace. Others, like Dixiana, once a great Saddlebred place and now breeding Thoroughbreds, covered a century of ups and downs, after each down rising again like the phoenix.

"I'm so happy the grapes are flourishing. Alicia said I won't believe how big they've grown when we get home."

"It will be interesting to see if the crop proves profitable."

"Not for three years," she quickly replied.

"I know that, honey. Remember, I heard the lead-up to this, then the purchase of rootstock, and, well, I'm probably as excited as you are." He inhaled the refreshing morning fragrance of dew, grass, horses in rich limestone-enriched fields.

·

"You're right. I get nervous about my grapes. I'm starting to wonder if I shouldn't have put more in when I did, but I could only afford a quarter of an acre. An acre would have cost fourteen thousand dollars. Of course now, given the hideous spike in oil prices, the cost would be fifteen thousand dollars. Every item that is transported by truck just goes up in price. Scares me."

"I told you to plant an entire acre. You're too conservative," declared Pewter, who really had tried to reach her human when Harry prepared the ground for her rootstock.

"She's brave about some things and cowardly about others." Mrs. Murphy also breathed in the wonderful summer odors. *"She gets scared about money, and that's not going to change."*

"But she has Fair, and he makes a good living." Pewter was quite happy that she didn't have to balance checkbooks.

"Years of living off a postmistress's salary." Tucker left it at that.

"Sunflowers look good, everything looks good. I'm so glad the girls are out there. Alicia said that Miranda has been the biggest help." Harry beamed at mentioning the older woman, a surrogate mother. "But then, Miranda is such a natural with plants."

Fair laughed. "She really is, and it plucks Big Mim's last nerve. All the thousands of dollars she spends on her gardens and gardeners, yet Miranda's outshines hers every year."

Big Mim, also known as the Queen of Crozet, had grown up with Miranda. They adored each other, but when it came to their gardens, each burned with competitive fire.

They reached Paris, passing the large courthouse. One could gauge the wealth of a county by the size of its courthouse in Kentucky. In Virginia, the telling detail was the size of the monument to the heroic Confederate dead.

Claiborne, a few minutes away, made Harry's heart skip a beat. Fair drove around the perimeter.

"Well?" Pewter, already bored with sightseeing, thought it was time for a crunchy treat, something with fish flavor today.

"Well what?" Mrs. Murphy, on the other hand, loved sightseeing.

"Did she see a horse for Alicia?" Pewter turned a circle on Harry's lap.

"No. Great horses in those pastures. Great prices." Mrs. Murphy, paws on the dash, noticed a redwing blackbird as they passed a low creek bed. She even spied a tanager in a bush by the same creek bed.

"Then why are we doing this if the horses are so expensive? Why can't she find one in Virginia?"

"Oh, she likes looking around." Tucker did, too.

"And you never know." Mrs. Murphy sounded hopeful.

"Got behind on this project." Harry stroked Pewter with her right hand; her left rested on Tucker's silky head as the corgi wedged between her and Fair.

Mrs. Murphy, hind paws on Harry's knees, intently watched everything.

"Extraordinary events." Fair headed west out of Paris.

"Sure have been, but it's starting to make sense, vaguely— I emphasize vaguely."

"What?" He turned a moment to stare at his wife.

"Renata succeeded. Publicity up the wazoo, and when she rides tonight, her class will be covered by news channels, entertainment channels, you name it. No fool, that one. But, no, that's not what I'm thinking about. It's Jorge."

"Ah." He, too, had fretted over the murder.

"I think it's connected to the raid, but I don't know why."

"How do you come up with that?"

"So far nothing has turned up—the usual causes of murder, you know, thwarted love, greed. The only thing I can think of is that he was somehow connected to the illegal workers." She bit her tongue, because she wanted to tell him about the diesel motor she'd heard in the middle of the night when she slipped out to the fairgrounds. The next day when Joan questioned Jorge he said he hadn't heard it. However, Fair still didn't know she'd gone out, and she thought it better to keep that to herself. The problem was, she still didn't know what cargo the truck had carried. She could only guess.

"What else? No women. No booze. No drugs. I mean, he might have visited prostitutes, but that wasn't going to get him killed. What could he do that would create that kind of danger?"

"That's a big jump, Harry."

"I know it is, but I believe his death is connected. I can't prove it, that's all."

Fair turned onto one of the north–south roads that would head back toward Lexington, which was now about forty minutes south. "Let's go by Payson Stud. They're real horse people. They understand bloodlines and stand some stallions that retired sound after years of racing. Then we can drive west to Paula's."

"Funny, isn't it, how the business has changed?"

"True everywhere. Saddlebreds have changed; the necks seem to get longer and longer. Thoroughbreds—well, we've discussed this ad infinitum—are bred for five to seven furlongs. I can't bear it." His voice carried more emotion than usual. "Even the black-and-tan coonhound. Now that the AKC recognizes them, they're being bred racier. Well, that may be pretty to a lot of people, but pretty is as pretty does. Whenever Americans start fiddling with breeds, they lighten them, lighten the bone most times. Look at the difference between a German shepherd from Germany and one from here."

"Kind of shocking." She agreed wholeheartedly with her husband.

"The fanciers ruin a breed, and then thirty or forty years later someone tries to revive it along proper lines. The worst thing that can happen to any dog is to become popular, and I tell you, it's not so good for horses, either, although, thank God, it's a lot more expensive to breed horses than dogs, so there aren't as many people mucking it up. You never, ever remove an animal from its purpose."

Delighted by his outburst, since he was usually buttoned up, she said, "Honey, you should go on television. You can make complicated matters easy to understand."

"Really?" He was flattered.

"You can." She paused. "That's what worries me about Ned a little bit. He does the reverse."

"He's a lawyer."

Ned, Susan Tucker's husband, had been elected to the Virginia assembly. As this was his first year, it meant many adjustments for him and for Susan, Harry's friend from cradle days.

"It's good that Alicia's given you this project."

"She'll even pay me a commission for finding the horse and then training it." Harry beamed. "I like earning my way."

"I know. Hey, that willow tree may be the largest I've ever seen." He pointed to a willow down near an old springhouse, with a creek running through it.

"Probably bodies buried underneath it."

"Harry." Fair shook his head.

"Well—" She couldn't explain why murders, crimes riveted her. "Joan told me all about the murder of Verna Garr Taylor, allegedly by General Denhardt, and then when he got off, how her three brothers gunned him down."

"No more murders in Shelbyville." He sighed. "Jorge was enough."

"You never know." Harry actually sounded hopeful.

"Harry." He reached over with his long arm to punch her left shoulder.

"I'm resting." Pewter opened her eyes when Harry rocked slightly to the right.

"I didn't say I was hoping for another murder. I'm hoping to find Joan's pin. I hope someone finds Jorge's murderer. I'm just saying," she slowed her words, "you never know."

She was right.

$$\boxed{23}$$

Because stall rents bit into Ward's slender budget, a horse finishing his or her class at the end of the evening would be driven back to the farm, unless a client was riding the animal the next night. Ward would sit down to figure out if the extra trips cost more than the stall rent for that day, given the horrendous increase in gas. He solved this problem by vanning other people's horses to the various stables when he took one of his own horses back to the farm. His van could carry six horses. Since clients paid by the mile the savings came out to be about thirteen dollars a day—pin money, but pin money was better than no money.

Prudently, Ward placed the cash from smuggling illegal workers in a half-size fireproof vault. He marked down these funds according to each transaction as profits from hauling mulch to landscape sites. Not that he expected anyone to break into his vault or authorities to sweep his records, but he thought ahead. His motto could well have been "Plan for the worst, hope for the best."

Ward intended to buy one young stallion and perhaps three exceptional broodmares when the sum reached four hundred thousand dollars. He wanted to play safe, so he was looking for just the right stallion from the Rex Denmark line. Since Supreme Sultan, foaled in 1966, led the list of sires of Hall of Fame broodmares, he wanted mares from that line. Whether or not he had the breeding gift would be apparent in a few years. One stallion would lead to more if he enjoyed any kind of success, and those stud fees would prove a nice augmentation to his training fees and board income.

He'd figured out the cost to put up six-board fencing for the first stallion's paddock, the cost of a clean but small breeding shed, and the costs for shipping semen.

Ward left nothing to chance save for the Russian roulette of breeding. It wasn't as easy as Mendel's peas. He envied Joan Hamilton her extraordinary success. Some people had the gift, just as Donna Moore of Versailles had the gift of finding incredible prospects and making them better.

He and Benny parked by the practice arena at ten-thirty in the morning to take home a gelding for an amateur owner in Barn Three and to take one of his clients' horses back to his barn. He'd already driven back to his farm in his pickup after breakfast, checked on everything, turned everyone out, then hopped in the van with Benny, who regaled him with stories of a busted date last night. She had a bust, all right, but the rest of her screamed nonstop neurosis. Benny could make Ward laugh, and the two of them had laughed all the way to Ward's rented stalls at Shelbyville.

Ward had two horses going tonight. It should be an easy day, more or less.

Harry and Fair pulled into the opposite lot near Route 60. Both were elated, since the gelding at Paula's Rose Haven farm impressed them. Fair did a thorough check, asking Paula to call in her vet for X-rays when possible. Fair didn't have his portable X-ray equipment with him.

Mrs. Murphy, Pewter, and Tucker strolled down to visit Spike. Cookie, still at Kalarama Farm, wouldn't come in until the evening's classes. This pleased Tucker, since she'd have gossip for the pretty little Jack Russell.

"Hope Spike has some dirt." Tucker snapped at a monarch butterfly who flew low.

"Wouldn't you rather he had bones?" Pewter, food never far from her mind, replied.

"Wouldn't mind, but I wouldn't give you any." Tucker smiled devilishly.

"Dog bones taste like cardboard." Pewter had gnawed a few Milk-Bones and overstated her case.

"Good, I don't have to share."

"But a knucklebone, a real true bone, that's a different story." Pewter's eyes half closed in remembered bliss.

"You two ate a big breakfast. How can you think about food?" Mrs. Murphy liked her tuna, chicken, and beef, but food wasn't her obsession.

"You need to surrender more to the rituals of pleasure," Pewter declared.

Both Mrs. Murphy and Tucker stopped for a moment to stare at each other. Where did Pewter come up with that? The large gray kitty sashayed on, her tummy swinging from side to side. She certainly indulged in her rituals of pleasure. The two friends lifted their silken eyebrows, then followed Pewter, in as good a mood as anyone had ever seen her.

Charly Trackwell was not yet in the barn. Carlos had watered the horses, checked everyone's feed, double-checked them after they'd eaten, and was now going from stall to stall lifting hooves. The barn cats reposed on the tack trunks, a mid-morning nap being just the thing on a day that promised to get into the nineties with high humidity.

Spike, on his side on an old saddle blanket in navy and red, snored. His paws twitched.

"Let's not wake him," Mrs. Murphy whispered.

A startled horse caused the ginger cat to open one eye, and then a hellacious shriek sent him bolt upright along with the other barn cats.

Mrs. Murphy, Pewter, and Tucker craned their necks to view Miss Nasty, in an orange and white polka-dot dress, swinging from a barn rafter. The horse eyed her with the greatest suspicion.

Carlos, hearing the horse shy, quickly looked into the stall but didn't see Miss Nasty at first. The monkey swung down, grabbing his grimy baseball cap. She then scurried across the beams, cap in one paw.

"Mine, mine, mine!" the brown creature triumphed.

Carlos, furious, ran under the beam. "Diablo!"

"Ha, ha."

"I hate that disgusting thing." Pewter curled her lip. *"So dirty."*

Spike, wasting no words, climbed up the stall post and hurried across the wide beam toward the monkey. *"You're on my turf, bitch. Get the hell out of my barn."*

Benny, walking by the barn, heard the monkey's shrieks. He stuck his head in.

"I'll shoot her," Carlos threatened.

"Don't do that, Carlos." Benny smiled. "Booty will shoot you. If you turn your back on her, she'll be disappointed and eventually drop your hat."

"No, I won't. I'll tear it to shreds," Miss Nasty boasted as she kept one jaundiced eye on a puffed-up, approaching Spike.

"You'll pee on it, Miss Nasty." Mrs. Murphy hoped to distract her so Spike could knock her hard. *"We know you pee on things."*

"And you don't?" Miss Nasty twirled the cap in her paws, then put it on her head, but it slipped over her eyes. She quickly pulled it off, then waved it at Spike.

Carlos walked with Benny to the end of the barn toward the parking lot. "Not working."

"Give it time." Benny took off his green ball cap with the white logo. "Use mine. Hate to see your bald spot."

"I don't have a bald spot."

"If you tear your hair out over that goddamned monkey you will." Benny laughed and headed toward the van.

The old van would grumble, belch, smoke, start, then cut off. He didn't know if it was the starter or the battery, and he'd attend to it later, but he wanted to get the motor turned over and let it run for a few minutes before putting the horses on.

As Carlos returned to his duties, Miss Nasty, having lost her human audience, waved the cap at Spike. *"Cats are stupid. Humans are descended from me. That's why I'm smart."*

"You have a lot to answer for," Mrs. Murphy sarcastically

said as she, too, climbed up on the opposite stall so the monkey would be between herself and Spike.

Seeing this, Spike advanced slowly. *"I'm descended from a saber-toothed tiger. You're lunch."*

"Don't forget to take off her ridiculous dress first," Mrs. Murphy reminded Spike.

Miss Nasty stood up as tall as she could on her hind legs. *"I look good in orange."*

"Dream on." Pewter laughed from down below as Tucker sat right underneath the chattering monkey.

"Yeah, you'd have to shop in plus size," Miss Nasty called down just as Spike leapt toward her.

The monkey emitted a shriek, jumped over the ginger cat, dropping the hat in the process. She ran hellbent for leather toward the other end of the barn. Spike gave chase.

Tucker picked up the ball cap and waited for Carlos to come out of the stall, which he did since the monkey created havoc.

"She keeps getting away from Booty." Pewter stated the obvious. *"And she steals things. Charly cussed a blue streak yesterday because she got into his barn and ran off with the colored brow bands he uses on his bridles."*

Mrs. Murphy, running on the opposite beam parallel with the monkey, yelled down, *"That's it!"*

"What?" Pewter asked as she tracked their progress from down below.

"She stole Joan's pin!" Mrs. Murphy hollered.

Tucker, silent because she had Carlos's hat in her mouth, dropped it. *"Miss Nasty, where's the pin?"*

"You'll never know!" The monkey slid down the end stall pole and, tail out, ran as fast as she could away from the barn.

Spike shimmied down and chased her to the end of the practice arena, then turned back just as Benny walked into the barn. The old van rumbled, warming up in the lot. Benny picked up Carlos's hat as the head groom stepped out of the stall, too slow to swat the monkey with a broom.

As the two men swapped hats, Spike, puffed up like a conquering hero, walked back into the barn. *"Showed her."*

"She admitted it! She has the pin." Mrs. Murphy was beside herself. *"We have to get it from her."*

An enormous explosion shook the rafters of the barn. Dust rose up, then fell below.

The animals flattened on their bellies. The horses whinnied, terrified. Carlos and Benny rocked sideways. They regained their equilibrium as the animals crept toward the parking-lot end of the barn.

Ward's green and white van, front torn off, engine parts scattered over the lot, burned, thick black clouds rising upward.

"Oh, my God." Benny put his right hand over his heart.

"God had nothing to do with it." Mrs. Murphy wanted more than anything to get her humans back to Crozet, Virginia.

24

*B*y the time Harry, Fair, Booty, and others reached the parking lot, the flames had engulfed the remains of the van. Fortunately the only other damage was to the windshield of a truck parked fifty yards from the van. A piece of debris had smashed through it.

As the people stood there helplessly watching, Benny ran for Ward, who upon hearing the explosion had put the horse to be moved back in a stall. He didn't know what had happened, but he figured the commotion would spook the horse.

The two men now ran to the parking lot.

Carlos, who'd been as close to the event as Benny, explained to the others what they heard, what they saw. Charly had pulled into the Route 60 parking lot minutes before the van blew apart. He ran down, too.

As Ward and Benny approached, Booty hurried to him. "Man, I'm sorry. What a goddamned mess."

Charly, hearing this, bluntly said, "Mess? Benny could be dead." He waited, then added, "I'll guarantee you when the cops finally finish crawling over what's left, they'll find it was a bomb."

"We're not in Baghdad." Booty frowned.

Ward, speechless, put his arm around Benny's shoulders.

Benny, voice low, whispered, "Someone wants us dead."

"Just me, I think." Ward's voice was even softer than Benny's.

Renata drove into the lot. She had seen the black smoke curling upward but couldn't have imagined the source. Upon seeing that this wasn't a brush fire, she turned around, but she heard fire engines and knew she couldn't get out, because they'd both reach the opened gate at about the same time. So she pulled a one-eighty and cautiously drove behind the long barn where Charly kept his horses. She, too, got out and ran to the scene.

She reached the small knot of people as the fire trucks and sheriff's squad car spit out small stones tearing into the parking lot.

"What happened?" Renata asked.

Charly simply said, "Ward's van was bombed."

"Oh, God." She quickly walked over to Ward but didn't really know what to say, so she hugged him, then Benny. Renata wondered if this show was cursed, but she kept her misgivings to herself. She could be emotional, but she could put other people's feelings first. Right now Ward needed consoling.

Booty snarled, "Charly, stop saying the van was bombed.

It could have been anything. I mean, these old jobs, the wires burn, touches grease or gas. Boom."

"Booty, my job was explosives." Charly referred to his combat service. "I'm telling you, someone planted a bomb in Ward's van. The kind that detonates a few minutes after ignition."

Harry asked the question on other minds, too. "Why?"

"How the hell do I know?" Charly, upset, growled.

Renata, voice quiet but commanding, said, "We're all upset, Charly, don't take it out on Harry."

"You're right. Harry, I apologize."

"That's okay." Harry's eyes watered as the wind blew the smoke their way.

"Let's move," Fair sensibly suggested. "Sheriff Howlett knows where to find everybody. We'll just add to the confusion."

Benny, shaking now that it had begun to sink in, said, "My favorite penknife was in that van."

Ward tried to think if he'd left anything valuable in the cab or in the box. Apart from two leather halters and lead shanks, he couldn't think of anything.

As Harry and Fair walked back to Barn Five, she touched Fair's forearm. "Where are the kids?"

"I expect the explosion scared the bejesus out of them. They'll be back at the barn."

They were chasing Miss Nasty through Booty's barn. The monkey squealed to high heaven. Given the commotion down in the parking lot, no one was paying attention to an irate monkey.

Mrs. Murphy kept up with her as she climbed rafters and dropped down to beams, but Pewter and Tucker shadowed her from the aisle. Miss Nasty finally squeezed out under an eave and climbed up to a large overhanging light fixture at the main entrance to the barn. There she sat howling obscenities and abuse. For good measure she tried to pee on Pewter and Tucker, who'd just emerged from the barn, but they ducked back in.

Mrs. Murphy backed down a stall post and walked to the large entrance. She called up to the monkey, *"Tell me where the pin is and I won't bother you."*

"Never! Never!"

"Why'd you take it?" Tucker asked, then dashed to the side.

As Miss Nasty had completely emptied herself, Tucker was safe. The two cats, realizing this, also walked outside and turned to view the monkey, who swung on the light fixture, then righted herself and sat on it. She sure wouldn't be doing that if it were night and the fixture were turned on.

"'Fess up, Miss Nasty." Pewter thought the animal even worse than the blue jay who dive-bombed her at home.

"Pretty things for pretty girls." Miss Nasty struck a pose.

"My, my, don't we think a lot of ourselves," Pewter purred maliciously.

Mrs. Murphy thought to change her tack. *"How do you keep getting away from Booty?"*

"Easy as pie." She puffed up, swung around again.

"Show me," Tucker egged her on.

Too smart for that, Miss Nasty just intoned, *"I have my ways."*

"I thought he locked you in that big gilded cage." Pewter slyly moved a little closer to the wooden side of the barn.

"Twit. It's painted white." Miss Nasty now contemplated her nails.

"But he locks it?" Pewter called up.

"Yes." She grinned, ear to ear. *"I can get into or out of anything."*

"You didn't get into the van that just blew up, did you?" Mrs. Murphy realized that Miss Nasty knew a lot more than she was telling.

"No." The monkey stared down, grinned again as she enjoyed her superior position. *"You can't trick me. I'm too smart."*

"You go with Booty everywhere, don't you?" Mrs. Murphy kept on.

" 'Cept on dates."

"With you along, the date would be a disaster." Pewter laughed.

Miss Nasty flipped her the bird, a gesture she'd studied from Booty. *"Fat fleabag."*

"You play with yourself," Pewter fired back.

"I have an itch." Miss Nasty bared her fangs.

"Gross." Pewter's pupils narrowed to slits.

Mrs. Murphy hissed quietly, *"Pewter, shut up. Let me handle this."*

Pewter glared at her tiger friend, but she piped down.

"You know about Booty's bringing in Mexicans," Mrs. Murphy flatly declared.

"How do you know that?"

"Saw you in Charly's barn in the middle of the night on Thursday."

"What were you doing there?" Miss Nasty was becoming intrigued.

"Harry couldn't sleep, so she came over to check on the horses. Was the night after Charly and Renata had the big fight. She took Queen Esther, Voodoo, and Shortro out of his barn."

Tucker smiled as she looked up. *"Good business."*

"Yeah, until all those goons showed up." Miss Nasty, spoiled,

wanted Booty to make lots of money, as then she'd get more toys, treats, and dresses.

"*Did you know Jorge?*" Mrs. Murphy asked.

"*Not really. He had something to do with that business, but I don't know what. Booty works with the people in Texas. Charly dealt with Jorge. All three of them hooked the workers up with their employers.*"

"Who took Booty's hair dye?" Tucker was sure those bottles had been used to blacken Queen Esther's neck and legs.

The monkey's eyes widened. "*Don't you ever mention that! Booty would die.*"

"Because he dyed the horse?" Pewter couldn't stand it any longer.

"*I'm not talking to you.*" Miss Nasty grimaced.

"Is it because he dyed Queen Esther?" Tucker reiterated Pewter's question.

"*No. He doesn't want anyone to know he's gray. He'd die.*" Miss Nasty was very loyal to Booty. "*He's afraid to get old.*"

"Who dyed Queen Esther?" Tucker asked. She knew, but she was testing the monkey.

"*Not Booty. But I'm not everywhere.*" She swung around again. "*I'm tired of talking about this. I want to talk about me. Did you know that I can eat a raspberry sherbet cone faster than Booty? I can. And I can use the can opener, too, so I can open any can in the kitchen if I'm hungry. I bet you can't do that.*" A malicious gleam enlivened her eye. "*Maybe Pewter.*"

"Eat you!" Pewter snarled, fangs at the ready.

Just as Harry and Fair walked up to Barn Five, Miss Nasty clapped her hands. The humans spied the animals at Barn One.

"Come on, kids," Harry called.

Reluctantly, the three friends turned from the monkey.

Calling after them, Miss Nasty yelled, *"I know things."*

"We just want Joan's pin," Mrs. Murphy called back.

"I want to kill her," Pewter threatened.

"Wouldn't mind that myself," Tucker agreed.

"Not until we find that pin," Mrs. Murphy paused, *"and the rest of it."*

"What rest of it?" Pewter thought the monkey was a blowhard.

"What she knows." Mrs. Murphy glanced over her shoulder as Miss Nasty hung from the light fixture with one hand and made an obscene gesture with the other.

25

The acrid smoke frightened many of the horses. Trainers and grooms did their best to comfort the animals. None of this boded well for those who needed to perform tonight, the last night.

The black billowing smoke spiraled upward as the firemen pumped water onto the van and the sizzling debris. Little by little the cloud flattened out, the flames subsided, but the smell of burned rubber and upholstery remained.

Fair called Larry, who was back at Kalarama working a horse from a jog cart, a light sulky used to develop an animal's stamina. Saddlebred training, like any type of equine training, demanded patience, knowledge, and a variety of methods. Harry didn't need a jog cart, since she could throw her leg over a horse and jog for miles across country. Saddlebred trainers worked on their farms, using outdoor tracks and indoor arenas. They rarely rode across country. Fair reassured Larry that everything was all right in Barn Five and that he, Harry, and Manuel and the other grooms would do whatever was necessary to calm the horses.

"Need to tranq?" Harry asked when Fair clicked off the cell.

"Let's see what we can do without," Fair told Harry and Manuel. "Hate to tranquilize them before a show, even if it is hours early."

With Mrs. Murphy, Pewter, and Tucker tagging along, the humans began visiting each stall.

Before Charly and Booty walked back to their barns, Ward pulled them aside. "I'm taking the big risk." He sneezed violently, and they moved farther away from the smoke. "It was my van, not yours, so someone knows."

"Don't jump to conclusions," Booty counseled.

"Easy for you to say. Not your van."

"We'll get you another van," Charly volunteered, patting Ward's shoulder once. "Blessing in disguise. You collect insurance. We buy you a brand-new, *reliable* van. Everyone's happy."

Ward's mouth twitched slightly. "It's got to be a three-way equal split. I'm the one carrying the freight. You two aren't. I'm the one with your workers still at my farm, Charly."

"We make the deals." Booty ran his hand over his hair. A thin, dark sheen appeared on his palm, which he wiped on his jeans.

"Soot," Charly generously said, checking his own hair.

"Ward, I understand your position. But Booty and I have the contacts. We make the payment to our man in Texas."

"Your man or an independent operator?" Ward's eyebrows rose.

"Independent."

"See, I don't think that's quite the way it goes." Ward was upset—after all, he or Benny or both could have been blown to bits. "I think Jorge was the go-between."

A moment passed, then Booty said, "He was sure helpful, but there's someone in Texas. We told you when we agreed to do business to let us," he nodded toward Charly, "take care of the setups, the pickups. You make the deliveries."

"I run my van to Memphis or Louisville. Hell, one time I had to go to St. Louis. I'm smart enough to know the rivers prove safer passage than roads, but I still make the last trip on the roads to pick up the boys off the river. It's me that will get stopped, not you. And I'm telling you, someone's on to us."

"I still say your van blowing up and burning could have been faulty wiring." Booty avoided the main question.

Charly said, "Booty, it was a bomb. I'd bet my life on it."

Churlish since he was being contradicted, Booty spat, "Let's hope you don't have to."

"No, it's me that's betting my life. If I have to take this risk, I want an equal third. If not, I'm out," Ward said.

"Out where?" Booty crossed his arms over his chest.

"In for a penny, in for a pound." Charly said this in a lighthearted manner.

"How do I know you won't run to the feds to save your skin?" Booty's eyes narrowed.

"Don't be an ass, Booty." Ward, emotions close to the surface, raised his voice.

"Shhh, shhh." Charly held his palms out toward the ground and made a slowing motion.

"Dammit!" Booty did keep his voice low.

"If I turned tail, if I double-crossed you all, I'd be in the slammer. They wouldn't let me walk free. Plea-bargaining is a crock of shit. I'd still get it." Ward's voice was urgent, worried.

"Not as many years," Booty shot back.

"I don't want any years. As I see it this is a needed business, supply and demand."

"Got that right." Charly agreed with Ward, which he hoped would help defuse the situation.

"The fact that this is illegal is ridiculous. The laws will change." Ward also lowered his voice. "They must. White folks ain't doin' this work." He half-smiled. "But in the meantime, we're breaking the law. I'll pay for it. You two will be safe. 'Course, while I'm in the slammer, maybe Congress will figure out a way to make these guys legal. Then you two have a head start on an upright business while I'm punching out license plates."

"If whoever blew up your van is the same person who killed Jorge," Charly hooked his thumb into his belt loop, "Booty and I won't be safe. I've been thinking about that."

"You think too much." Booty, exasperated, threw up his hands. "Looks to me like Jorge's regrettable murder was a crime of passion."

"You think a woman slit his throat?" Ward was incredulous.

"No, a brother, another lover. Too violent." Booty pondered this. "Too violent to just be business."

"Never stopped the Mafia." Charly stated the obvious, which only made Booty angrier. Charly noticed and added, "But you might have a point."

Booty checked out the firemen, the sheriff. "We need to wrap up this meeting. I need to get to my horses. My advice, especially to you, Charly, is for God's sake don't mention a bomb. Let them figure it out. If it is, we'll think of something else and try to find out what's going on. Maybe Ward's right, maybe someone is on to us."

"What I can't fathom is, why try to scare us? That's what drug czars do. Doesn't fit." Charly stifled his worry, hoping it wouldn't show on his face.

"Fit or not, one man is dead, my van is cinders."

"We'll buy you a new van." Charly repeated this as though to a child.

"An equal third and a van." Ward looked each man square in the eye, then returned his gaze to his van.

"Charly and I need to talk about it." Booty played for time.

"Now or never, Booty. I'm not the fool you take me to be."

"I say we let him in as an equal partner. He's proven himself these last two years, and he does risk more," Charly paused, "initially."

Booty was livid that, as he saw it, Charly had given in, but he agreed through gritted teeth. "Fine."

"And we'd better start sniffing around." Ward's shoulders dropped a little, he'd been so tense. "You might be next."

"Shit." Booty spat on the ground.

"Booty, don't be so sure you won't wind up with your throat slit. We're all marked, I swear it." Ward's voice wavered slightly.

"Oh, hell, Booty will be killed by his ex-wife. She'll start lower with the knife, then work her way up to his throat." Charly couldn't suppress a laugh.

"Kill Miss Nasty, too," Ward, enjoying Booty's sudden look of discomfort, added.

26

As the smoke slowly dissipated, the horses calmed down. No matter what happens, even in war, horse chores must get done. Manuel kept everyone moving once the worst had passed, so Fair and Harry could attend to other things.

No sooner had Fair stepped out of Barn Five than Booty waved for him to come over to his barn. Miss Nasty, on his shoulder, waved, too. "Mare cast."

Fair strode toward the barn, daylight so bright he squinted. "Harry, shouldn't take long," he called over his shoulder.

A horse who is cast has laid down in his or her stall and can't get up again. Sometimes it's foolishness; they literally get stuck in a corner and then become frightened. Other times, they're down and appear cast but are sick, even though they showed no prior signs of illness. You didn't know until you got into the stall with the horse.

Booty, taking no chances, for it had already been a bad day from his point of view, hailed Fair.

If the horse was simply cast, the men could raise her up. Even then, Booty wanted Fair to examine her. She'd probably flopped down in a fit over the smoke, fire, and hollering.

Harry, left to her own devices, headed toward the practice ring, then noticed it was empty. Given the proximity of the incinerated van, that made sense.

People were working their horses in the main show ring with the blessing of the fairground officials.

In an impromptu meeting, the officials, some on a speakerphone, deliberated whether to cancel Saturday's events and send everyone home. After viewing this from every single angle, they chose to go forward. They deliberated more because the next proposed step was costly, but they finally agreed to hire extra security. Under other circumstances this might offend the sheriff's department. As it was, Sheriff Howlett was overstretched, so he felt relief. This had turned into one hell of a week for the department.

Harry observed the manager striding down to the parking lot, so she turned toward the show ring. Mrs. Murphy, Pewter, and Tucker tagged along. The sun high overhead encouraged her to duck under the covered arena on the eastern side of the ring. Sitting in the front was Renata.

"May I join you?" Harry inquired.

Harry, even though she was pretty sure Renata had "stolen" her own horse, liked her more each day. Renata wasn't silly, she loved horses, and, given all that had happened apart from Queen Esther, Renata stayed grounded.

"Please."

The two women watched as three good horses, each with little dangling chains like bracelets on their long hooves, trotted.

"Hot. Hope those trainers have sense enough to shorten this." Harry hated to see a horse ill-used or pushed too hard.

"Think they will." Renata leaned forward, elbows on knees. "More than anything I think this was to give them a positive focus—you know, take their minds off the explosion." She paused. "Charly swears it was a bomb."

"He would know." Harry leaned forward, as well, since the bleachers had no backs on them.

Mrs. Murphy and Pewter climbed to the top of the bleachers because birds made nests under the eaves. They couldn't reach them, but they could listen and dream. Tucker stayed with Harry.

"You're talking to Charly again?"

"Sort of." Renata tugged at the ends of her cowboy neckerchief, which she'd tied around her neck.

Neckerchiefs proved useful when the dust kicked up. Slip one up over your nose and you could breathe better than without.

"I'm surprised you're not at Kalarama with Queen Esther. Don't you ride tonight?"

She turned her beautiful face toward Harry. "I'm chicken."

" 'Cause you haven't worked her much?"

"No. Too many terrible things going on around here. I don't want my mare hurt. I don't want to bring her back here." She inhaled deeply. "And I don't want to get hurt, either. Publicity may be good, but I care about Queen Esther more than that." Renata now regretted generating that publicity, although she couldn't say as much.

"Understand that." Harry breathed in, the sticky air coating her throat. "You are the main attraction, though."

"No." Renata smiled disarmingly. "The main attraction is the five-gaited stake, Charly and Booty going head to head."

"Don't forget Larry."

"Point Guard should do well, but it really is between Frederick the Great and Senator. Point Guard is young. Lots of time."

Charly came into the ring, with Carlos leading a light-brown gelding with a high head carriage. The horse possessed the desired Saddlebred attributes: long neck, good head set and carriage, longish strong back, powerful hindquarters. He threw his right foreleg out a bit to the side. This small flaw would in no way compromise his performance, but if in a class with a horse who was equal to him in presentation, he'd be pinned beneath that horse. Still, he'd be in the ribbons.

"Haven't seen that horse before." Harry remembered horses, dogs, and cats the way most people remembered human faces.

"Charly brought him in from Indiana. He's just starting his career. He goes right back to the farm after this. But we agreed to meet here so I could watch him—easier for both of us today and, well, who knew?" She threw up her hands.

Charly tipped his Panama hat at the ladies while slowly walking the gelding around, giving the animal time to relax, stretch his legs. Even at the walk, the horse exhibited a big, fluid stride.

"Nice mover." Harry studied intently.

"Charly says he's easy to ride."

"How much?"

"Today, forty thousand. If he starts the bigger show circuit and does well, that will double fast enough." She rested her chin on her fist. "I need more horses, horses I can ride. I'm not paying all this money to watch someone else ride my horses."

Harry laughed. "You start out with one or two; two's better since horses shouldn't be alone, they need a friend. Next thing you know, you've got a herd."

"I can do the job." Tucker could, too. *"I can move them in and out of the barn all by myself. You just get a herd."*

"He says he likes the horse." Harry smiled at Tucker.

The youngster started his trot, extraordinary action, his knees about touching his chin.

Harry sat up straight. "Holy cow."

"I know. That's why I need to buy him now."

"Renata, if you've got the money, why not?" Harry couldn't imagine being able to dash off a check that large. "Guess you've patched it up with Charly?"

Sighing, Renata lifted her chin off her fist, exhaling loudly. "I don't know what to do with myself. Or with him. I'm embarrassed at the scene I made Wednesday, but he drove me to it. He sets me off, gets under my skin."

"Some people do that."

"But I can't stay away. He's so gifted, and when you spend time with him away from everyone else, he's funny and kind. Around other men he puts on a show."

"I noticed."

"Booty's as bad." Renata half-laughed. "The two of them are like bulls in a china shop when they're together. Nonstop competition."

"Two successful men with successful egos, hey." Harry shrugged.

Renata blushed slightly as Charly winked at her. Now astride, he walked the gelding in front of her, then continued to the other side of the arena, where the horse would be silhouetted against the rail.

"Booty did get one up on him." Renata smiled. "Charly still talks about the time Booty milked a rattlesnake. Booty called Charly a chicken since he wouldn't hold the rattler." She wrinkled her lips in disgust.

"Joan told me he keeps snakes."

"Too weird."

"Useful, I guess. Fair said venom can immunize horses in the production of antivenin serums."

"What's that?"

"I forgot to ask him." Harry smiled. "But whatever it is, it's good. He did say that the venom dries into yellow crystals and can stay toxic for a really long time."

"Well, I still don't like snakes and I think Booty's weird. Miss Nasty proves that."

"Aptly named."

"Fair seems to have his ego in check." Renata returned to men and their egos.

"He's an amazing man. His love is his work, and he thinks about the horses, not himself. He doesn't really care if anyone pays attention to him or not, but I think maybe because he's so tall and powerfully built, he doesn't have to care. Who is going to challenge him?"

"That's a thought. Can you imagine if women worried about how tall we were? Stood next to one another and looked down, that sort of thing?" Renata laughed lightly.

"We compete in other ways, I expect."

With an unexpected vehemence Renata said, "I'm over it. I'm sick of the A-list parties. I'm sick of the PR firm I had to hire to keep me in the news in a positive light. Harry, it's such utter and complete bullshit. I'm not a person, I'm a brand, a piece of merchandise. This may surprise you, but I actually like acting, although I hate the rest of it. I don't know how much longer I can do it."

"Kind of what Alicia says."

"She could walk back into a studio today and get a great role." Renata thought a minute. "Not many good lead roles for older women, but if she'd play a supporting role, she could have anything she wanted. Look at the work Julie Christie gets when she wants it."

"Alicia doesn't care. She made a lot of money and inherited a lot, too, from her first lover," Harry said.

"Didn't she have three husbands?"

"Did. But her first lover, Mary Pat Reines, left her everything. I think she taught Alicia a great deal about being a lady and about life. Not that any of this came to light in Hollywood."

"It's chic to be gay now."

"I don't think so," Harry countered. "A few get away with it, but—" She watched as the gelding stepped into a canter. "Smooth. Ah, well, as I was saying, our country is odd, you know. We go through economic cycles, fashion cycles, and, what would you call it, tolerant cycles? Right now we aren't exactly in a tolerant cycle."

"I think all countries are that way. There are two opposing points of view, and they can never be reconciled."

"Which are?" Harry turned to look Renata full in the face, enjoying a real conversation with someone, not idle social chat.

"The first is you take people as they are. Sure, you have

laws to curb the worst excesses, but you go about your business and other people go about theirs. The other point of view is that humans are evil and must be controlled, watched, hammered. The real problem there is the definition of evil changes according to who is in power. However, they always claim they are following old laws or God's word or decency."

"The twain shall never meet," Harry replied.

"Never. Not here. Not in Iran. Not in China. Wherever people are, these two views are opposed, sometimes violently."

"I'm glad I'm a corgi," Tucker rightfully said.

Harry dropped her hand on Tucker's head, stroking her friend. "I can see why you're sick of Hollywood, Renata."

"Two more years, Harry, two more years, and if I'm lucky two good pictures so I can cash in and come home. I belong in Kentucky."

"I understand." She did, too. "Do you think you belong with Charly?"

New though Harry was to her life, Renata instinctively trusted her. She knew she wouldn't gossip. Better yet, Harry approached her as a horsewoman, not a movie star.

"He asked me to marry him."

"Ah." Harry didn't pry as to her reply.

"I don't know what to do. I said I'd think about it and I'd give him my answer at the close of the show. Tonight."

"You'd never be bored."

"No, but I might like to kill him sometimes."

Harry laughed. "Renata, every woman feels that way about the man she loves."

Renata frowned, then smiled. "Guess we do."

"You'll make the right decision."

"Thank you, Harry. What I don't look forward to is telling Joan and Larry that I'm moving Queen Esther back to Charly's. They've been very good to me, and they're the ones who have had to put up with the press as well as my behavior."

"You've been fine."

"I think I got a little emotional there, particularly when I found Jorge."

"You're human, Renata. Joan and Larry will understand. They're wise in many ways."

"Yes, I think they are, and when you look at Joan's parents it all falls into place, doesn't it?"

"You can't pick your parents, so if you get a good pair, you're very lucky." Harry smiled.

"You?"

"Oh, good. Mother could be tough, very intellectual and strict. Maybe 'intellectual' is the wrong word. Her mind was very practical. She read all the time. When I majored in art history at Smith, she was one step ahead of a running fit. She wanted me to apply myself to a field where I could make a good living. Dad took life as it came. He told me to be happy."

"Lucky you. Mine left a lot to be desired." A flicker of pain crossed her face. "I did learn to forgive. They did what they could. They shouldn't have married and they shouldn't have had children. Both could suck a river dry, if you know what I mean. I think that's why I've sidestepped marriage. I'm afraid. Why I don't drink, too."

"Like I said, you'll do the right thing."

"Harry, you don't know how good you've made me feel." She stood up, motioning Charly to the rail. "I'll buy him. I'll buy the filly and colt, too. How's that?"

Charly tipped his hat again, his face radiant. "Madam, I'll hop to it." He then nodded to Harry and walked toward Carlos at the gate. He called back, "Remember my offer to get the filly and colt free."

She nodded. "Right. I'll tell you tonight."

"Are you still going to show Shortro?" Harry adored the young game gelding. He was all heart.

"You know, Shelbyville was a fine hour for him. He's a good three-gaited horse; he'll probably get even better. I thought about selling him after the show. I've had inquiries, but he's so kind, takes care of his rider..." She reached for Harry's hand. "But I don't need the money. I love the horse. I want him to be happy. I'm giving him to you."

Stunned, Harry could only say, "Renata."

"You're not showing Saddlebreds, I know, but I think Shortro would like to be in the country. I bet he'd be a good foxhunter. He's the most willing horse I have ever owned, and I want him to be where he'll be loved and where he can just be a horse. I'm impulsive, I know, but you've made me feel so good and, well, I do love Shortro. He'll be happy with you."

Harry hugged Renata. "I promise I'll send you monthly reports."

"And I will come foxhunt."

As the two women walked toward the steps, the cats rumbled down from the top, each row reverberating as they thumped down.

"Life's funny, isn't it?" Harry beamed.

"If it's not, we are." Renata laughed, feeling so light and carefree, despite it all.

27

I'll call Horsin' Around." Fair named an equine-shipping company that he recommended to "patients" and their owners. "They can pick up Shortro and Indian Summer." He was amazed that Renata had given Harry the wonderful gelding.

Indian Summer was the Thoroughbred at Paula Cline's Rose Haven. Alicia had agreed to make a donation to the Thoroughbred Retirement Fund after discussing the horse with Harry. Her donation would exceed Paula's request.

Booty, stripped to a T-shirt and jeans and sweating, overheard the conversation as they were outside his barn. He stepped into the sunlight, Miss Nasty on his shoulder. He filled that T-shirt right well.

Wearing a lime-green short skirt, a matching halter top, and her floppy straw hat to ward off the sun's rays, Miss

Nasty peered down at Pewter and curled back her lips. She then turned around on Booty's shoulder to flip up the back of her skirt.

"If my rear end were that ugly I wouldn't show it to anyone," Pewter sassed.

"You're so ugly you should put a paper sack over your head. Don't cats like paper sacks?" Miss Nasty whirled around.

"Nasty, keep still." Booty patted her head.

"That revolting gray cat insulted me."

"Monkey hamburger. Yum." Pewter's deep-pink tongue licked her gray lips, her whiskers forward.

"My bite is bad. Don't delude yourself. You can't hurt me."

"She can try." Mrs. Murphy sounded conciliatory. *"Miss Nasty, have you thought about the pin? I'll make it worth your while."* She gave Pewter a dirty look to stop the insult about to pop out of the cat's mouth. *"That pin has sentimental value. It belonged to Joan's grandmother."*

"So?" The monkey held up her palms.

"Bananas—we could get you a cart full of them." Tucker had no idea how to buy bananas, but it sounded good.

"What do you take me for? A monkey?" Miss Nasty laughed. *"Anyway, I can eat bananas whenever I want."*

"What if we found you another pin even prettier?" The tiger figured the longer she kept Miss Nasty talking, the closer she would get to discovering what the monkey would take in trade.

"How pretty?"

"Lots of diamonds to show off your color." Mrs. Murphy smiled.

"Yes, that beautiful shade of poop brown," Pewter venomously said.

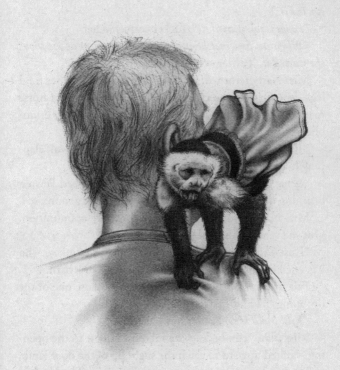

Miss Nasty flew off Booty's shoulder, running into the barn.

"Dammit, Pewter, you've upset her. She's run away." Tucker wanted to find the pin as much as Mrs. Murphy did.

"If she's that sensitive, she should stay in her cage. Besides, she started it."

"Pewter, you started it," Tucker corrected her.

"When we first met her on the rail, first night of the show, she started it." Pewter was adamant.

Miss Nasty returned, running then hopping on her hind legs. In each paw she carefully held a large dollop of horse manure. Taking aim, she pelted Pewter, the droppings crumbling on contact.

"Who's the color of poop?" She hopped up and down, clapping her hands as Pewter puffed up in total rage.

"What's gotten into these guys?" Harry grabbed Pewter, brushing off the manure, which was dry, thank goodness.

Miss Nasty returned to the barn for more ammunition. Out she came. This time she nailed Harry.

"Nasty!" Booty took a stride toward the monkey, who hastened out of reach by retreating back into the barn.

Fair brushed off his wife and Pewter, because one of the droppings had hit Pewter again.

"Kill! I will kill!" Pewter howled.

Miss Nasty climbed up the tall post closest to the opening, vaulted upward to catch the slight lip of the door jamb, and swung herself up on the protruding light. The sun had heated the metal; it was hotter than the last time she was up there. She burned her paws a touch and dropped straight down to the ground. Pewter launched herself out of Harry's arms, narrowly missing smashing onto the monkey by inches.

Miss Nasty, her paws smarting, tore back into the barn, Pewter hard on her heels. Fortunately, the humans hadn't a clue.

"Maybe we should separate them." Booty turned toward the aisle.

Fair replied, "We can follow, but I bet you Miss Nasty can stay out of Pewter's reach."

Mrs. Murphy and Tucker had the good sense not to participate in the chase. The monkey perched on a rafter as Pewter, on top of a stall beam below, hurled insult after insult.

Booty repeated an offer he'd made to Harry when the animals were carrying on. "Because Shortro is Renata's horse, I can get more money for him if you want to sell. He's a good horse, personality plus. Fifty thousand for you." And ten for him, which he kept to himself. His fee should have been five thousand.

Harry and Fair knew how that worked, which was one of the reasons they put every sale or purchase in writing.

"Thank you, Booty. I know a person should take the money and run, but Renata expressly stated she wanted to retire Shortro from showing, young though he is. She wants me to have him. I look forward to working with him, really."

"Well, if you change your mind..." Booty smiled, oblivious to the fact that Harry had given her word to Renata. He turned to Fair. "Miss Nasty isn't being very nice, especially after you helped me with the cast mare. She suffers from temper tantrums."

"Pewter can provoke them in anyone," Tucker said.

"Some friend you are." Pewter looked up again at the

monkey licking its paws. *"I hope you get hemorrhoids. I hope they crack open. I hope you sit in turpentine!"*

"Next time I throw a cow pie."

Booty called Miss Nasty, to no avail. He shook his head. "Well, she'll come down when she's ready. I've got to get back to work. Thanks to the INS, we're going around the clock. What do they expect us to do?"

"I don't know, but we'd better figure it out." Fair felt great sympathy for people who needed physical labor performed by reliable individuals. And he understood the illegal worker's desire to improve his or her life by working in America. "We've got about eleven and a half million illegal immigrants. Send them away and the economy will go down like a B-52 with its tail shot off."

Exasperated, Booty raised his voice. "Help them become citizens. They work, they buy stuff like milk and shoes. I know they use our social services and schools, so help them become citizens and they'll pay taxes for those services."

"Good reason not to become a citizen," Harry ruefully commented.

"Ever think about how much money we throw away? What will those INS stooges do? Write reports. What does any public official do? Write reports." Booty snarled, a real flash of anger.

Fair, more balanced in his outlook: "Booty, depends on the public official. The closer someone is to their people, the better job they do most times. Sheriff Howlett knows everyone, the fire chief knows everyone, plus they know how important this show in particular and the fairgrounds in general are to Shelby County. To someone from the INS, Shelbyville is a place to raid, not a place to live. That's the problem with large state agencies. Put it on the federal level and the disregard for local sentiment reaches gargantuan proportions."

Booty nodded. "What's the expression, 'You rise to your level of incompetence'?" He brightened a moment. "I've risen to mine."

They laughed.

As Harry and Fair left the barn, Booty returned to checking harnesses. Tucker and Mrs. Murphy pondered a moment.

"Don't go," Pewter begged.

"Why?" Mrs. Murphy asked.

"If I wait long enough, hunger and thirst will bring this little bitch down."

"Bring you down first, Tub." Miss Nasty felt bored up there, and she wanted Bag Balm on her paws. She knew right where Booty kept it. She liked a little pinch of the other substance, too, since Booty used his Bag Balm tin to store a bit of cocaine. Miss Nasty also enjoyed a sip of spirits occasionally.

"Come on, Pewter. This solves nothing," Tucker reasonably said.

A flash of indignation illuminated Mrs. Murphy's countenance. "Miss Nasty, you brag. You don't have the pin. You can't even describe it."

"Oh, yes, I can. It's a sparkly diamond horseshoe with a ruby and sapphire riding crop through it."

Tucker, often in tune with her friend, called up, "You probably noticed it when you were on the rail of the Kalarama box. You sat right in front of Joan."

"I have it!"

Mrs. Murphy shrugged, turned to leave. "You almost had us there, Miss Nasty."

"You'll see," the monkey, stung, promised.

Pewter, realizing she'd better join her pals, backed down the stall pole. The three reached the end of the aisle.

Following them overhead on the high rafter, Miss Nasty shouted, *"You'll see!"*

28

The day, sultry, kept everyone sweating. Harry could smell the salt on her own body as well as on other humans and horses. She wanted to drive over to Lexington to Fennell's, a marvelous tack shop at Red Mile, the harness racetrack right smack in the middle of town. Whenever she'd get a little money to the good, she would order one of their bridles. The leather and workmanship held up for decades if properly cleaned. Harry wanted value for her dollar, and Fennell's couldn't be beat.

The drive over would take an hour, and the heat and excitement over Shortro had already tired her a little. The van explosion upset her more than she realized, as well.

For a moment she stood in the Kalarama temporary tack room, studying the bits and equipment used, much of it different from what she used. Saddlebreds achieved a stylish tail carriage, the top of the thick tail rising above the rounded hindquarters by use of a tail set. This light harness utilized a padded crupper, which went right under the tail to elevate it. Sometimes a vet would cut the ventral tail muscles, a simple procedure, which allowed the tail more movement without harming it. Thoroughbreds and hunters bypassed these refinements, for they had no need of them. The tail carriage was the reason hunter–jumper people dubbed Saddlebreds "shaky tails."

Each type of equine sport developed its own tools, although the basic principles remained the same. Saddlebreds generally used longer-shanked bits than foxhunters, who often rode out in a simple snaffle bit or Tom Thumb Pelham, so named because the shank was short.

Bitting, a discipline in itself, required wisdom. Many a poor trainer made up for his or her inadequacies by overbitting the horse—using too much bit because they didn't know how to achieve the result with patient training. That was an excellent way to ruin a horse's mouth, but the short-term result might be that the animal showed well, the trainer snared his fee as the animal sold, and the new owner soon discovered all was not as it seemed.

Much as Harry deplored this, as well as running Thoroughbreds too early, she knew in her heart it would probably get worse. The tax laws forced most professional horse people to get quick results from young horses.

Laws reflected the needs of city people to the detriment of country people, which isn't to say that city people received adequate funding for their needs, either. A law that on the books might make perfect sense to someone in the depths of Houston could hurt the horsemen. Something as simple as removing income-averaging for farmers drove everyone to their knees when it happened. People lost farms; those that hung on battled the arbitrary rule that you had to show a profit every four years. Sounds so easy unless you're a horseman. A quarter horse might mentally mature, understand its training, and be sold by age three or four. A Warmblood would take six or seven years to be fully made. No way to sell the slower-developing animals within the unrealistic time frame. If the horsemen diversified and grew corn, that took money as well as time away from the horse operation.

Harry sighed deeply. "Try telling that to someone who graduated from law school and is currently honing their mastery of the sound bite." She half-whispered this, but her animals overheard.

"Talking to herself again." Pewter, still fuming over her encounter with Miss Nasty, sniffed.

"Mind goes a mile a minute." Mrs. Murphy understood Harry and loved that the human often understood her intent, although she rarely knew what Mrs. Murphy was saying.

Harry inhaled the heady perfume of leather and oil; the steel of the bits even gave off a light odor. She could smell the hay in the hayracks in the stalls, coupled with the sweetest aroma of all—horses. She looked down at her friends. "Sometimes this wave washes over me and I feel like I will live to see our way of life vanish." Tears filled her eyes.

"Don't worry, Mom. People can't be that dumb." Tucker smiled, her pink tongue hanging out.

"Are you kidding?" Pewter, still sour, replied. *"Think about the revolutions. Everything goes. People die by the millions and so do cats, dogs, and horses. Humans have no more sense than*

that horrible, stinky monkey." She puffed out her chest. "*Figures.*"

"*When an ear of corn costs fifty dollars, when mulch and manure for those suburban gardens climbs to thirty bucks a bag, they'll wake up fast enough,*" Mrs. Murphy predicted.

"*Well, that's it, isn't it? Agribusiness keeps the cost down.*" Tucker followed Harry everywhere and overheard her conversations with other humans who farmed.

Mrs. Murphy, swaying back and forth in a hypnotic manner, said, "*Until a virus hits a crop. It's one-crop farming; genetic diversity has been removed. It's bound to happen, Tucker. And with oil being volatile, no one can keep prices down, because it takes gas to ship the crops, right? Sooner or later they're loaded on a truck.*"

"*Bring horses back in a big way. Then maybe people will appreciate animals again.*" Tucker laughed with delight at the thought, not considering the potential abuse from people who had no feelings for animals.

Overhearing the animals, Point Guard nickered, "*When the automobile became affordable, the horse population dwindled to the point where we were afraid we'd become extinct. Thank God, some humans still loved us. My mother told me what her mother told her and so on down the line. Do you know that today there are more horses than since before World War One?*"

"*Still rather use draft horses to timber and plow on steep hills.*" Pewter was finally settling herself. "*Safer.*"

"*Doesn't suck up gas, either,*" Point Guard called over his stall.

Rousing herself at the horse's nicker, Harry told her friends, "Sorry, guys. Gave in to the slough of despondency. Too much happening. I don't have it figured out. Scares me.

And it's odd, but being given such a big present kind of knocks me out, too. I'll be all right." She walked into the hospitality room, pulled a can of lemonade out of the small fridge, downed it as she watched the cats and dog drink from the water bowl. "Okay, I'm better." She walked back out, down the aisle to Shortro.

He turned his lovely gray head when she came into the stall. "Buddy Bud, you and I are going to become very good friends."

His large kind eyes promised sweetness and fun. *"What do I have to do?"*

Mrs. Murphy climbed up the wooden side, stepping onto his back since he was against the stall.

"Shortro, you're coming with us to Virginia."

"Do they have Saddlebred shows there?"

"They do," Tucker answered. *"There's a big one down in Lexington, Virginia, called the Bonnie Bell, but you're coming home to be a foxhunter. You'll love it."*

"I don't want to kill anything," Shortro, troubled, replied as Harry stroked his long, glossy neck.

"Don't kill 'em. You just chase them." Pewter preferred to watch the hunt. She wasn't going to run around after foxes. Actually, Pewter wasn't going to run after anything if she could help it.

"Is Renata going to hunt?" the gelding inquired.

"Says she is, but she's given you to Harry because Harry will love you and you can play in pastures a lot, too," Tucker said. *"There are other nice horses there. You'll make friends."*

"I'll miss Renata." Shortro hung his head, then lifted it to look Harry full in the face. *"But you look kind."*

Harry rubbed his ears. "We'll have a lot of fun, you beautiful guy." She looked down at his tail. He'd be the only horse in the hunt field with his tail up like that, but, hey, if folks could ride mules and draft horses out there, she could go on a horse with a shaky tail. The more she touched Shortro and talked to him, the happier she felt. Him, too. So many times when she was distressed, words didn't lift Harry, but touching her horses, her cats and dog brought her back to a good place. She thought that humans didn't touch enough. When they did, the purpose was usually sex or violence. No wonder so many people felt disconnected.

Her cell rang. She pulled it out of her hip pocket. "Hi."

"Harry." Joan's voice was excited.

Before Joan said more, Harry spoke. "I didn't call you about Ward's van because I figured everyone else had."

"Did. I called you because I found out—took a little wooing of the Shelby County sheriff, but I found out—that Jorge withdrew his money from his savings account on the day he was murdered. He wired it to his mother in Mexico."

"Jeez." Harry felt the net closing.

"Seventy-five thousand dollars." Joan paused. "That's a lot of money. It's really a lot of money for a groom."

"You said he didn't spend much."

"He didn't, but he still couldn't have saved that much in two years. No way."

"He sure was smart enough to hide it." Harry lowered her voice.

Everyone in the barn was at late lunch or taking a siesta before the madness of the final night, but still, she half-whispered.

Joan's tone was definitive. "I ask myself what could Jorge do that someone else couldn't."

"And?"

"He could go back and forth to Mexico. He had his green

card. He could speak to people on the phone from Mexico or Arizona or wherever. He was learning a lot from Manuel, he was becoming a good horseman, but that's not special enough. This has to do with his background."

"You're right." A lightbulb turned on in Harry's head, although the wattage was still pitifully low. "INS."

"Or against them."

"What do you mean, Joan?"

"I mean, what if he was bringing people here?"

"I considered that, but wouldn't he have been off the farm more? How could he do that? Did he go back to Mexico a lot?"

"Christmas, but he could leave in the middle of the night. Larry and I wouldn't know. We're down at the end of the road, and Mom and Dad wouldn't know. Their bedroom doesn't face the farm road. It's possible."

"Did he have a cell phone?"

"No one can find it. He had one. I saw it enough times."

"Ah. Well, now what?" Harry reached up to scratch Mrs. Murphy's ears.

"I don't know."

"Larry still showing tonight?"

"Yes. I'm nervous, but he said we have to go on. We owe it to Shelbyville. They've been good to all Saddlebred people."

"Joan, you don't think all this is some kind of effort to destroy the show?"

"No. Every county has their date. Hurting Shelbyville would only hurt them. People use those shows to prepare for this one and for Louisville."

"What if a county wanted to get as fancy as Shelbyville?"

"Sure brings in the horsemen's dollars, and the tourists,

too. Nothing to stop county commissioners from building up a show, a fairgrounds. The trick is getting the residents to pay for it via taxes, but, hey, the fairgrounds here are used nearly every week of the year. It generates revenue and pays for itself. That's a long-winded answer, but there's no gain for anyone to hurt this show."

"What about the animal-rights nuts? They like to stir up trouble and they don't mind twisting the facts."

"They'd go right after us straight up. This isn't direct. They'd take public credit for the disruption." Joan, always three steps ahead, had considered that. "We aren't abusive." She paused. "Not that that matters."

"Weird, isn't it? No one loves animals more than you and me, and now there are people actually saying we shouldn't domesticate them. Hell, they've domesticated us. Well, I'm off the track and I'm sorry. It's been pretty intense here."

"You saw the explosion?"

"Heard it and ran right out. If Ward, Benny, or horses had been there, they'd be in pieces all over the parking lot. It was by the grace of God that Benny left the van once he cranked it to warm up. He walked over to Charly's barn to talk to Carlos."

"Whoever did this wanted them dead just like Jorge."

"Connected?" Harry thought so.

"I believe it is, but I don't know why. Something to do with the illegal workers. It's the only thing that makes sense."

"I think about illegal workers, but Ward works like a slave. It's only himself and Benny. If he were part of some kind of smuggling ring, wouldn't he have help at his own barn? He could afford grooms. Maybe he's getting close to whoever did kill Jorge."

"That's what I've come to think, but..." She took a

while. "I don't know. I don't think I'll relax until the five-gaited class is over, and Larry, Manuel, the boys, and the horses are back at Kalarama. Harry, I'm not sure I want to know."

"You do."

"Well, then I don't want anyone else to know I know except you, of course."

"One other thing." Harry scrupulously did not spill the beans about Renata leaving, but she did say, "Renata gave me Shortro."

"She did!"

"She's grateful I found Queen Esther. She promised to help me with my wine if it turns out potable. 'Course, that's three years down the road. Guess she wanted to do something now."

"How good of her. He's a great guy. The Shortros of the world should be gold-plated. That wonderful mind."

"You'll lose a boarder. Sorry."

Joan laughed. "He wouldn't stay long. She'll wind up back with Charly. Too much emotion there. Takes a woman to know a woman."

"Yes." Harry bit her lip.

"I expect her to pull Queen Esther after the show. She did call and say she wasn't showing the mare tonight. I wanted to make sure—after all, this is her last prep before Louisville. She'll be up against even more horses at Louisville. Said she didn't trust whatever was happening, so she wasn't going to show her. I thought she'd do it for the publicity."

"Can't blame her."

"No. Well, does this mean you're going to show a Saddlebred?" A merry tone lifted Joan's voice.

"Actually, Joan, I'll just walk him under tack, then see if he's willing to do more."

"I knew it. I knew you'd turn him into a foxhunter."

Harry laughed. "He'll tell me what he wants to do."

"That's why you're a good horseman."

"I'll do anything," Shortro promised.

As Harry and Joan finished up their conversation, Fair stood in the aisle of Charly's barn. The smoke finally was dissipating and wafting eastward. The smell of it, the burned oil and metal, still hung over the place.

"Seeing more of it." Charly walked the aisle with Fair as they looked in on each horse. "More shows. More pressure. And if you have a client who has a four-hundred-thousand-dollar horse and they tell you not to turn him out in the pasture because they're afraid of an injury, what do you do?"

"I know it takes patience, but you need to show them what gastric ulcers are and how they affect an animal. Keep a horse in a stall with limited turnout, cram them full of high-energy food, subject them to high stress, you're going to get ulcers. Performance drops. Once the ulcers are diagnosed, it takes twenty-eight days of a full tube of Ulcergard every day. And after that it's a quarter tube a day. Don't change the regimen and the ulcers return. People have to learn these are living, breathing, emotional creatures. They aren't cars."

"I know. I know. Had five horses in my barn suffer from them."

"How many horses at the farm?"

"Sixty. Give or take."

"How many in work?"

"Well, horses come in and out. Some are there for specific training, a course, and they're gone in a month, say, but on average, twenty-five."

"If you only have five with ulcers, you have a good program. Some people don't use Ulcergard, by the way. They use papaya juice. I prefer Ulcergard. Ulcers are a bitch."

"Now if I could calm mine." Charly smiled ruefully. "It's feast or famine in this business."

"This last week can't have helped."

"Never been through anything like it." Charly folded his arms across his chest. "Well, the first Gulf War was bad, but we knew what we were about. This," he held out one hand, keeping the other arm across his chest, "I don't know. I feel like there's someone behind every bush. That damned raid, along with Jorge's murder, has everyone looking over their shoulders. Now this." He shook his head, then stood straighter. "I'll worry about it after the show. I will beat Booty if it kills me."

"Or him."

"Given all that's happened, I probably shouldn't say that, but I really do want to wipe his face in the dirt. Frederick the Great is going to win Shelbyville, and Louisville, too. He's a world champion."

"For my part, I hope there's good competition tonight." Fair smiled at him and said, "No glory in a walkover."

Charly smiled, too. "They'll make it hard for me. You'll see a pretty damned exciting class."

29

*A*s if the portents since August 2 hadn't filled people with wonder and anxiety, the yellow stakeout around the debris of the van completed the aura of incipient danger.

The show officials wanted the bits hauled off, but the sheriff declared they had to stay. Plus, they still were warm. Bomb experts called in from Louisville needed time to consider the pattern of debris.

The result of this wise decision on the part of young Sheriff Howlett caused the officials consternation. Half of the main parking lot would be cordoned off, so they petitioned the sheriff and the mayor to allow them to mark the westbound shoulder of Route 60 for parking, as well as side streets closest to the fairgrounds. Residents didn't complain about Route 60, but having their streets clogged up proved a major irritant. The smarter ones parked their cars at the foot of their driveway so no one could block them. Windows had been smashed for less.

As for Route 60, traffic to the show from both east and west would need to be rerouted to park along the curb of town streets.

Many of the officials feared that spectators would remain home after the week of wild events; after all, how many Saddlebred shows endured a murder, a van blowing up, and a horse being stolen, and then recovered? The reverse proved true. What is it about the human race that draws it to danger, drama? Let there be a car crash, a house fire, a bridge collapse, and folks will travel for miles to view the disaster. The final night of the horse show was no exception. People started pouring in two hours before the first class.

The grooms feverishly worked to prepare the horses and riders, bringing extra water for themselves as the heat remained unabated; the trainers all dodged the unbelievable press of flesh. By five, two hours before the first class, all prior attendance records had been shattered. Despite the expense for extra security and the anticipated cost of extra cleanup of the grounds, the coffers would overflow.

Ward, hearing the sounds of cars, people, feet, quipped to Benny, bridle over his shoulder, "This proves there is no such thing as bad publicity."

Ward no sooner got the words out of his mouth than Booty appeared, in the company of Miss Nasty.

"Benny, take a hike," Booty ordered.

"Hike, hike, hike," Miss Nasty echoed Booty, and for whatever reason this put her in an especially good mood.

Benny shifted the bridle to his other shoulder, looking to Ward.

"He stays right here, Booty. What the hell is this about? I've been through as much as I care to handle today."

Booty half-smiled. "I won't be as tedious as your insurance agent." He glanced at Benny, deciding to go forward. "Here's the deal. I know you serviced Renata, so to speak. You carried the mare to your farm." Ward stayed expressionless as Booty kept on. "I don't mind. She got what she wanted out of it. I don't even want to know what she paid you. But I want to know two things. Did Jorge bring Queen Esther to you?"

"I told you he did." Ward ignored Miss Nasty, who left Booty's shoulder and now pulled on the hem of his jeans.

"I don't remember you telling me that."

"Alzheimer's," Ward joked, but Booty didn't laugh. "What's the next question?"

"Did Charly pay you, too?"

"What's Charly got to do with it?"

"Oh, come on, Ward, don't play me for a fool. You're smarter than that and so am I. Renata doesn't breathe without Charly."

"What are you talking about?" Ward raised his voice. "I don't know what Renata and Charly are doing, but I can tell you I didn't talk to him. The only person I talked to was Renata."

"He's behind it."

"Well, go talk to him. I don't know anything about it."

Booty clucked to Miss Nasty.

"I don't want to leave yet." The monkey dropped Ward's hem to snoop in the hospitality room. Might be something scrumptious in there.

Checking his watch, Booty's eyebrows raised. "Damn, time gets away from me." Two long strides and he entered the hospitality room, just as Miss Nasty unwrapped a cold Reese's peanut butter cup. She left the small refrigerator door open, which Booty closed. "Miss Nasty, no sugar."

She popped it in her mouth, trying to swallow it whole. With tremendous effort and a few chews while eluding Booty, she managed.

Booty came out with Miss Nasty in tow.

Ward stepped closer to Booty. "I don't know what your worry is about Charly. Seems to me I have more to worry about than you do. Benny and I could have been blown to kingdom come, and, well, Charly knows all about explosives."

Booty, holding the monkey's paw as she walked along with him, her eyes watering from swallowing such a big hunk of candy, said, "Don't do business behind my back."

"I don't think doing business with Renata is doing business behind your back. I've kept up my end of the bargain concerning you."

Booty's tone dripped sarcasm. "Everything concerns me. If Charly did set up the so-called theft of the horse with you, then how do I know you aren't siphoning off money elsewhere? Maybe you bring in a load of merchandise on the QT."

"I wouldn't do that. I've been straight up." Ward's jaw jutted out.

"Good." Booty's tone improved. "If there's one thing I hate it's a double cross."

Ward and Benny watched him as he strutted toward his barn, nodding and smiling to all and sundry, Miss Nasty waving, too.

"Peculiar mind," Benny intoned.

"I'll say, but he's one hell of an organizer. I learned that going for the pickups."

"Yep. Booty succeeds at what he does." Benny said no more. He kept his personal feelings to himself, a habit learned the hard way.

"Whenever you get that flat sound in your voice, I know you're not telling me what you're thinking."

"What I'm thinking is, what the hell is he worried about? No one has tried to kill him."

"Maybe he thinks he's next." Ward watched as Booty disappeared into the mass of people.

"Be a blessing." Benny couldn't help it, it slipped out.

"Sometimes I think that myself." Ward picked up a can of hoof dressing and entered a stall.

Booty walked into Charly's barn, finding Charly back in the small dressing room. Carlos was in one of the stalls.

Booty pulled aside the curtain as Spike hollered to the other cats, *"That damned monkey is in here."*

"Shut up," Miss Nasty called back, then ran out into the aisle to irritate the cats, an activity in which she richly succeeded.

"I've been thinking." Booty sat on a navy and red tack trunk. "You sure let Ward off the hook easy."

"Did we have any choice?"

"Yeah, we could have cut him out."

Charly shook his head. "Too risky. Plus he does good work, and he is the one who will get arrested first."

"Well, I'm not overfond of reducing my own profit."

"Half a loaf is better than no loaf. Ward's tight-lipped, does what he's told, and he's bright enough. He can learn more of the business and hopefully create more profit, which will offset our slight loss in making him a full partner. Plus we don't have to pay Jorge anymore. There's a penny saved."

"There is that." Booty leaned in toward him. "I figure you and Renata contacted him to steal Queen Esther."

"The hell I did." Charly's face turned bright crimson. "That was her idea."

"I don't believe you. She's an actress. Playing a public scene with you is her bread and butter. Why should I believe you? You both get something out of it."

"What do I get out of it?"

"Renata." Booty listened for a moment to one of Miss Nasty's shrieks and decided it wasn't life-threatening, since she was cussing cats.

"My relationship with Renata has been rocky, but relationships between trainers and clients can be that way. She's wound tight."

"Then let me just say this: if you and Ward are running a little sideline behind my back, I'm going to get really angry."

"I would, too." Charly, irritated, rested his hand on the metal crossbar of the portable clothes rack. "Look, I've got to get ready. I have a boatload of clients going this last night, and there is the five-gaited stakes, which I'll be winning."

Silky smooth, Booty said, "I've given that a lot of thought. I'll be winning that class, Charly, because if you don't bring Frederick the Great down just enough to come in second, I'm telling the press about Renata stealing her own horse. Might even tell them you were in on it."

Charly, for a second, didn't move a muscle. "You son of a bitch."

"I don't like a double cross. For all I know you killed that Mexican, too."

"You're out of your mind. Out of it! I wouldn't kill Jorge."

"Well, you damned well blew up Ward's van. You're the only one who could do it. Eliminate someone who knew too much, not just about our business but about Renata. Also increases your profit."

"Come on, anyone can find information on the Internet about how to build and plant a car bomb."

"Maybe so, but I know you have that skill, thanks to the United States Army. You've even got the medals to prove it, and," he drew this out, "I know you're in love with Renata."

"For Christ's sake, Booty, Ward's no threat to Renata."

"No?" Booty's eyebrows rose. "He stuck us for a full third of a share. Blackmailing Renata could be very lucrative. She oozes money."

"You're crazy." Charly's lips turned white with rage.

"You made a mistake, buddy, a tiny mistake, but I picked up on it."

"Oh, and what might that be?" Charly wanted to hit Booty so badly he was shaking.

"When you and Renata performed your screaming match at Kalarama's barn, you pointed a finger at her and said, 'I know about you.'" Charly's face was blank. Booty continued, "A comment like that stays with people. Now, most folks when they heard about it assumed you meant she was sleeping with you. Me, I'm a little different. I investigated. I've got more friends than you think."

"If you pay them enough," Charly hissed through gritted teeth.

Booty leaned right toward him and lied through his teeth to shake up Charly. "She worked as a call girl before she hit it big. Worked in New York City and Los Angeles."

Charly, with a vicious left hook, hit Booty like thunder.

Rocked back on his feet, Booty instantly crouched low, then sprang up in Charly's face. He hit him in the mouth, loosening a tooth.

As blood trickled from Charly's mouth, he blocked another blow from the slighter man, then smashed him hard with a punishing straight right to his gut, followed by a left uppercut.

Booty sprawled on the ground but made no more attempt to defend himself.

Charly straddled him, daring him to raise up. "Get up, you slimy bastard."

"Before you hit me again, let me drop this tidbit into your overheated brain. If you don't take it down tonight just a notch, a tiny notch, Charly, then I go to the press about Renata's past and about stealing her own horse for publicity."

"I'll kill you first."

Booty, still down, looked at his expensive watch. "Got about two hours to do it. After that we'll be pushing those clients into the ring."

Charly stepped back and Booty got up, sauntering off, although he did rub his jaw.

Miss Nasty trundled after him as Spike called down, *"Your days are numbered, Nasty. Every cat on this show grounds hates your guts."*

"Oh la." She lifted her shoulders insouciantly and kept right on truckin'.

Carlos, who'd heard the crunch of fist on jaw, waited until Booty left the barn, then walked into the changing room where Charly was massaging his hand.

Charly looked at him. "I will kill that walking piece of feces."

30

*J*oan felt like she stood at a turnstile, so many people passed through Barn Five, most of them clients, friends of clients, prospective clients. By five-thirty, even before the greatest crush of people, she felt slightly wilted.

"I'll do the shake-and-howdy for twenty minutes," Harry offered. "You sneak off and drink a nice tall iced tea with a sprig of mint. That will refresh your spirits."

Joan wryly smiled. "You sound like my mother."

"How is Mother?"

"Hasn't spoken to me since she learned about the pin." Joan brightly smiled as another person came forward. "Well, Mr. Thompson—"

"John, please."

"This is Mrs. Haristeen, and there are drinks and sandwiches in the hospitality room. Dad will be here shortly."

The square-built, middle-aged man smiled back. "Thank you."

As he walked into the room, Joan whispered, "Looking for a roadster. Dad called me and told me he'd be here probably before Dad and Mom got here. I don't have but so many roadsters. That's Dad's thing."

From time to time, Paul enjoyed donning the silks to whiz around the ring, although he'd decided to take it easy this Shelbyville, which proved a prescient decision.

As if on cue, both women looked down toward Charly's barn by the practice ring. They saw Charly, his hand wrapped in Vetrap, a sky-blue thin ice pack underneath. He and Renata stood just outside the barn to the side.

"Hmm." Joan squinted. "Looks intense."

Harry noticed their shoulders raised up, faces flushed. "Yes, it does."

Spike, sitting behind them on the grass for a breath of fresh air, heard the whole thing.

"Shouldn't you put that in a bucket of ice?"

"I need to use my hand, Renata. Remember, there's only Carlos. The rest of the help ran like rabbits when INS raided."

"Guess I would, too." She reached for his hand, gently looking at it. "Good you put the Vetrap on, it will keep the swelling down. Charly, how can you ride like this?"

"I have to. I have to win." His chest expanded and he breathed hard, for it hurt even to have her hold his hand. "Look, this can't wait. I have to know something. Did you work as a call girl in New York and L.A.?"

Stunned, she stammered, "No. I was a messenger. I rode a bike. Whatever gave you that idea?"

"Booty. When I threatened you Wednesday and said, 'I

know about you,' he called in some chits. He said you worked for a high-class escort service."

"Charly, if that were the case, don't you think it would have hit the tabloids sometime during my career? It's ridiculous."

"You could have paid people off."

"Not the tabloids." She dropped his hand. "How could you even listen to such trash?"

"You're in a hard business, and thousands of beautiful women think they can achieve what you've achieved, Renata. And most of them don't come from solid backgrounds, if you know what I mean."

Fire flashed in her eyes. "You mean they're poor, they're from broken homes—like me. Trash, in fact. You think because someone started life on the short end they have no morals?"

"I think the kind of narcissistic ambition it takes to be an actress could lead any woman into anything."

"Jesus Christ, look who's talking. Narcissus!"

"Oh, come on. It's not the same. I would never have had to rent my body to get ahead in this world."

"Well, Charly Trackwell, I never did, either, and I come from hunger. I worked hard. I took jobs that allowed me to study, but I never sold my body, and I never would. I can't believe you. I can't believe you would even consider such slander." She told the truth.

He wavered. "It's been a rough week. Maybe my judgment is shaky. But he seemed so sure."

"Then tell him to give you names and numbers. I will call them myself. Actually, I won't. I'll have my lawyers call them, and I will sue their sorry asses into next week. I wouldn't mind suing Booty, either, but he needs to say it to my face." Her face, crimson, betrayed her emotions.

Spike moved forward until he was three feet behind Charly.

"You'd sue?"

"You bet."

Charly exhaled deeply. "I'm sorry."

The fact that she would sue convinced him Booty did make it up.

"Have you thought that he's trying to throw you off tonight? He wants this win."

"He also threatened to tell everyone, media included, about that and that you stole your own horse for publicity's sake."

A long cold moment followed. "Did he?"

"Said he'd tie you, me, and Ward up together. Ruin your career."

"He can try." Renata had steel in her spine. "He has to prove it. If he doesn't, he winds up in court. Do you need me to help you since you can't use your right hand?"

Surprised at this shift of subject matter, Charly blinked, then shook his head. "I can manage."

"Good. I'm going to pay a call on Booty Pollard, and when I'm finished, he'll have lost his focus for the five-gaited stake."

Charly smiled slowly. "Renata, you could make any man lose his focus."

"Only if he has a set of balls," Renata sharply replied, then added, "Would you have honored your proposal if I had been a call girl?"

His eyes looked downward, then up to hers. "No. I can't

have a whore for a wife." He didn't consider that he was a thief.

"There are all kinds of whores, Charly. You might qualify yourself. I wouldn't marry you if you were the last man on earth."

Now his face turned red. "Because I thought you were? Come on, it's not such a far putt."

"No, that doesn't upset me as much as the fact that you wouldn't marry me if I had made a mistake like that." She glanced down at Spike, who was paying rapt attention, then up to Charly. "To love is to forgive, to accept. You don't truly love me. You only love yourself. I deserve better."

She left him standing there, his hand throbbing even more, and she moved fast toward Booty's barn.

Joan said to Harry as they watched her, "Trouble in paradise."

"I'd say that Charly's goose is cooked." Harry still hadn't mentioned Renata's intent to move back to Charly's barn and was glad she hadn't.

"From the looks of it, Booty's in for a blast." A devilish moment overtook Joan. "I can't stand it. I'm going to have to promenade by Booty's barn."

Just then Mrs. Murphy and Pewter shot out in front of them, Tucker and Cookie immediately behind.

"Curiosity killed the cat," Cookie opined, her little tail nub straight up.

"It's Mom and Joan who are curious. I'm going as a guard," Pewter half-fibbed.

The small contingent, twenty yards from the front of Booty's barn, heard Renata's rising tone. Booty's responses were lower.

The two women looked at each other, the corners of

their mouths turning upward. If nothing else, it would be a reprieve from the week's events, a comical interlude, so they thought.

"Oh, come on, I was trying to rattle his cage," Booty said soothingly.

"By throwing filth at me?" Renata was so angry that Miss Nasty cowered on Booty's shoulder.

"He's in love with you. What better way to hurt him?" Booty didn't smile when he said this.

"First of all, you disgusting toad, he is not in love with me. He's only in love with himself. Secondly, you've slandered me, and if you ever say anything like that again, I will sue you. I will drive you to your knees, because I won't give up. I keep a powerful law firm on retainer for just these kinds of cheap shots. So, Booty, you either give me your sources or you get down on your knees."

By now Joan and Harry stood at the door. They couldn't help themselves.

Booty, facing outward, saw them, and a helpless look crossed his face.

Miss Nasty was so scared, she threw her skirt over her face.

"If you wear a paper bag with holes in it for your eyes it would be easier," Pewter jeered.

The monkey pulled down her skirt, glared at the gray cat. Anger overcame fear. *"I hope you eat poisoned mice."*

"Who cares what you think or say? Liar. Big liar. You don't have Joan's pin. You don't have any sparkles. All you have is a bunch of dumb dresses and hats."

Before Miss Nasty could respond with an appropriate vulgarity, Renata pulled out her silvered cell phone and hit a button for automatic dial.

"Who are you calling?"

"My lawyer. You have three rings before she picks up. So on your knees or you'll be in court, and I swear, Booty, I will drag it on and on until I bleed every penny out of you. You forget, I have the resources to do it, and the will."

Too late, Booty realized he'd underestimated Renata. He dropped like a sack of grain. "I'm sorry. I was wrong. I made it all up. I don't have any contacts. I will never say anything like that again."

She stepped toward him, placing her forefinger hard on his Adam's apple, pressing as he choked. "Keep your word, fool."

Tears welled in his eyes from the soreness at that pressure point. He coughed as Miss Nasty threw her arms around his neck.

Spinning on her heel, Renata beheld Harry, Joan, Mrs. Murphy, Pewter, Tucker, and Cookie. "I have witnesses. He slandered me. He apologized. If he reneges, I'll have him for breakfast."

She walked by them with such energy the little group felt a breeze.

Booty, hand to his throat, stood up.

Harry noticed a darkening mark on his jaw. "You're toast." At that moment her admiration for Renata reached the stratosphere.

Tears still in his eyes—he had no idea that one finger could hurt so much—he shook his head, rasping, "It was a joke."

"Booty, you aren't Mr. Popularity today." Joan put her hands on her hips.

"Screwed up." He wiped away his tears.

"Big-time." Joan left and the rest with her.

Pewter called over her shoulder, *"Liar, liar."*

Miss Nasty, still hugging Booty, didn't reply.

It took two minutes to get back to Barn Five, where Harry and Joan found Renata calmly drinking a Schweppes tonic water, popping a quinine pill with it.

She lowered the bottle. "I'm glad you saw that."

"I am, too." Joan laughed. "I only wish I'd had a picture."

"He accused me to Charly of being a call girl before I made it. And you know what else?" She laughed derisively. "Charly believed him. Believed him!" Her magical hazel eyes seemed lit from within, the contained emotion was so strong.

"I'm sorry." Harry couldn't think of anything else to say.

Joan did. "He's a shit and you're well rid of him."

As Joan rarely used profanity, this electrified the women and animals.

Paul, hearing this, stuck his head out of the hospitality room. "Joan."

"Sorry, Daddy. I'm glad you're here."

He nodded to the others, then turned back to Joan. "You weren't raised with loose talk, girlie." He then ducked back in to Mr. Thompson.

Joan whistled low and walked toward the back end of the barn, the rest in tow. "Glad Mother wasn't in there. I'd have to put smelling salts under her nose."

"Being a Southern lady takes a boatload of discipline." Harry laughed, for she, too, had been strictly brought up.

Renata, on the other hand, heard profanity on a daily basis and had to learn to talk and act like a lady. She made a telling comment. "At least someone loved you enough to correct you."

"I was loved a lot!" Harry laughed, lightening the mood.

"Renata, you know how much is at stake in this show. Booty and Charly fight at every show. Maybe they don't hit each other, but they try to get under each other's skin, push the other into a bad ride. It's silly, but then again, it provides entertainment back at the barns and practice ring, as well as the show ring."

"Got that right, but I'll be damned if Booty is going to smear my name to do it."

"Would you sue him?" Harry was leery of lawyers and courtrooms. She believed the Spanish proverb "Better to fall into the hands of the devil than lawyers."

"Unto my last breath, and I would hurt him in other ways. I'd take every client he had out of that barn, one way or the other. His revenue stream would become a trickle and then dry to dust." She stopped a moment. "I'm sorry. I'm sorry on a lot of levels. I've caused you both time and trouble. I'm not always like this. These last couple of years I've been slipping and sliding. Not just in my career. I need to come back to my real self."

"Your real self is pretty impressive," Joan wryly commented.

Renata tossed her head; her hair swung back over her shoulders. "I come from a different place than you all do. It taught me a couple of things that maybe you know and maybe you don't. But I'll tell you, if you let one person push you around, sooner or later everyone will try. It's harder being a woman. You have to bite a man bad, then he realizes you've got fangs and he backs off. We're just a bunch of animals. If you look weak, you die. That's how I see it."

"*Truth to that.*" Mrs. Murphy closely observed the great beauty.

"Most humans don't want to deal with it. They think they can negotiate things." Tucker was thoughtful.

"I reckon for most Americans that works. We live good lives, soft even." Cookie, too, was thoughtful.

"Yep, but when the trappings of civilization are stripped away, it's kill or be killed." Pewter was adamant. *"And I will kill Miss Nasty."*

Mrs. Murphy, Tucker, and Cookie chose to say nothing about Miss Nasty. There'd been enough fits already.

Joan took out the handkerchief from the pocket of her linen jacket, to fan herself. "That's why we need good friends. Friends protect one another. The government doesn't do squat." She shrugged. "It's friends that save you. And if you have a good family, they save you, too. Once people start talking about the big things, I can care but I don't see that I can do much." She looked straight at Renata. "But I can do for you, for Larry, for Harry, and what I tell you, Renata, is keep riding. Make movies until you're sick of it, but don't let people know what you really think like you just told us. People live in a bubble. They see the world the way they want to see it, not the way it is."

"I know." Renata nodded. "I do know that."

"Anything or anyone that disturbs the bubble becomes a bad person. You're in the public eye, so you have to be a good person." Joan fanned Renata, then Harry.

"You don't think we can work together? I mean, work together as a nation?" Harry plaintively asked.

"Daddy's generation did. His father and mother did. World War One and World War Two pulled people together, but nothing's pulled us together since then, really. Even September eleventh hasn't pulled us together." She stopped. "Maybe it has, maybe it's underneath all this ugliness in Frankfort," she named the town in which Kentucky's state government was located, "and Washington is on the surface. Maybe underneath, we'll do what we have to when the time comes. I don't know, and no one cares what I think, anyway."

"I do," Harry said.

Joan threw her arm around Harry's shoulder. "Harry, you can be so sweet."

Renata added, "I work in a profession that sells illusions. And you know, we're pikers out there in Hollywood. Can't hold a candle to Washington." She sighed long. "God, it's been a day. What's the night going to bring?"

"A good end to the show," Joan replied. "Then we can all go home and get a good night's sleep."

"You'll have a barn full of customers tomorrow." Harry knew the drill after a big show.

"Good." Joan brightened. "But I need one good night's sleep."

"I swear I won't cause more uproar," Renata promised.

Harry thought a moment. "Are you still going to buy that horse Charly showed you earlier?"

"Not only am I going to buy the gelding, I'm buying two yearlings he's bred. I will write the check after the show and I'll have them moved over to Kalarama." She turned to Joan. "With your permission. I will beat that creep with horses he bred. He's such a fool. He'll be happy with the checks, but year after year as I beat him at his own game, that smile will be wiped right off his face."

"He's good," Joan quietly cautioned.

"Joan, I didn't get from a trailer park in Lincoln County to Hollywood without something extra. I will beat him. I don't care how hard I have to work. I will do it, and you'll be on the rail cheering when I do."

"All right, then." Joan smiled, and the three women turned to walk back to the hospitality room, arm in arm. They needed a cooling drink.

Renata said, "I'm done with men."

Neither Harry nor Joan answered, since there wasn't a woman in the world who hadn't said this at least once in her life.

31

The organ played "New York, New York," the strains floating over the entire fairgrounds. The first class, equitation championship, which judged the riders' ability, started. Ward trotted beside his client, a middle-aged man who came late to riding but who found a new reason for living because of it.

As he stopped at the in-gate and the gentleman trotted into the ring, Ward panted a bit. Benny, back in the barn, was preparing the next horse for the amateur three-gaited stake, the stake being five hundred dollars.

Despite all, the show ran like clockwork. Ward, grateful since he felt comfort in routine, regained his breath as he walked along behind the western boxes to the spot where they ended. He stood there so his client could clearly see him, the double-decker grandstand just behind him, people already eating at tables on the top level.

The heat hung over central Kentucky like a wet shawl. The sun wouldn't set until about eight forty-five P.M. A whole lot of classes would go before sunset, but perhaps the mercury would drop just a bit to help people breathe, for it was so close. He glanced to the west when it felt stifling like a storm was brewing, but no telltale clouds presaged relief. Given the grisly discovery in the last storm, Ward figured it was better to sweat.

The boxes were filled up. The grandstands, too. Those spectators who had friends in the first class cheered vigorously each time a buddy swept by, their number, in black on a white square, hanging from the collar of their jacket by means of a thin, unobtrusive wire.

Hundreds of other spectators, famished, chose the early classes to cram into the main grandstand for some of the enticing food. Those who couldn't purchase a ticket to this exclusive setting stuffed themselves with the goodies on the midway behind the western stands, where the shops had patrons standing four deep. After all, this was the last night of the show, and each person hoped perhaps he could make a good deal with the proprietor of the shop. Horse traders are horse traders, regardless of what they're buying. The incredible aroma of barbecued ribs, pork, beef, and chicken wafted over the stands, as did the distinctive odor of funnel cakes, that downfall of many a diet.

Ward inhaled deeply to calm himself. Every now and then he'd get the shakes, the morning's near brush with death haunting him. Try as he might, he couldn't think why anyone would want to kill him. Although rising in the world, he hadn't amassed enough wealth yet to be worth knocking off. He was unmarried, no children nor wife to fight over his worldly goods, and much of his blood family had succumbed to heart disease. That frightened him, too. Each time his heart raced due to today's events, he'd fret that he'd come down with the family curse, as well.

Harry, on her way to the Kalarama box with Tucker on a leash right behind her, stopped by him for some reason known not even to her. When he encouraged his client, who was riding well, Harry smiled. As the client swept by, his number reading 303, Harry put her hand lightly on Ward's shoulder. He turned, she smiled at him, and he felt his troubles melt away. Touch has great power, especially from a sympathetic, pretty woman.

"Good luck tonight, Ward."

"Thank you."

She continued on to the box where Fair, coming from the opposite direction of the in-gate, carried a small hamper for Frances, who was dressed to the nines, the heat be damned. Frances always looked good, but on the final night she appeared in a light pink organdy dress, quite cooling, and a pretty pink straw hat, which she would remove when she sat down. Her jewelry bespoke her status in life without shouting it. Frances knew better than that. She smiled, chatted along the way, and gloried in being on the arm of a six-foot-four-inch blond man, all muscle. Marriage is one thing, male attention is quite another, and Fair paid all the courtesies.

Harry beamed when she saw them, and thought to herself, "He truly is the most handsome man."

Paul Hamilton was standing outside the entrance to the main grandstand, with Mr. Thompson glued to his side. A platoon of cronies hovered there, men who'd fought in

World War II and Korea, men who'd known one another all their lives. Paul possessed magnetism undimmed by years. If he stood in the middle of an empty pasture, soon enough people would be there talking to him. He exuded confidence, control, and good humor, and he exuded it in spades this evening because people needed to believe all would be well. The men laughed, cigars filling most mouths but Paul's. He checked to see just where Frances was and then copped a big puff from one of his friends. A look of sublime contentment filled his face. He handed it back, said something, and all the men laughed.

Mr. Thompson ventured to query, "Any prediction for the five-gaited?"

Paul slapped him on the back. "If Point Guard doesn't win this time, he'll win every year after."

As the first class wrapped up, Ward's client snagged third, the huge yellow ribbon in his hand, a giant smile on his face. Third at Shelbyville meant something.

Ward ran down to the gate as the gentleman rode out, and he said, "Well done, Mr. Carter, well done. You keep riding like that and you'll be in the blues in no time."

Mr. Carter, widowed two years ago, was too happy to speak. Without being fully aware, the last of his grief leached away in that moment. Life does go on.

They passed Booty leading a client out of his barn. Ward waved. Booty waved back, although clearly he was distracted.

Miss Nasty sat in her cage, but not for long. The instant she saw Booty's back, she undid the little lock with a client's hairpin she'd fashioned for the task.

Humans, in their arrogance, believe they are the only higher vertebrate to make and use tools. Obviously they spent little time with their monkey cousins, nor did they

observe ravens and blackbirds, who displayed similar abilities.

Miss Nasty swung open her cage door and lifted her little ecru-and-black-striped skirt to step out. She leapt over to the tack room, swung up on a saddle rack, perched on the saddle, and fiddled with a broken board. She slid it open, revealing a cubbyhole behind, no doubt originally made by enterprising mice. The Spikes of Shelbyville's fairgrounds slaughtered them mercilessly if they could catch them. Miss Nasty reached in, feeling around. Out came Joan's pin. She hopped down, rubbed it on a grooming rag, then neatly pinned it on her bodice, which was ecru without black stripes. She walked into the changing room, grabbed her straw boater, ribbons trailing down the back, and clapped it on her head. Miss Nasty was ready for life.

Charly also walked alongside a client for this second class. He had farther to go coming from down below the in-gate, which was one reason he reserved that barn each year. He thought the long walk helped the rider and horse focus. The young lady up top wore a cerise coat and a dashing black derby, her hands poised in the correct position, showing off beautiful kid gloves.

Charly's hand, still wrapped in Vetrap with the sky-blue ice pack, hung by his side. He walked on the right of the horse so he could use his left hand. More than anything he had to keep the swelling down or he wouldn't be able to pull on his gloves for the last class.

Boxes overflowed with people and color. Pinks, yellows from lemon to cadmium, all manner of reds, purples, lilacs, sky blues, greens from electric lime to soft shades—every color of the rainbow appeared on the human form.

The crowd had settled into deep enjoyment. Perhaps all would be well.

Frances told those in her box that bad things happen in threes so they'd be fine.

Renata, not riding, as she promised, had changed in the dressing room into a dress. She sat between Frances and Joan in the front row. She wore white, which offset her tan, her flashing teeth, her lustrous eyes. Keeping it simple—a good pair of emerald and diamond earrings, one divine marquise diamond on her hand—drew attention to her commanding physical assets. No wonder the woman was a movie star.

Harry, not beautiful but attractive, never minded being with beautiful women. Her sturdy sense of self-regard served her well.

Paul sauntered back, free of Mr. Thompson at last, to sit in the rear of the box just behind Fair and Harry.

"Mr. Hamilton, please take my seat," Fair offered.

"No, no, you drove a long way and I'll be up walking about." He smiled genially. "First class was good, and this one is shaping up."

Joan turned. "Daddy, after the class tell me what you think of that gray."

"Donna Moore's horse?" Paul mentioned a famous horsewoman—a colorful personality, too.

"Yes."

The folks in Kalarama's box focused on the gray as the gelding swept by.

Back at the hospitality suite, Mrs. Murphy and Pewter waited with Cookie for the humans to return when the ring was tidied and fluffed after their class. The two cats smoldered with anger. They had been placed in a large dog crate.

True, they had extra food treats, fresh water, and a small dirt box, but this hardly offset the insult.

Cookie, on the other hand, snored in the little sheepskin bed next to the cage.

"How can she sleep at a time like this?" Mrs. Murphy groused.

"Jack Russells are a law unto themselves. I don't understand anything they do," Pewter said.

As the cats grumbled, they were surprised by Ward ducking into the hospitality suite. He looked around, then left. They heard him walk down the barn aisle, greet Manuel, then leave.

Within five minutes, Harry, Fair, and Joan returned during the brief interlude between classes.

Renata, trailing fans, ducked in shortly afterward.

Harry let the cats out of their crate.

Cookie opened one eye, then fell back to sleep.

"Did we miss anything?" the two cats asked Tucker.

"Good classes."

"Where's that disgusting monkey?" Pewter irritably inquired.

"Haven't seen Miss Nasty. If she shows up, that ought to enliven the evening," Tucker replied. *"We'll see if she's a blowhard or not."*

Just then Booty came into the barn. "Anyone see Miss Nasty?" He avoided Renata's eye.

"No," everyone answered.

Booty, without further comment, left.

Harry idly mentioned to Fair, "Stopped by the jewelry booth before I came to the box. They sold that ring I loved. Good thing. Now I'm not tempted."

"That's one way to look at it." Fair had locked the ring in the glove compartment of his truck last night.

Joan left to join Larry as they both helped a client from Illinois, who would ride next. Joan checked out her habit, while Larry double-checked her tack. The extra attention pleased her before competition, so she'd put in a better ride.

As the group fanned themselves and drank something cool, Booty was popping into Charly's barn. "Seen Miss Nasty?" He carried a chilled bottle of Jacquart La Cuvee Nominee 1988 champagne along with two long fluted glasses.

"Get out of here," Charly growled low.

"Hey, I was wrong. I'm really sorry." Booty sounded semisincere.

"Get out."

Booty turned to leave and nearly collided with Ward heading into Charly's barn. "He's in a black mood."

"You have that effect on people." Ward breezed right past him.

Booty said loud enough for Ward to hear, "You're gettin' too big for your britches, Ward."

"Shut up, Booty," Ward called over his shoulder, assuming Booty wouldn't follow him inside.

Charly looked up at Ward; he and Carlos were grooming a muscular gelding who'd be in the fourth class, junior exhibition five-gaited stake.

Charly winced as he tried to use his hand. "Damn the INS. I need hands, literally."

"I can see that." Ward reached up to fasten the throatlatch on the bridle, since Charly couldn't use his fingers on such a small buckle. "Had a thought."

"That's scary." Charly's humor was returning.

"Can someone really find instructions for making a car bomb off the Internet?"

"Yes, and I can show you. After the show."

"I'm not asking for it now, but you are the person who knows about these things and"—he didn't sound accusatory, just factual—"you had incentive."

They both looked at the doorway at once, because Booty had walked back in. He held up one hand, two glasses between his fingers, bottle of powerhouse champagne in the other. "Wait, Charly, before you blow up." Neither Charly, Ward, nor Carlos moved. "I was wrong. Renata nailed me. I was wrong to make up something like that about her. I want to win this class, and I lost my compass, kind of."

"That it?" Charly had figured Booty might apologize, but he still had a hand with probably a broken bone or two in it because of Booty's smart mouth.

"What do you want me to do, grovel?"

"I don't know what I want from you, and right now I don't care. I do know I'm not doing business with you anymore, Booty." He looked at Ward. "If you think I blew up your van, then I expect I'm out of the game. I didn't. I have no reason to kill you."

Carlos, on hearing "kill," prudently left for the tack room. While he knew about his fellow countrymen being trucked in, he didn't want to know anything more. Ignorance might not be bliss, but in this case it was safety.

"Maybe. But dividing the profit two ways instead of three would be incentive enough for some people. You can find someone to do pickups, drop-offs. But can you trust them?" Ward challenged them both.

"How do I know I can trust you? You put my feet to the fire over money," Booty said.

"And so will another driver in time. I'm willing to do

more. I told you, I want to learn." Ward defended himself. "And, Booty, no one has tried to kill you."

"Renata would if she could." He frowned.

"She's not the only one." Charly leaned his arm over the horse's neck.

"Annie here?" Booty made light of it.

"Let's sort this out some other time." Charly returned his attention to the horse. "I've got a horse in the fifth class and, Booty, I'm going to win the five-gaited. I don't care what you tell the press." He and Booty might be in business together, but when it came to riding in the big class, their only desire was to win.

Ward froze. "Tell what?"

Booty shrugged. "That Charly, Renata, and you stole Queen Esther."

"Booty, add me to the list of people who want to kill you." Ward checked the bridle buckles for Charly. "You do something like that and you won't walk out of here tonight."

"Like Jorge?" Booty challenged.

"You would know," Ward fired right back. "I didn't touch him."

Booty's lower lip jutted out. "Seems to me one of us killed him. He was getting a little like you, Ward—greedy. He pressured Charly and me for a bigger cut."

"No one knows about greed better than you." Charly felt his anger rising, but he didn't want to hit Booty with his left hand. He'd have to hold the reins in his teeth.

"One or both of you are lying, so let me say this: I came down here to apologize, Charly. I was wrong. I'm sorry. If either of you has seen Miss Nasty, let me know. That's all I ask." Booty put down the champagne. "I was going to drink this after I won the five-gaited, but I brought it as a peace of-fering. Maybe you'll feel more forgiving once it works its magic." Booty left the barn, taking one glass with him. He called over his shoulder, "You'll drink alone, I reckon, be-cause you won't win."

Ward waited for him to get far enough ahead on the path before he left, too.

Carlos came back out for last-minute touches on the horse. "If you hurt your hand more, you won't be able to ride in the last class."

"I'll be fine," Charly replied, "but you'll have to help me with my coat and tie. I hope I can get the damned glove on, that's all." He picked up the champagne and walked it to the fridge in the hospitality suite. He read the label. "Bastard does have good taste."

$$\boxed{32}$$

*A*part from being a monkey, Miss Nasty would be conspicuous by her ensemble graced by the very expensive pin she had hooked through her bodice. Knowing Booty's habits, she laid low—or rather, high, since she rested on the top limb of one of the large trees off the midway. Her commanding view allowed her to keep tabs on Booty's movements. She knew that when he mounted up and rode into the ring, he couldn't stop her from what she perceived as her frolic. If she broke cover before that, he'd nab her and her party would be over.

More than anything, she wanted to display her treasure in front of those snotty cats. It was worth the wait as she watched classes, listening to the cheers. Occasionally someone walking under the tree would feel the light tap of a

pistachio hull on their head. Miss Nasty had taken the pre-
caution of grabbing a big bag of pistachios from Booty's
hospitality suite. However, the small hull posed no danger,
so no one peered upward into the thick foliage to behold the
well-dressed monkey on the top limb.

Having demolished the entire bag, Miss Nasty felt a
powerful thirst. It overcame her prudence, what little there
was of it. She climbed down the tree and scurried behind
the shops on the midway until she found the back of one of
the food booths stacked with soft drinks. Snagging one, she
popped the top straight off. The two ladies, as members of a
Shelbyville farm club, were serving hot dogs, hamburgers,
and French fries and didn't notice the monkey chugging behind them. Having finished that off, Miss Nasty felt much
better. The sugar and caffeine in the soft drink energized her.

What if Booty did see her? She'd climb to the top of another tree. He'd have to go back to work. She intended to
have her moment, so she loped along amid the cries of children and adults.

Every resident of the 385 square miles of Shelby County
had to be at the show grounds. The horsemen knew Miss
Nasty. First-timers did not, so she caused a sensation, much
to her delight. She even stood on her hind legs, sweeping off
her lovely straw hat to a few. They'd approach; she'd fly away.
Couldn't be too sure. Anyone could be an agent of Booty's.
She wanted to parade before Pewter and Mrs. Murphy. Of
the two, Pewter sent her blood pressure through the stratosphere.

She climbed up the rear of the western grandstand. Perching on the high backrest, built so no one would tip over
backward, she peeped over the heads down to the Kalarama
box, again filling after another sweeping of the ring. The sun

had set, and the powerful lights circling the show ring were so bright she could see the tiny dust specks floating upward.

Night birds bestirred themselves, calling to one another. Moths danced around the softer barn lights, a few immolated on the show-ring lights.

Miss Nasty climbed back down since people noticed her. She knew her safety rested in height, so she rapidly climbed back up a tree, which afforded her a view. The minute she saw those cats she was going to cavort in front of them.

The ring, pristine now, filled the air with the aroma of dark loam, the last whiff of tractor gas disappearing. The flowers, dusted off after the dragging of the ring, seemed extra beautiful. The ringmaster strode to the middle, the organist hit the notes, and the two judges—one a silver-haired man in a tuxedo, the other a lady in a flowing dress—stood on the dais, ready to watch each five-gaited horse as it entered the ring.

The lady judge—a horsewoman, obviously—knew not to wear materials that reflected light, since this caused some horses to shy. Often ladies presenting the trophies wore shiny jackets or glittering evening gowns, and the horse wouldn't stand still to be pinned or to have the silver trophy raised by its head.

The crowd held its breath, for this was it. The entire week culminated in the five-gaited open stake. The winner would be the favorite for the World Championship in Louisville, two weeks hence.

Betting isn't allowed at Saddlebred shows. No tickets for win, place, or show litter grounds after a class. However, gambling proceeds apace. Is there a horseman anywhere in the world who can resist laying down a wager?

Money changed hands, as did chits. The extra security

hired by the officials patrolled to keep order, not to dampen betting. Good thing, too, or they'd have had to arrest and hold the participants at the high-school football field. No jail would be large enough to contain the multitudes.

Ward was first in the ring, riding a large, somewhat unrefined bay with great action, Shaq Attack. He smiled to the cheers. Ward wore a tuxedo and looked very handsome.

Charly, slowed by having to split open the palm of his right glove to make it fit, didn't worry about time. He'd be up there in two minutes. Before he mounted up, he had Carlos pop the cork of the Jacquart La Cuvee Nominee 1988. Carlos poured the Baccarat fluted glass full, handing it to Charly.

"I'll celebrate before I ride and then after." He knocked it back, handing the glass back to Carlos. The bubbles soothed his cut gums and loose tooth. "It will pick me up and kill some of this pain." He swung a long leg over Frederick the Great. "My God, that's good champagne." He felt better already.

Harry, Fair, Joan, and Renata filed into the box. Paul and Frances were already there, as were most of Joan's sisters and brothers, which meant it was a full box indeed. The men stood so the ladies could sit.

Miss Nasty spied the cats, Mrs. Murphy in Harry's lap and Pewter in Joan's. Cookie sat with Frances, and Tucker sat by Fair's foot, until he picked up the dog so she could see.

Miss Nasty hurried down the tree just as Booty entered the ring on the brilliant chestnut, Callaway's Senator, who was on tonight.

Larry followed on Point Guard, who gleamed like black patent leather, serving notice that the two favored horses couldn't rest on their laurels.

The ring filled until, lastly, with an actor's sense of timing, Charly blasted in, hands high but quiet and a brilliant smile under his perfect dark navy homburg, with small red-colored feathers stuck in the grosgrain hatband. Frederick the Great, a light bay, groomed to perfection, hooves glistening, two red braided ribbons sailing, one from his forelock, one up behind his poll, promised to match Senator stride for stride.

Before the class completed one round of the ring, the crowd was screaming.

Much as Renata loathed Charly right now, she had to admit he looked divine showing a horse.

The announcer allowed another lap at the trot, then called out, "Walk, please, walk."

Larry moved closer to the rail, which, while farther from the judges, set off black Point Guard against the white boards.

As he moved away, Charly and Booty, now in the ring, jostled for position in front of the judges, each trying to block out the other. Ward hung back, slowed Shaq Attack, then asked the horse to walk out. The huge fellow ate up the ground effortlessly. While he lacked refinement, his motion compensated. Shaq should pin well and with any luck would retire to stud. Ward hoped the owners would keep the horse with him. He believed if the horse were crossed with refined mares, good things would follow, and he intended to show this horse at his best. Shaq wanted to show.

"Reverse, please, reverse."

The contestants reversed direction, walked a bit, and the announcer called out, "Trot, please, trot."

Deep in the curve of the ring, Charly cut off Booty, laughing as he passed. Booty nearly broke stride, only managing to pull it out in the nick of time by squeezing Senator hard, which then made the flashy fellow surge forward.

As the announcer called out the canter, Miss Nasty hopped through the now-empty midway, zoomed around the path in front of the western grandstand, vaulted onto the back of a chair in the Kalarama box, and jumped to the top rail.

Renata flinched as the monkey flew past her.

Miss Nasty sneered down at Pewter and Mrs. Murphy. *"See! Worthless cats. Fish breath!"* She pointed to Joan's pin on her ecru bodice.

Mrs. Murphy, grasped firmly by Harry, could do little but thrash her tail. Pewter, catching Joan unaware, lunged at the monkey, who easily eluded her. The cat then pulled back, slipping off her turquoise collar in a move worthy of the monkey. Pewter, now free, stalked the monkey. Then Miss Nasty jumped onto Joan's lap. The monkey, thrilled at her disruption, jumped from lap to lap. Fair put Tucker down to grab Pewter, an exercise in futility.

"My pin!" Joan finally had a second to concentrate on Miss Nasty, as the cat and monkey verbally abused each other.

Frances, hands to her face, pleaded, "Miss Nasty, you be a good girl. Give us the pin."

"I'll kill her," Pewter promised, claws out.

As this transpired, the announcer called the slow rack, a beautiful, controlled gait.

Booty bumped Charly when both judges were looking the other way. Larry, three strides behind, with quick reflexes, steered clear. He concentrated that much harder. Nothing was going to deter him from making Point Guard's debut memorable. Well, it would be for many reasons, not least because Miss Nasty jumped into the ring, followed by Pewter.

Joan's eyes were darting to the drama in the ring, then back at the monkey. She knew Larry would skin Booty and Charly alive after this class. Competitive as he was, Larry would never stoop to anything like their hijinks. She thought she could see smoke coming out of her husband's ears, but she smiled when she saw how readily Point Guard responded, how fluid his movement. He didn't shy even when passing Miss Nasty and Pewter, who both prudently returned to the Kalarama box amid gasps from the crowd.

"This pin is mine!" Miss Nasty touched the pin as she perched on the rail.

Pewter lurked under the rail.

"Give Joan the pin." Mrs. Murphy puffed out her fur while being firmly held by Harry.

"Or what? What can you do? Ha! Ha!" Miss Nasty turned a somersault on the rail, dropped under, and swung around then back up.

Pewter grabbed Miss Nasty's tail, but the monkey jerked free. The cat then bounded into Joan's lap to face her opponent.

Paul clucked to the monkey, who clucked back but eluded his reach.

"Maybe if we ignore her," Joan suggested.

"I'll kill her!" Pewter became repetitive.

"Rack on, ladies and gentlemen, rack on." The announcer called for the most physically demanding gait, the rack.

The speed of the rack is much faster than a non-Saddlebred horseman can imagine, until he or she sits on top. It's like driving a mighty racing Ferrari with a long hood, yet you feel the rear wheels grip the road.

Point Guard lifted his forelegs effortlessly while driving from behind. His hindquarters were not as big as Shaq's. Ward made the most of that, using Shaq's muscle to drive and fly. The rack was Shaq's best gait.

Point Guard would develop further and his motion was truly flawless, although the rack wasn't his best gait. Right now his trot was his best gait, his balance flawless, but his rack was showy enough.

Accustomed to the competition, Senator and Frederick went at it hammer and tongs. Each horse has a gait where they excel, and it's a rare horse that's equally fabulous at all gaits. Senator, like Shaq, excelled at the rack.

Charly and Booty wanted these horses, at the height of their careers, to win big. Then the animals could be sold at a huge price or retired to stud if the current owners were willing. Each time a horse sold, the commission slipped right into the seller's pocket.

As for Ward, he didn't want Shaq's owner to sell, but he was tired of eating Booty and Charly's dirt, so his competitive fires burned high.

For a split second Booty was distracted when he passed by the Kalarama box to behold Miss Nasty carrying on. He immediately refocused because Charly passed him, obscuring him exactly when he was distracted by his beloved monkey. Cursing under his breath, Booty pulled away from Charly to give the judges a clear view of Senator.

The crowd, many on their feet, bellowed to high heaven.

"Walk, please, walk." The announcer had sense enough not to keep the rack going for long, as it was brutally strenuous.

After a brief walk the announcer called, "Trot, please, trot."

The judges, watching intently, could still see out of the corners of their eyes the japes of Miss Nasty. Even the organ couldn't drown out her obscenities.

The two judges conferred briefly. They agreed to call in the horses after this trot for the conformation exam.

In the five-gaited grand championship, the tally for each horse was based seventy-five percent on performance, presence, quality, and manners; twenty-five percent on conformation.

They figured while the horses stood in the lineup, stripped, someone could bag Miss Nasty.

The male judge stayed on the west side of the center dais; the lady crossed over to the east side as the horses continued to trot counterclockwise.

Charly, in front of the Kalarama box and pointedly ignoring the ravishing Renata, felt the muscles in his throat go numb just as Miss Nasty leapt onto Frederick's hindquarters, which caused the highly strung stallion to rear up. Pewter elected to stay in the box, for as much as she vowed to kill Miss Nasty, she wasn't going to get trampled.

Charly's lips, tightly compressed and a touch blue, only made spectators think his concentration during this unpredictable moment was ultra intense. He pulled the left rein down, since his right hand was useless. Down came Frederick, but as Charly loosened the left rein, the horse swung his head to the right, irritated by the monkey. Charly saw Renata staring at him, and for a flash he knew he'd been a complete fool to disregard her. Another sharp pain followed, and he gasped for breath, but his legs, strong and trained, kept the right pressure on the horse. He couldn't get air into his lungs. He couldn't breathe at all.

Charly died just as the announcer called, "Line up,

please, facing the east." His legs closed on the horse and he sat bolt upright, Miss Nasty still on Frederick's hindquarters. Then, to the shock of everyone watching, he keeled over and off the horse in front of the main grandstand, ten strides from the Kalarama box.

The crowd screamed and Renata stood silent. No one knew he was dead. They only knew he'd slid off Frederick, which was odd for such a skilled horseman.

The announcer didn't see, but the male judge did. He called to the other judge, who calmly ordered the horses to go to the lineup and remain there. The announcer called again, "Bring your horses to the center, ladies and gentlemen. Center, please."

Carlos, one hand on the top rail, swung over, reaching Charly first. Benny, at the other end of the ring, caught Frederick, who was moving to the lineup but bucking to dump Miss Nasty. The monkey proved quite the little jockey as she moved up to the saddle.

Charly lay flat on his back, eyes skyward, as fleecy pink and lavender clouds with a touch of gold rolled over. His face was blueing.

A doctor hurried out of the main grandstand, knelt down, took his pulse but betrayed nothing. No sense in adding to the tension.

The ringmaster puffed up, a bit heavy to run.

The doctor looked up and said, "Call the ambulance."

Nobody moved. Nobody spoke. Then a low murmur circled the ring. The contestants now dismounted, looked to their left. No one knew exactly what to do. The riders, at the head of each horse, had a clear view of Charly. Benny handed off Frederick to another groom, since he needed to be with Ward and Shaq.

The ringmaster flipped open his cell phone, calling for the ambulance crew parked behind the main grandstand. "No sirens."

As it was, they had been watching. They ran back for a gurney. They reached Charly in less than two minutes, carefully loading him up. For form's sake, one ambulance attendant clapped an oxygen mask over Charly's face.

Carlos, walking beside Charly, kept talking to him, although he feared his boss was dead.

The ringmaster walked back to the dais. He conferred with the two judges and the announcer.

The organist, a quick thinker, played slow tunes.

The announcer, voice appropriate to the circumstances, said, "We will keep you updated on Mr. Trackwell's condition."

Struggling to wipe the grim look from their visages, the judges started at the northern end of the line to begin the conformation part of the class.

Miss Nasty, still in the saddle, expected cheers, not gasps. She let her guard down. The second groom who came in to help the first reached for her. She jumped off Frederick to scamper out of the ring.

Larry, next to Ward, said nothing, but the two men looked at each other; they both felt Charly was dead. Booty, farther down the row, still angry at his lapse in concentration, held the reins up when the judges approached. Senator reached forward with his front legs and backward with his hind in what's called "parked out."

After the conformation exam, the grooms put the saddles back on and held their hands for those riders who needed a boost to mount. The horses went through a few more paces, but no one's heart was in it.

When Senator won first, applause was polite. When Point Guard pulled second, there was a bit more enthusiasm, and quite a bit for Shaq, who needed and earned the third.

Senator performed a victory lap as the organ played a jaunty tune while the other horses filed out.

Harry, Fair, Joan, Renata, and the animals were already at Barn Five.

Renata, ashen-faced, said outside of eavesdroppers' earshot to Harry, "He looked awful."

"He did." Harry put her hand on Renata's shoulder. "Do you want to go to the hospital? I'll drive you."

The siren started when the ambulance reached Route 60.

"No. It's over between us." Renata breathed deeply. "I don't wish this on him, but I don't belong there." Her eyes filled with tears.

Renata reached up and put her hand over Harry's on her shoulder, but she said no more.

Larry rode up to the entrance, dismounted, and Joan kissed him. "Those two were trying to kill each other." His face, red, showed his high emotion.

"Point Guard okay?" Joan thought first of the horse.

"Joan, if he could win second in tonight's class with everything that was going on in that ring, he'll never turn a hair at anything." Larry sank heavily into a director's chair as Manuel and the men quickly stripped Point Guard, wiping him down. Sweat rolled down Larry's brow, both from exertion and emotion. "They were crazy."

"I know," Joan simply said, as Frances and Paul came into the barn.

Paul quietly said, "I think we'd better pack up and go home a little faster than normal."

"You're right, Daddy." Joan didn't know what was going on, but she didn't want to be around if there was more of it.

"Can I help with anything?" Fair asked.

"No, but I think you should get out while the gettin's good," Joan said. "We can link up tomorrow."

Harry turned to Fair and said, "Give me a minute."

"Why?"

"The pin."

"Oh." He'd forgotten all about it.

Harry ran over to Booty's barn. Booty and Senator hadn't yet returned. Miss Nasty hadn't, either. Small wonder. She knew she was in big trouble.

Fair had put the two cats in their crate—a good thing, since they'd only set off Miss Nasty again—but Tucker and Cookie followed Harry as she ran, faster this time, to Charly's barn. Yes, she was looking for Miss Nasty, but she wanted a peek at Charly's barn before Carlos and others arrived.

As she entered the barn, she couldn't miss the monkey sitting in the rafters.

No one was in the barn—no human, anyway.

Tucker called out, *"Spike."*

"Yo!" Spike stuck his head out of the hospitality tent, where he and the others had sampled the food, finding it delicious.

"Charly's dead."

"Ah." Spike neither liked nor disliked Charly, although he liked his food. Too much drama surrounded Charly for Spike's exquisite feline sensibility.

"Anything weird happen here before the class?"

"Booty brought champagne as a peace offering. Charly

wouldn't make peace. Ward came in. A go-round, if you know what I mean."

Tucker sniffed deeply, then saw the sweating champagne bottle on the navy and red tack trunk in the aisle. A single fluted glass lay on its side. The corgi walked up to the glass as Harry investigated the tack room and the hospitality room. She returned to behold her dog standing at the glass, whimpering.

Harry went to Tucker, glad for the indoor lights as it was now truly dark outside. She touched the champagne bottle but, not being an aficionado, she had no idea how special it was.

"Smell the glass, Mom," Tucker barked softly.

Harry pinched the stem of the glass between her forefinger and thumb, lifting it to her nose. Then she blinked, putting it back down. "Odd." She didn't smell too much, but she noticed some yellow crystals on the bottom, where the slight bit of liquid remaining had dried in the heat.

Just to be sure, she picked up the champagne bottle and inhaled the aroma. She could almost taste the toasty, fruity liquid, a deep enticing blend of other elements she couldn't place adding to the bouquet. Then she smelled the glass again, wrinkled her nose, coughed once, and put it back.

She ran for a deputy, the sheriff, anyone in law enforcement. She forgot all about Miss Nasty, who had observed everything.

33

The hospitality suite in Barn Five was overflowing when Harry burst in, motioning for Fair to come outside. Joan and Larry, surrounded by guests, watched out of the corners of their eyes.

Frances finally spoke to Joan as she, too, had noticed Harry's flushed face, and Harry was usually a cool customer. "Joan, you should see to Harry."

Renata, surrounded by people, started to wiggle free.

"What's up, honey?" Fair asked.

"I can't find a cop."

"They're probably down at the show ring or," he paused, "at the celebrations after the show. A lot to contend with."

"Fair, Charly was poisoned. I'm pretty sure."

"What?"

"Come with me."

Joan and Renata came out together just as someone—well-meaning, probably—let Pewter and Mrs. Murphy out of their crate.

The two cats shot out, skidding into the main aisle.

"Follow Mom!" Mrs. Murphy headed after Harry, Fair, and Tucker.

Cookie waited for Joan, saying, *"Come on, come on!"* To emphasize her point, the Jack Russell ran circles around both Joan and Renata.

Joan took the hint, hurrying after Harry and Fair.

As the little half platoon moved on to Charly's barn, Booty was regaling a large number of well-wishers. Booty, Senator in his groom's hands with a monstrously large tricolor ribbon hanging for all to see, was in his glory.

Ward popped in to congratulate him. "Hear anything about Charly?" Booty asked loud and clear.

"No, but Charly's too mean to die." People laughed, and Ward continued, "I wouldn't be surprised, though, if Charly was on the operating table at this moment getting some kind of bypass surgery or a little balloon in an artery. He blued up on us there."

"Charly doesn't have a heart," someone said jokingly but with a bite.

"Well, he sure tried to knock me in the dirt tonight." Booty smiled triumphantly. "Hey, it's competition that makes a good horse race, right? I bet you he'll be back at it at Louisville. By the way, anyone see Miss Nasty after her disgraceful conduct?"

"No."

Benny piped up. "Last I saw her, she was heading down to Charly's barn."

A panicked look crossed Booty's face. "She's always where

she shouldn't be. One of the really great things about Miss Nasty, as opposed to the real Miss Nasty, is she can't use my credit cards."

This called forth an uproar of mirth, so Booty continued in this vein. He did, however, want his monkey.

Spike retreated when the humans came into Charly's barn, but he then came out to sit on a director's chair.

"Smell the champagne." Harry pointed to the bottle.

One by one, Fair, Joan, and then Renata smelled the champagne, still inviting.

"No wonder he fell off his horse," Joan joked.

"Does he usually drink before a big class? Calm his nerves?" Fair wondered.

"I've never seen him take a drink, smoke a cigarette, or take a toke before a class," Renata offered. "He was in pain, though. His right hand might have been broken."

"Well, smell this." Harry pointed to the glass, took a red grooming rag, and picked it up by the stem.

Fair gingerly took the glass and rag from her first. "Doesn't smell like champagne." He noted the yellow crystals still forming. "Smells like poison."

Joan, next, inhaled. "I don't know what it is."

Renata then inhaled. "How do you know it's poison?"

Fair answered, "I'm around a lot of substances that can kill horses, remember. I'm pretty sure this is poison, natural poison. He didn't clutch at his heart. Charly's face blued up a little, and my hunch is he was either bitten or drank snake poison. It stops your respiratory system if you're full of a fatal dose. And when snake venom dries, it crystallizes. Pour liquid on it and it will melt again."

"I didn't see a deputy anywhere. I wanted Fair to smell it because, well, because I didn't want to make a mistake," Harry said. She knew Booty kept snakes, as did the others. Now it was a game of flushing out your quarry.

"You didn't. Anyone have a cell phone? I left mine in the truck. Maybe we can call the sheriff down here."

The ladies didn't have their cell phones, either, as they didn't fit in their dresses.

Miss Nasty called down, *"I know where there's a cell phone."*

Joan looked up and wondered if she'd ever get that pin back, although given the immediate circumstances the fluted champagne glass was more important. "I'll walk up to the barn and get mine. It's in the changing room."

"Where's the cell phone?" Tucker asked the monkey, sidling down the rafters to reach the top of a stall beam.

"I told you I had the pin." Thrilled with herself, Miss Nasty strutted, ignoring the request.

"Where's the phone?" Mrs. Murphy inquired.

"I said I knew where it was, I didn't say I'd tell you." Miss Nasty grinned.

"I'll kill her." Pewter danced on her hind paws.

"Shut up," the tiger cat advised. *"And don't climb up the stall post."*

Joan, moving through all the people back at Barn Five, smiled and kept saying, "Excuse me, I'm on a mission." She finally stepped into the changing room, took her purse from the tack trunk, grabbed her thin phone.

Her mother ducked her head in and said, "Joan, what's wrong?"

Joan's polite behavior to the crowd didn't fool Mom. "Found Miss Nasty. I've got to get that pin, Mom."

Frances looked at Joan's face, looked at the phone. "With a phone?"

"I'll explain later." Joan left the room, saying to people who stopped her for a chat, "I'll be right back, right back."

Frances left the room and found Paul standing out in the main aisle with sixty other people. She pointed toward Joan, who was already heading down the slight slope to Charly's barn, and said, "Paul, something's not right."

Paul observed, then said, "Wait and see. Got a whole lot of people here, honey." They returned to the responsibilities of being host and hostess.

As Joan briskly walked away, Booty, needing a breath of air from the hordes in his own main aisle and hospitality suite, stepped outside for a moment, although still surrounded by people. "Seen Miss Nasty?" he called to Joan.

"She's in Charly's barn."

Now it was Booty's turn to promise he'd be right back.

No fool, Joan flipped open her cell and called the sheriff before she even reached the barn. This Shelbyville week had kept her on pins and needles. The hair rose on the back of her neck. She didn't know why, but she trusted her instincts.

Ward and Benny, who were putting up Shaq, had seen Harry, Fair, Joan, and Renata go by first. Then Joan came back up the hill. Now Joan was going back down, Booty trailing.

"Benny, something tells me we're in the ninth inning and it's a tie game. Come on."

Benny double-checked Shaq and the other horse there, then both men headed down the path.

Joan entered the barn. "Called Sheriff Cody. Said he'd be here in a minute."

"Good." Renata seemed especially relieved.

Carlos came into the barn, looked at everyone in surprise and weariness.

Joan, always thoughtful, said, "Carlos, can we do anything for you?"

He shook his head. To keep from crying—for he liked Charly, who was a good boss—he went into Frederick the Great's stall and rubbed down the horse, who kept casting his big eyes up at Miss Nasty. The ignominy of carrying that monkey on his back grated on his nerves. As for Charly, Frederick could smell he was dead when he fell off and hit the ground. He wouldn't miss Charly, for he worked him too hard. In fact, Frederick was rather glad he was dead.

Booty came in, then Ward and Benny followed.

The others looked at them but said nothing.

Booty picked up the bottle of champagne. "Let's drink to Charly's recovery. He'd hate it if we let this go to waste." He handed the bottle to Joan, but she politely declined.

Harry, Fair, and Renata also passed.

"I don't think Charly's health can be restored," Renata claimed.

"He'll be fine." Booty offered the bottle to Ward, who took a swig. "He's tough as bad weather."

Benny then took a sip of the wonderful champagne.

"He's dead," Renata said.

"How do you know?" Booty didn't want the mood to

further plummet. He took a deep drink when Benny handed the bottle back. "Did you call the hospital? Actually, they wouldn't tell you, because you're not family."

"I just know." She was beyond tears, feeling a bit numb.

"Now, Renata, he'll be fine. I know you're mad at him and—"

"What about me!" Miss Nasty shrieked.

"There you are, my pretty." Booty pretended that he wasn't mad at her.

"ME, ME, ME, and I have this sparkle on my chest!"

She crept down, her eyes on Pewter, but she kept just out of Booty's reach. Bottle in hand, he coaxed her. "Good girl." Then he saw the Baccarat fluted glass on its side. "That was dumb. Could have used the glass." He picked it up and poured a little champagne in it before anyone could stop him.

He held out the champagne glass to Miss Nasty to tempt her, but he had no intention of giving it to her. Being much faster and stronger than Booty imagined, she eagerly grabbed the glass with both paws and yanked it from his fingers. She gulped down half the contents, spilling the rest.

"No!" Booty yelled. Then she hopped around in circles, defying the cats, just beyond Booty's grasp or anyone else's. They kept still, both out of horror and because she'd race up to the rafters again.

She swaggered near Pewter. *"I told you I had the pin. What do you have? Worms!"* Shrieking with delight, she sped around the gray cat as Mrs. Murphy, Tucker, and Cookie tensed to grab her if they could.

"Dungdot," Pewter hissed.

"You were the dungdot. You looked lovely in horse poop. You

should wear more." Miss Nasty spun around to dash into a stall to find a suitably large piece of poop.

She spun smack into Spike, who had been silently creeping up behind her.

"Hello, my pretty," he said with menace, echoing Booty's name for her, as he pounced, both paws around the monkey, fangs sunk in her neck.

She howled, her arms and legs, even her tail, standing stiff, then she died.

"Hooray," Pewter cheered.

Spike shook her like a rag doll, breaking her neck, then dropped her. *"Death to vermin!"*

Booty, distraught, ran to his pet, as Pewter did, too.

"Pewter, you get back here," Harry ordered.

"I want to make sure she's dead." Pewter stopped midway to her goal.

"Let's drive a stake through her heart," Cookie suggested.

Booty picked up the lifeless monkey and said, "Oh, Miss Nasty."

Sheriff Cody finally appeared. Renata and Ward noticed him as he was making his way down from the other barns.

"What's the sheriff want?" Ward wondered.

Harry should have kept her mouth shut, but she blurted out, "Booty, you tried to stop Miss Nasty from drinking out of the glass."

Holding Miss Nasty in his arms like a baby, he looked hard at Harry. "I—"

"You knew the glass was coated in poison." She let her anger get the better of her.

Ward suddenly got it and said, "You son of a bitch, you tried to kill me!" He lunged for Booty.

Much as Booty loved Miss Nasty, dead was dead. He

needed to save himself. He flung her body hard in Ward's face, then turned to run out the back of the barn.

Cookie and Tucker easily kept apace with him, biting his ankles as he ran.

"Death from the ankles down." Joan couldn't help it, she burst out laughing.

Benny tore after Ward, who had regained his balance to chase Booty.

Sheriff Cody walked into the barn, looked down at Miss Nasty, and just caught sight of Benny at the far entrance to the barn.

Fair said, "Booty. It's Booty. They're after him."

The sheriff pulled out his gun but walked the length of the barn as he called his men on his phone. Sooner or later, Booty would be trapped.

Pewter pounced on Miss Nasty's body. *"Dead! Whoopee."*

Spike grinned his snaggle-toothed grin.

The cats didn't need to pretend they weren't thrilled at Miss Nasty being dispatched by Spike and the poison. Mrs. Murphy, Pewter, Spike, and the barn cats surrounded the hateful creature.

Harry strode over. "Leave her alone." She unfastened Joan's pin and handed it back to her.

Renata said, "That ginger cat won't die, will he? I mean, he bit into Miss Nasty."

"He'll be fine." Fair figured Spike didn't chew her or bite deep.

A shot rang out in the parking lot. Everyone ran to the far end of the barn in time to see Booty, blood pouring down his leg, hopping away. Ward and Benny tackled him, Ward pulling his right arm up behind his back. Sheriff Cody walked up, as did the deputy who'd shot Booty, moving from the opposite direction.

Pewter, Mrs. Murphy, Spike, and the barn cats had run down to that end of the barn, too.

Mrs. Murphy looked from Booty to Miss Nasty. *"No more monkey business."*

34

*T*he white truck, loaded and ready to go, sat in the Kalarama drive.

Harry and Fair had come to say good-bye to Joan and Larry at nine A.M. on Sunday morning. Clients and customers would start showing up around ten. The two weeks between Shelbyville and Louisville heated up business, as did the weeks following the Kentucky State Fair.

Krista, on deck, had the sitting room clean. A small breakfast buffet had been squeezed on the coffee counter, pot already bubbling outside her office door.

Harry, Fair, Joan, and Larry were drinking coffee and tea and eating doughnuts. Harry, not much for sweets, found she craved sugar this morning.

Harry and Fair sat on the sofa, Mrs. Murphy, Pewter, and Tucker right with them. Joan sat opposite, and Larry kept popping in and out from the long main aisle to confer with Manuel.

"Would you have guessed?" Harry asked Joan, since Joan knew the people involved better than Harry did. They both had run out to the parking lot last night when Booty bolted for his freedom. Once shot, Booty couldn't move. They heard everything as they drew close to him.

Joan tapped the edge of the heavy mug, maroon with "Kalarama" emblazoned on its side in gold. "I thought it was Ward at first. He's young, needs money, and he did take Queen Esther from Jorge—that was conjecture, but I was pretty sure that's how it happened, and now we know."

In pain and knowing the game was up, Booty confessed at the parking lot while waiting for the medics. Like many people, when hope was lost he just babbled. Ward, standing right there, didn't deny that he was in business with Booty and Charly, especially since Booty pointed the finger at him. Better to confess to smuggling illegal workers than be thought a murderer. Ward came clean about stealing, so to speak, Queen Esther.

"I'm sorry Ward was part of it," Harry said. "Whatever money he's made will go to lawyers."

"Think he'll go to jail?" Fair asked. "I don't know Kentucky judges. Virginia's are pretty conservative."

"Most are here, too." Joan thought a long time. "I don't think he'll go to jail. He'll pay a fine, be sentenced to community service, but Ward was the driver, not the mastermind. He's already exonerated Benny, who he said knew nothing."

"Ah, good for Ward," Fair said.

"Good for Benny." Harry laughed.

"And Renata says she will stand by Ward about Queen Esther. Of course, that cat is out of the bag."

"I resent that," Pewter grumbled.

"How bad will it be for her?" Fair asked.

Larry popped back in, heard the question, leaned over the divider, and said, "More publicity, wrong kind."

Just then Renata drove up, parked, and walked in. She poured coffee, snagged a doughnut, and leaned over the divider, as well.

"We were talking about you," Joan said.

"I deserve what I get." She started to bite the doughnut, then stopped for a second. "Charly didn't deserve to die, though."

"Booty sure thought he did." Harry leaned back.

"'What a tangled web we weave when first we practice to deceive.'" Joan put down her mug. "Booty claims Jorge wanted more money, so he made calls to whoever it is in Texas. Booty says Jorge knew the man, who is a Mexican himself."

"The smuggling agent? I mean, what do you call someone like that?" Renata wondered.

"'Agent' sounds good." Joan smiled at Renata. "Same function, different business than yours."

"Not by much." Sarcasm dripped off Renata's tongue.

"So Jorge didn't talk to Charly or Ward?" Larry was so tired last night that he wasn't sure what he remembered and what he didn't.

"Ward was the driver; pretty much that was it. Booty and Charly both handled the money, but Booty directed Jorge, and Charly contacted people receiving the workers. Division of labor," Joan said. "Jorge went to Booty. That was his big mistake. If he'd asked all of them for more money, he might be alive today. Charly wouldn't have agreed to murder. He just wouldn't. Carlos may have known about the smuggling, but he wasn't implicated. He was smart enough not to talk, but then, Booty talked so much who could get a word in edgewise? Guess the pain got to him, too. Funny, he really thought he could get away with it."

"Booty killed Jorge." Larry rested his chin on the palm of his hand, his elbow on the divider. "He could have found an easier way."

"That was the point," Harry filled in. "Booty wanted it to be gruesome and dramatic. The double cross on the palm was a theatrical touch."

"Charly then knew Jorge had double-crossed them. Naturally, he figured Jorge had talked to Booty, but he couldn't be sure that he hadn't also talked to Ward. Charly was too smart to confront Booty, at least during the show." He might have questioned Booty and Ward afterward, but he tried to keep things level during Shelbyville. He had a lot riding on the show, one of the reasons why he was stunned at Jorge's murder. Could Booty or Ward be that cold-blooded? Joan added, "It's strange how someone can put up walls around themselves like Booty did and then the walls come tumbling down. He couldn't shut up last night. It was kind of embarrassing."

"He's lucky Ward didn't kill him." Renata had polished off her doughnut, not having eaten since lunch yesterday. "After all, Booty tried to kill Ward and make it look like Charly did it. He really was cold-blooded. He could go right out in the ring and put in a great ride."

"That seems so stupid to me." Harry threw up her hands. "Hadn't enough gone wrong? I mean, after Jorge pushed Booty for more money and Booty refused, Jorge threatened to call the INS. You should have heard Booty about that. He thought he'd killed Jorge in time, even though it might have been an empty threat. Well, he found out differently the next night."

"Maybe your mind goes." Joan spoke slowly. "Maybe because what you're doing is criminal, even if a lot of people don't think it is—bringing in illegal workers, I mean. But anyone involved in crime leads a double life. That's the real double cross. You get locked inside your mind, in a way. And then how can you really grasp what's real and what's your fear? Booty didn't have to kill Jorge. Even though the INS did raid the show, Booty and Charly had enough money to hire good lawyers. The show was raided; no one said they smuggled in illegal workers, only that they used them. I think he just lost it." She tapped her temple with her right forefinger.

"See, I think it was greed." Harry shrugged. "The business had run smoothly up to Shelbyville. Booty wanted all the profits."

"Or a combination. I think Joan's right; Booty's judgment did fail." Fair interlocked his fingers.

"What a waste." Larry put it in a nutshell, then turned to Renata. "What are you going to do?"

"Pay for Ward's legal fees regarding Queen Esther if that becomes an issue. I don't think it will. But I won't leave him in the lurch. He made one mistake, egged on by Charly and myself. As to driving in the workers, well, that was a bigger mistake, and he'd better learn from it. I'm not paying those legal fees."

"But what are you going to do about you?" Harry followed up on Larry's intent.

"Oh." She blew air out of her full lips. "I'll be a laughingstock for a while, but I haven't smashed liquor bottles over anyone's head or taken videos having sex, stuff like that. It appears the American public laps up this kind of tripe." She stopped suddenly. "What I am is sick of myself. If I had to do something as absurd as stealing Queen Esther to bump myself back up, you know, I need to leave. I don't like myself."

"You don't mean leave Earth, you mean leave Hollywood, right?" Harry had a nervous moment.

"Right. Harry, I'm not the suicide type. And," she drew in a deep breath, "I've always been hostile and pooh-poohed it, but I think I need to get some help, therapy. That's number one. Number two is coming back home. I won't be able to put myself together back there on the meat rack."

"Good for you." Fair turned around to look upward. "I went into therapy for three years, and it was the best thing I ever did for myself. Jesus, it can be painful, though."

"No pain, no gain." Larry summed it up, using the line espoused by the health guru Jack La Lanne.

"And who would have thought this would start with Grandmother's pin being stolen and end up with it being found?" Joan mused, then looked at Harry. "Remember I said I didn't think I'd like what we found if we found the pin?"

"Do." Harry nodded.

"Honey, it's an eight-hour haul." Fair smiled at Harry.

"Wait one minute. Birthday present." Joan rose and went into the office, returning with a dark green plastic bag with a big pink ribbon on it. "Happy birthday from Larry, Mom, Dad, and myself. I hope you have at least forty more." She handed the bag to Harry, who could feel what it was.

Opening the bag, Harry held up a beautiful bridle from Fennell's. "Just what I wanted. Oh, you all." She dropped the oiled bridle back in the bag and got up to kiss Joan, then Larry. "I'll kiss you, too. Thanks again for Shortro." She kissed Renata.

"That was one thing I did right." Renata smiled. "Happy birthday, Harry."

Fair stood up. "This is your last day to be thirty-nine. Tomorrow I'll give you your birthday present."

"How can it top my bridle or Shortro?" she teased him.

"Well," he rolled his eyes up to the ceiling, then back to meet hers, "it comes along with me."

"I like it already."

The animals roused themselves, and Cookie walked out to the truck to say her good-byes.

"Don't guess we'll ever see the likes of Miss Nasty again. Imagine how Booty felt when she grabbed that glass from him that he'd loaded with snake poison. She was faster and stronger than he realized," Cookie said.

Mrs. Murphy recalled the sight. *"Funny, isn't it, the look on his face when she grabbed the glass and how he picked her up when she died. He loved her."*

"They're family." Pewter giggled.

Dear Reader,

Don't you just love Miss Nasty? Karin Slaughter likes monkeys, so I created Miss Nasty for her.

I hate monkeys, myself, but I do love horses. Mostly I play with Thoroughbreds, but there is a young Saddlebred on the farm, Blue Sky, and he's such a sweetheart. For one thing he recognizes that I am far more intelligent than the human around here.

Hope all is well in your world. Don't forget to give to your local animal shelter.

Yours in Catitude,

Sneaky Pie

Dear Reader,

There's no point in responding to Sneaky's gargantuan ego. I actually do some of the work around here.

Ever and Always,

Rita

About the Authors

RITA MAE BROWN is a bestselling author, an Emmy-nominated screenwriter, and a poet. She lives in Afton, Virginia. Her website is www.ritamaebrown.com.

SNEAKY PIE BROWN, a tiger cat born somewhere in Albemarle County, Virginia, was discovered by Rita Mae Brown at her local SPCA. They have collaborated on fourteen previous Mrs. Murphy mysteries: *Wish You Were Here; Rest in Pieces; Murder at Monticello; Pay Dirt; Murder, She Meowed; Murder on the Prowl; Cat on the Scent; Pawing Through the Past; Claws and Effect; Catch as Cat Can; The Tail of the Tip-Off; Whisker of Evil; Cat's Eyewitness;* and *Sour Puss,* in addition to *Sneaky Pie's Cookbook for Mystery Lovers.* She uses the above website, although she threatens to develop her own since she is much more exciting than her human.

If you enjoyed *Puss 'n Cahoots,* read on for a
taste of the next Mrs. Murphy mystery

The Purrfect Murder

RITA MAE BROWN
&
SNEAKY PIE BROWN

On sale February 2008

RITA MAE BROWN

& SNEAKY PIE BROWN

The Purrfect Murder

A MRS. MURPHY
MYSTERY

It Takes a Cat to Write the *Purr*-fect Mystery

The Purrfect Murder

ON SALE FEBRUARY 2008

1

Morning light, which looked like thin spun gold, reminded Harry Haristeen why she loved September so much. The light softened, the nights grew crisp, while the days remained warm. This Thursday, September 18, there was only a vague tinge of yellow at the top of the willow trees, which would become a cascade of color by mid-October.

The old 1978 Ford F-150 rumbled along the macadam road. The big engine's sound thrilled Harry. If it had a motor in it, she liked it.

Her two cats, Mrs. Murphy, a tiger, and Pewter, a gray cat, along with her corgi, Tee Tucker, also enjoyed the rumble, which often put them to sleep. Today, all sitting on the bench seat, they were wide awake. A trip to town meant treats and visiting other animals, plus one never knew what would happen.

Harry had just turned forty on August 7, and she declared it didn't faze her. Maybe. Maybe not. Fair, her adored husband, threw a big surprise birthday party and she reveled in being the center of attention, even though it was for entering her Middle Ages. She wore the gorgeous horseshoe ring her husband had bought her at the Shelbyville Horse Show. She wasn't much for display or girly things, but every time she looked down at the glitter, she grinned.

"All right, kids, you behave. You hear me? I don't want you jumping on Tazio's blueprints. No knocking erasers on the floor. No chewing the rubber ends of pencils. Tucker." Harry's voice kept the command tone. "Don't you dare steal Brinkley's bones. I mean it."

The three animals cast their eyes at her, those eyes brimming with love and the promise of obedience.

Tazio Chappars, a young architect in Crozet, won large commissions for public buildings, but she also accepted a healthy string of commissions for beautiful, expensive homes, most paid for by non-Virginians. The houses were too flashy for a blue-blood Virginian. However, Tazio, like all of us in this world, needed to make a living, so if the client wanted a marble-clad bathroom as big as most people's garages, so be it.

As Harry parked, she noticed a brand-new Range

Rover in the small lot. Painted a burnt orange, she walked over to admire it.

"Good wheels," she muttered to herself.

Good indeed, but the closest dealer was ninety miles away in Richmond, which somewhat dimmed the appeal. If that didn't do it, the price did.

Before she reached the door, a stream of invective assaulted her ears. When she opened the door, the blast hit her.

"Wormwood! I don't care what it costs and I don't care if termites get in it. I want wormwood!" An extremely well cared for woman in her mid-forties shook colored plans in Tazio's face.

"Mrs. Paulson, I understand. But it's going to slow down the library because it takes months to secure it."

"I don't care. You'll do what I tell you."

Tazio, face darkening, said nothing.

Mrs. Paulson spun around on her bright aqua three-hundred-dollar shoes to glare at Harry. Harry's white T-shirt revealed an ample chest, and her jeans hugged a trim body with a healthy tan. Mrs. Paulson paused for a minute because, even though not of Virginia, she had divined that often the richest people or the ones with the oldest blood wore what to her were migrant-labor fashions. Carla Paulson wouldn't be caught dead in a white T-shirt and Wranglers. She couldn't fathom why Harry would appear in public looking like a farmhand.

She knew Harry in passing, so she switched into "lunch lady" mode.

Tazio stepped around her drafting table. "Mrs.

Paulson, you remember Harry Haristeen; her mother was a Hepworth. Her father, a Minor." Tazio knew perfectly well that Mrs. Paulson didn't know the bloodlines, but the simple fact that Tazio recited them meant "important person."

Not that Harry gave a damn.

Extending her hand, radiating a smile, the well-groomed woman purred, "Of course I remember."

Harry politely took her hand, using the exact amount of pressure all those battleaxes at cotillion drilled into her year after year. "I can see you've hired the most talented architect in the state." She paused. "Love your new wheels."

"Isn't the interior beautiful? Just bought it last week." Carla Paulson brightened. She checked her diamond-encrusted Rolex. "Well, I'll call later for another appointment. Oh, before I forget, Michael McElvoy said he'd be out at the site tomorrow at eleven."

Tazio wanted to say she had an appointment then, which she did, but if one of the county building inspectors was going to be at the construction site, then she'd better be there, too. Michael lived to find fault.

"Fine. I'll be there." Tazio smiled and walked Mrs. Paulson to the door, while Mrs. Murphy and Pewter jumped on the high chair and onto the drafting table. Those pink erasers thrilled the cats. Tazio even had special white square ones that squeaked when bitten.

Brinkley, a young yellow lab rescued by Tazio during a snowstorm at a half-completed building site, chewed his bone. Tucker lay down in front of the wonderful creature and put her head on her paws to stare longingly at the bone.

Once Carla Paulson exited, Tazio exhaled loudly.

"Murphy, Pewter, what did I tell you?" Harry warned.

Murphy batted the square white eraser off the table. Both cats sailed after it.

"Don't worry about it. I have a carton full of them back in the supply closet. In fact, I'll give you one." She took another breath. "That woman is plucking my last nerve. I thought Folly Steinhauser was high maintenance and Penny Lattimore a diva, but Carla is in a class by herself."

"I can see that."

Tazio slyly smiled. "The diamond Rolex watch is so over the top."

"Better to wear plain platinum. Worth more and not showy. In fact, most people think it's steel." Harry leaned on the drafting table. "But if Carla owned a platinum Rolex, she'd have to tell everyone it wasn't steel and ruin it, of course."

"Harry," Tazio laughed, "you're so Virginia."

"Oh, look who's talking."

"I'm from St. Louis, remember."

"Doesn't matter. You mentioned that gaudy watch. I didn't."

Tazio was half Italian, half African-American, and all gorgeous. Her family, prominent in St. Louis, had provided her with the best education as well as a great deal of social poise, since her mother was on every committee imaginable. From the time she was small, her mother had marched her to different parties, balls, fund-raisers.

"I'm worn out, because she keeps changing her mind. Well, I'll grant, she's been consistent about the wormwood, but every time she changes something the cost spirals upward. It's not my money, but you move a window an inch and either Orrie"— she named the head of construction by his nickname—"or I have to call the building inspector. Michael McElvoy, as you heard."

Harry started to giggle. "Lucky you."

"Oh, well, everyone has their problems. You came to pick up the numbers on the different heating systems for St. Luke's. Got 'em." She walked back to her large, polished mahogany desk, about ten feet from the drafting table. Picking up a folder, she said, "Here. Digest it, then let's go over it before the next vestry meeting."

Harry flipped open the folder. "Jeez."

"Lots of choices, and each one has pluses and minuses."

"Herb have a copy?" Harry mentioned the pastor of St. Luke's, Rev. Herb Jones.

"I thought we should put our heads together first. Anyway, he's on overload because of the St. Luke's reunion next month."

The reunion would be Saturday, October 25. Each October, St. Luke's held a gathering of all its members. Many who had moved away from central Virginia returned, so the numbers ran to about three hundred.

"Okay. I'll get right on this. Be nice to have this

installed before the reunion, just in case the weather does turn cold."

"With luck the old boiler ought to hold out for another month or two. First frost usually hits us mid-October. We'll make it, I hope. You know, that old furnace is cast iron. A welder will need to dismantle it to get it out of there. That will take days. They don't build things like they used to," Tazio said with a big grin.

Harry finally noticed Tucker. "What did I tell you?"

Tazio walked back to the supply room, returning with a dog treat called a Greenies. She handed it to a grateful Tucker. "Made in Missouri."

"Well, then it has to be good." Harry laughed. "Come on, kids."

"I want the eraser." Mrs. Murphy carried the item in her mouth.

Harry had reached down to pluck it from those jaws when Tazio said, "Keep it. Really. I have a carton."

"Thanks. You spoil my buddies."

"You don't?" An eyebrow arched over one green eye.

"Well..."

"If you spoiled Fair like you spoil these three, he'd be fat as a tick." Tazio mentioned Harry's husband, who was six five, all muscle.

"You know, I don't think Fair will ever get fat. For one thing, if he doesn't work it off, he'll worry it off."

"He doesn't strike me as a worrier."

"Maybe not in the traditional sense, but he's always thinking about the future, investigating new technology and medications. His mind never stops."

"Neither does yours. That's why you were made for each other."

"Guess so. All right, madam. I'll get back to you." She paused. "Speaking of made for each other, you and Paul seem to be."

Tazio shrugged and blushed.

Harry opened the door and the three happy friends scooted out ahead of her. She got in the Ford, ran a few errands, then turned west toward the farm. Once down the long driveway, she could see her field of sunflowers, heads straight up to the sun, her quarter acre of Petit Manseng grapes ripening. How perfect.

2

*O*ne acre of sunflowers towered over another acre of Italian sunflowers, their beautiful heads turned toward the sun. The centers, heavy with seeds, barely moved in the light breeze, which lifted the leaves on the wide, hollow stalks.

Harry pulled the truck alongside the barn, cut the motor, and hopped out. Before returning to her chores, she stood, hands on hips, admiring the rich yellows of the big sunflowers and the subtle greenish white of the Italian variety. A twelve-foot grass swath ran between the sunflower acres and the grapes, pendulous beauties drooping on the vine. Since this was their first year, the grapes would not be picked but allowed to winter on the vine. This would thrill the foxes and birds.

"Come on."

Mrs. Murphy and Tucker followed.

"I need a nap." Pewter hesitated.

"I'm sure you do," Mrs. Murphy agreed.

The tiger's ready reply made Pewter suspicious. Mrs. Murphy and Tucker must be hiding something.

Harry walked along, Tucker alongside her, Mrs. Murphy behind, and Pewter bringing up the rear.

"Thought you wanted a nap," Tucker called over her shoulder.

"Decided I needed the exercise." Pewter's dark-gray fur shone, a sign of her overall health.

As they walked through the sunflower rows, insects buzzing, Harry paused, ran her fingers over a large head, then moved on. "Time for some rain."

A huge fake owl on a stake had thwarted some birds, but the blue jay paid no mind. Consequently, he'd eaten so much over the last month that his speed suffered. A red oak in the pasture next to the sunflower acre provided him with a refuge. He unfurled his topknot once the cats came into view. Lifting off, he circled the party once.

"Pissants."

Pewter glanced up. *"Butt ugly."*

The jay swooped low, just missing Pewter as he emitted what he'd eaten earlier. Satisfied, he returned to the red oak.

"One day," Pewter grumbled.

"Least it wasn't a direct hit." Tucker tried to look

on the bright side. The dog swiveled her large ears, then barked, *"Susan."*

The cats stopped, turning their heads to listen for the Audi station wagon. It was a quarter mile from the house, but they, too, could hear the motor. Few humans can distinguish the unique sounds each set of tires produces, but for the dog and cats this was as easy as identifying someone wearing squeaky shoes.

As the wagon approached the house, Harry finally heard it and turned to behold an arching plume of dust. "Damn, we really do need rain."

They walked briskly toward the house.

Susan met them halfway. "Hey, sugar."

Sweeping her arm wide, Harry beamed. "Can you believe it?"

Susan stopped, putting her hands on her hips. "Promiscuous in fertility and abundance."

"Worried about rain."

"Me, me, me." Susan bent down to scratch Tucker's ears.

"More."

"Me, too." Pewter rubbed against Susan's leg, so she petted the gray cannonball.

Harry slipped her arm through Susan's as they stood there for a moment admiring the yield. "Agriculture is still the basis of all wealth. Can't have industry or high tech if people can't eat."

Susan nodded. " 'Course, most people have forgotten that."

Harry smiled as they walked back to the house, the blue jay squawking after them.

As they passed the barn, Simon, the possum, stuck his head out of the open loft barn doors. *"Save me some cookies."*

Harry and Susan looked up at him, for he was semitame.

"If I don't eat them first." Pewter giggled.

"You need a diet, girl." Mrs. Murphy arched an eyebrow.

"Shut up." Pewter shot in front of everyone to push open the screen, then squeezed through the animal door in the kitchen door.